THE CESSION

THE AFTERMATH

The Cession

Part 2

The Aftermath

Copyright © 2024 by John Thornton

Book Cover by John Thornton

Publisher's Name: John Thornton

Publisher's Email: kbatto@ymail.com

Cover and Interior Design: John Thornton

ISBN: 979-8-218-47809-4

Contents

Dedication

This book is dedicated to my wife Kathleen, who tolerates me while I write it for reasons that escape me.

Acknowledgement

This book would not have been possible if it weren't for my mother's influence. She taught me never to take myself too seriously and respect everyone who deserves it. Of course, identifying the people who deserve respect is a challenge, but I work through it when possible. She informed me every day that something would happen, and she has always been right. When things went wrong, she readily identified it as "bad shit," and when something went well, that was just to be expected. She possessed the gift of simplifying complex things by stating, "Always start at the beginning." And in tough times, you could still find something to laugh about even when things went wrong.

Please Enjoy — The Cession – Part 2 — The Aftermath

CHAPTER ONE

The Only Man for the Job

As Congressman Harris sat on the corner of his daughter's head marker in prayer, his memories of the past year drifted by, filled with the good, the bad, and the ugly. The good was when his wife, daughter, and he traveled and sent their daughter to college. The bad was when a man driving a pickup truck killed his wife in a car crash. Only to discover later that the driver of the other vehicle was illegally in the country and deported nine times before that fateful night. The ugly was the assault and death of his daughter at the hands of another illegal immigrant while she attended college and was out for a morning jog.

He closed his eyes and scanned his last ten years in Congress, mediocre at best, he thought. His thoughts then turned to the events that followed the death of his daughter. The images of the past year flashed through his head. His formation of a secret committee led to the creation of the Republic of Sanctuary. He created the Black Ice group to remove dangerous immigrants and deport them to that Republic. In his meeting with Professor Norris, he embraced the conspiracy theory of foreign governments' takeover of the United States. The meeting of the crackpot Ken, the systems programmer who decoded the book "We Are the Dragons," to discover it filled with hacker code to destroy the United States infrastructure. And, of course, the meeting with representatives of South America, Mexico, and China to confront them with the evidence that revealed their plan to execute the takeover. He lifted his head, shaking it as it rose. I have accomplished so much this last year and dedicated it all to you, my wife, and my daughter.

The Congressman slowly stood and turned, walking down the stoney path to the cemetery's exit. As he walked, his mind again filled with images, not of the past but of the challenges ahead. The Congressman's work was unfinished, and he needed to return to his office in Washington for whatever lay ahead.

He arrived at his office an hour and a half later that day to be greeted by Bill, his Secretary, at the door. "You received a message from the White House while you were out today," stated Bill. Congressman Harris paused before speaking, "What was the message about?" Bill replies, "The President has requested a meeting with you tomorrow morning at ten. They will send a limo for you around nine to transport you to the White House. They did not give me a reason for the meeting, but it sounded important." The Congressman smiles before replying, "Bill, when the President of the United States requests a meeting with you, it is always important." Bill smiles back before responding, "Sir, I stand corrected. When the President of the United States calls and requests a meeting. It is always important."

The Congressman entered his office and sat down in his oversized desk chair. He turned to his computer and started to read the long list of e-mails displayed on the screen. Trying to stay focused on the e-mails, he could not help but wonder why the President requested a meeting at the White House. What could a lone Congressman have done so poorly that the President has asked for a meeting? Or maybe he needs something done and wants to keep a lid on it. I don't think I deserve a medal for anything. Why couldn't they tell Bill they would impeach me or something else wrong so I could sleep tonight? I cannot believe the President is meeting me to wish me a good day. What the hell does he want?

His eyes returned to the computer screen, and he half-heartedly continued to read the e-mails. The few telephone calls that afternoon briefly interrupted the reading of the e-mails, leaving the only thing that re-mained was what was on the President's mind, some-thing so important to request an in-person meeting at the White House the following morning. Reviewing his thoughts, they gave the Congressman no answers or even a good question about what the President could want on his drive home.

Even as he ascended the stairs leading to his bed-room, he could not find a reason for a meeting with the President. As he lay in bed, sleep came slowly. But even well-earned sleep could not stop the nightmare of stand-ing against a wall and hearing the voice of the President yelling "fire." Awaken from the sound of gunshots in his dream; the Congressman lay staring at the ceiling for the rest of the night. He surrendered to the fate he would need to attend the meeting with the President with very little sleep and turned on the television for the comfort of some noise in the room.

Arriving at his office shortly before nine a.m. with black coffee held tightly in his right hand the next day, he wait-ed for transportation to the White House. As promised, at nine a.m. sharp, a large black limo parked in front of the Congressman's office opened the rear door and directed him to enter the vehicle. With the Congressman safely in the back, the limo and driver sped away to sixteen hundred Pennsylvania Avenue to meet with the President of the United States without a word. The Congressman envisioned this was more like a scene from a 'Godfather movie' than real life.

As expected, the security at the White House is tight. There are multiple security checkpoints before you can enter the building. The first checkpoint is the name check, where you will show your photo ID, and the Secret Service will check your name off the reservation list. Even the limo driver needed to present proper identification to the Secret Service officer. No one, not even a sitting Congressman, can access the premises without identifying and stating their business. After entering the building, you must pass through an airport-style metal detector. Every item in your possession is cataloged and inspected. Nothing goes in or out without proper inspection by the Secret Service.

Twenty minutes after the Congressman arrived, he was finally escorted to the Oval Office to meet with the President. As he walked through the sizeable white-framed door, he could see the President of the United States oversized desk in front of a large curved window. Continuing to walk forward, he found himself standing in the center of the office of the most powerful man, the President of the United States. Sounds coming from behind him, followed by the announcement, "Mr. President, this is Congressman Harris." The President responds, "Damnit, I know who he is. Close the door when you leave so we can speak in private."

As the door closes, the President approaches the Congressman, extends his hand, and speaks, "Good to see you again, Harris." Congressman Harris replies, "And good to see you again, Sir." As they moved toward the large window, the President asked the Congressman to sit beside his desk.

White House Oval Office

Once seated, the President speaks, "I know you are wondering why I called you here today. We need each other, and I feel you may be the one person I can trust. I am not saying this because you are from the same party as I am. Frankly, I would not care if you were in the other party. The country needs someone who has paid the price for the mistakes made by both parties. You are that person.

I have lost some critical top-secret documents that include information that could place the world on a path of nuclear war. I sure wish I could remember what I did with them. Oh, on your way out, take that briefcase that belongs to you on the table. I don't know what is in it, but you must think it is vital for your upcoming actions. Is that your briefcase key on the floor over by the table? Please go and pick it up right now. It would be best to be more careful about dropping things like that. Now get out of here. I am sure you have things to do."

The President waits for the Congressman to recover and place the key in his pocket. Lifting the heavy briefcase, he moves back to the center of the room. The President presses a button to alert the Secret Service the Congressman's business has concluded and is about to leave. Secret Service agent Anderson enters the room to escort the Congressman from the White House. As Anderson looks at the Congressman, he speaks, "Excuse me, Congressman, you can not take that briefcase with you. Sorry, it did not come in with you, and can not leave with you." The President interrupts, "Agent Anderson, I saw the Congressman carry that case into this room. Congressman, show the Agent you have the key to open your case." The Congressman slowly reached into his pocket, removed the key, and unlocked the briefcase.

Agent Anderson watched closely as the lock opened. The President speaks again, "Now, Agent Anderson, you see, it is his briefcase, and you missed it when allowing entry into the White House. I hope I do not need to report this grave error." Agent Anderson replies, "No, Sir. I must have missed it somehow." The President looks directly at Agent Anderson before speaking, "Agent Anderson, you are to personally escort Congressman Harris through security and place him in the waiting limo. You will personally direct the limo driver to take Congressman Harris back to his office or any other location he wants to go. Is that understood?" "Yes, Sir," Anderson replies. The President continues, "After Congressman Harris has been cleared and left the White House grounds, I would like you to come back here and inform me he is safely on his way. Is that also understood?" "Yes, Sir," Anderson replies. The President finishes, "Remember, Agent Anderson, I want you to make this happen." Anderson replies, "I understand, Sir, and I am sorry for the mistake concerning the briefcase. It will not happen again."

Agent Anderson and Congressman Harris turned and left the office without speaking. Agent Anderson walked before the Congressman, assuring other security that everything was in order and allowing them to pass without intervention. When they reached the waiting limo, Agent Anderson directed the driver to go wherever the Congressman directed him to go before issuing a final apology concerning the briefcase to the Congressman. Congressman Harris lifted his hand to acknowledge the apology and slid into the rear seat of the limo.

As the limo exited the final security gate of the White House, the driver spoke, "Where do you want to go, Sir?" Congressman Harris replies, "Please just take me back to my office. I have some things I need to do there today."

As the Congressman pushed back into the deep limo seat, he stared at the locked briefcase given to him by the President. His thoughts ran riot, thinking about what happened to others with secret documents in their possession. Faces plastered all over the television news, lengthy prison sentences, and other untold horrors. This case should have been labeled 'Bad News' on the side because whatever it contained could be a problem for anyone with possession.

Arriving at his office, he exited the limo and walked straight into the main office area. "Bill," he said to his Secretary, "call security and have them send over two agents." Bill responds, "Two agents, Sir?" "That's right, Bill. I want two agents today. I want them to sit in this office and not let anyone in without my approval." The Congressman replied. Bill asks, "Is there something wrong, Sir?" Harris replies, "Nothing wrong. Some unsavory characters are around, and I would feel better with security here today. Please make the call and let me know when they arrive."

As the Congressman walks through the door into his private office, Bill lifts the phone and calls security. Twenty minutes later, two security agents were sitting in the office's central area with side arms and a shotgun. The Congressman opens his office door slightly to see the agents in place. He closed the door and walked over to his desk, where the briefcase lay. Slowly moving around his desk, he dropped into his oversized chair, thinking, 'What have I got myself into now.'

For ten minutes, he sat without motion and finally reached into his pocket to retrieve the key to the case. Cautiously, he unlocked the two latches and lifted the cover. Looking inside, he found two piles of documents marked, 'Top Secret' and 'For Your Eyes Only." He had broken every rule for handling classified documents and knew he would get twenty years in prison for having them. Why would the President want him to have these piles of documents? What could he need, in this case? The Congressman was not even sure what the President wanted him to do. He reached into the case, removed the piles of documents, and began scanning them for the answers.

It was getting late in the day, and he still could not find the answer to what the President wanted him to do. Too tired to continue, he replaced the documents in the briefcase and locked them in the private office safe. He spun the combination lock to secure the door before pressing the intercom button to summon Bill. When Bill entered the room, the Congressman said, "Bill, I think someone was outside my office window and may be trying to break in. Could you alert security and have them station someone in this office tonight?"

Bill looked out the window before responding, "I don't see anyone out there now." The Congressman replies, "I don't either, not now, but I would feel better if security stationed someone in this office tonight. Just a precaution. Better safe than sorry." Bill continues looking out the window and says, "I will ensure someone is here all night, Sir. You need to go home and get a good night's sleep. Sometimes, when you are tired, your mind can play tricks on you, and you are working too hard." The Congressman responds, "You are probably right, Bill, but it would make me sleep much better knowing we had security in this office tonight. Please do not leave before someone is here, and call me on my cell after they arrive. If you don't call me, I probably will not sleep well. Please call."

The Congressman grabbed a few items off his desk and headed to the office's front door. As he passed through the door, he heard Bill yell, "I got this, Sir. Get a good night's sleep, and things will be better in the morning." Without turning around, the Congressman yelled, "I know I can trust you, Bill, and I will see you in the morning." Congressman Harris strolled to his car for the trip home, thinking as he went, what the hell is in that damn case that is so vital for me to do?

Shortly before arriving home, his cell phone rang, and Bill informed him that security would remain in his office until nine a.m. the next day. Perfect, the Congressman thought. I do not have the answers yet, but at least I will get a good night's sleep knowing someone is looking over the office. As he opened the front door, he dropped the items taken from the office on a chair and ascended the stairs to go to bed. Sleep would not be an issue tonight, and he fell into a deep sleep within minutes. He was too tired to dream or have a nightmare and finally achieved a good night's sleep. Whatever was in that case would need to wait until tomorrow, no matter how good or bad.

CHAPTER TWO

The First Team Member

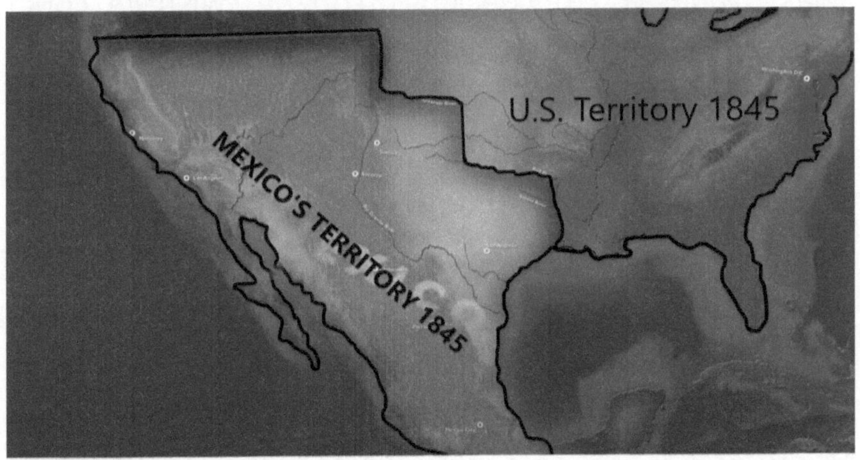

The seven a.m. alarm alerted the Congressman it was time to start his day. He slowly opened his eyes and looked out the bedroom window to witness the sun peeking through the dense tree limbs. As his eyes cleared, he saw two bright red cardinals perched on the window sill. They were standing side by side, heads moving quickly back and forth as if looking to see if he had awakened. His thoughts returned to something his mother had told him as a young boy. His mother would say, "Cardinals signify loved ones returning to show they are always with you. They return to give support when you are in need or unable to decide the correct thing to do." The Congressman paused before speaking, "Good morning, girls. I am glad I spent time with you guys the other day. Yes, I am awake. Thank you for checking up on me. I wish you could speak to me and tell me what I need to do and why the President selected me to do it. But whatever is needed, I will do it because of you two." As the Congressman finished the sentence, the two cardinals looked directly at him, turned, and flew away.

The Congressman climbed out of bed and headed to the shower to prepare for the upcoming day. Strange as it may seem, the two cardinals had somehow changed his outlook. Maybe that briefcase had intimidated him or threatened him in some way. Besides, how often does the President of the United States give you a case full of secret documents if he believes you are not the right person to do what is needed? If the President of the United States believes I am the right person, then I am the right person, and I will not fail him.

The drive to the office gave the Congressman time to sort through the things flying about his head. From his experience, he knew the limitations of a single person. Simultaneously, too many irons in the fire would produce less than desirable results. He would need help, and that help would need to start today. He tried to develop a story to cover the briefcase full of classified documents. Let me see. 'I found this briefcase on the sidewalk full of stuff. Can you help me figure out what it is?' No, he thought, that even sounded ridiculous to him. How about, 'I accidentally picked this case up at the White House and found it full of secret documents.' People would advise me to call the F.B.I. and turn in the case immediately, so that won't work. I can't tell them the President gave it to me. That would break the trust of the President.

Congressman Harris was in the wrong place with the briefcase and documents. He needed help, but without a plausible story for the existence of the case, what was he to do? As he parked his car in the office parking lot, he could hear a flashback story on a news channel. The announcer said, "This is a Watergate update. According to Bob Woodward, the information was provided to him by a person called 'Deep Throat,' and he shared it with Carl Bernstein of The Washington Post." The Congressman turns off the car's ignition and opens his car door. He places both feet on the blacktop pavement and says, 'Deep Throat gave me the briefcase. It worked once; it is going to have to work again.'

Reaching the main door of his office, he placed his hand on the handle to open the door. One last deep breath and the story' Deep Throat' was engraved in stone. He entered the office's central area and found his secretary, Bill, at his desk. "Good morning, Bill," he said. Bill responds, "Good morning to you, Sir. Good night's sleep has helped you look more alert today." The Congressman replies, "You were right. I needed a good night of rest to clear my head and get back on track. I need you in my office first, so we should latch the front door until our meeting ends." His secretary answers, "I will be done here in one minute. I will lock the door and be right in." The Congressman replies, "Thank you," as he enters his private office.

The Congressman heard the lock on the front door just before Bill walked through the private office door. He looked toward Bill before speaking, "Please close the door, Bill. This conversation will only be between us." Bill answers, "Yes, Sir," And pushes the door closed, securing the office.

"Bill," the Congressman starts, "How long have you been here working with me?" Bill looks toward the ceiling before answering, "Let me see, you have just finished your tenth year in Congress. And I have been with you since the start. So that must make it ten years." The Congressman responds, "That's correct. And do you re-member why I hired you?" Bill smiles before answering, "Yes, it was because you thought the young red-headed girl you liked might have caused a problem with your wife." The Congressman shakes his head and says, "Bill, that is untrue. You were the better choice and the more qualified person for the job." Bill replies, "I guess I need to take your word for that, Sir."

The Congressman pauses and continues, "I believe you have a current security clearance. What level is it at?" Bill replies, "Well, Sir, as you know, all Congressional staff must have a 'Top Secret' security clearance now. It is reviewed constantly and renewed unless an investigation discloses a problem. My clearance allows me to handle and review classified documents as needed and transport them within a secured facility." The Congressman interrupts, "That is why I hired you, Bill. You know the regulations and can recite them whenever I need information. The red-headed girl could not do that." Bill began to laugh.

The Congressman continues, "In my opinion, this office is a secure facility." Bill replies, "Well, we could consider it a secure facility. It is in a secure government area, and security guards protect the building around the clock." The Congressman interrupts again, "Great, we agree. Now that we have resolved the technical part, I need to know if you trust me completely." Bill looks puzzled before answering, " I trust you completely, Sir. I hope we are not planning a bank robbery or something, are we?" The Congressman folds his hand before answering, "No, Bill, nothing as easy as that. I need help, uh, well, saving the world from a nuclear war or something along those lines."

Bill does not speak momentarily and replies, "Are you sure, Sir, you would not rather plan a bank robbery? Nuclear war prevention seems above my pay grade." Congressman Harris sits deep into his chair and begins to laugh before replying, "Bill, I do not think there is a pay grade labeled prevent nuclear war, but pay grade or not, we may be in that position. The question I need answered today is whether you are in for the challenge of a lifetime or want to pass. Either way, I will not hold anything against you." Bill momentarily delayed before asking, "Sir, do you believe this, whatever it is, is that important? It sounds like it could be dangerous." The Congressman looks directly at Bill before answering, "Bill, dangerous is when you bury your wife and only daughter. Dangerous is when you have a loving family that someone could threaten. I am beyond the threat of danger. I am just asking for someone, you, to help me do what must be done to protect others. Bill, I need an answer." Bill smiles and replies, "Of course I'm in. Will I get a big gun like the one on 'Dirty Harry?' The Congressman shakes his head and then replies, "No guns. We are going to use pens and pencils to save the world."

The Congressman walks to the office safe, opens it, and removes the briefcase. Placing it on the desk in front of Bill, he unlocks the latches and lifts the cover, revealing the contents. Bill does not say a word for several moments. He stares into the case containing the documents marked 'Top Secret' and 'For Your Eyes Only.' "Well, Bill," The Congressman starts, "What do you see?" Looking over the top of the briefcase, Bill replies, "I see U.S.P. Leavenworth, twenty years, written all over them."

There was another pause before Bill questioned, "Where did you get this briefcase full of classified documents?" The Congressman takes a deep breath and replies, "Deep Throat." Bill, looking puzzled, replies, "But 'Deep Throat' was from the Nixon era, and I believe he is dead." Congressman Harris looks directly at Bill and states, "No doubt it is his son who gave the case to me. That is all I can tell you at this time. Are you still in?" Bill does not hesitate before speaking, "Sir, I have never known you to do something to hurt anyone. Let's get started. If you say it needs to be done, let's go. What do you need me to do?"

The Congressman speaks slowly, "We must ensure this office is always secure. Somehow, we need to get round-the-clock security for this office. I will leave that to you to figure out. Once we have security, we must review these documents to understand their meaning. 'Deep Throat' put them in this case for some reason that makes sense, and we must figure out why they are in the case. Let me relock the case and return it to the safe while you arrange security. Please advise me when we can review the documents after the security is in place. I hate to push, but this is a priority and needs to be done this morning. Bill, I am counting on you and need your help."

As the Congressman places the briefcase in the safe, Bill leaves the office to make security arrangements. The Congressman could hear Bill's conversation with security claiming the existence of unsavory people around the office and asking for office protection. Bill peaked into the private office to inform the Congressman that security would be there within the hour and that they could start work on the 'Deep Throat' documents.

The Congressman replies, "Thank you. See you in an hour." A long hour passed before the Congressman could hear the voices of the security agents in the main office area as Bill described what they needed to do. He could hear the offices answering a "Yes Sir" as he sat at his desk. Five minutes later, Bill walked through the private office door, closed it, and stood before the Congressman's large office desk.

The Congressman requested that Bill move the six-foot flat office table into the middle of the office under the bright lights. He was retrieving the briefcase from the office safe and placing it on the table while giving Bill instructions not to intermix the enclosed documents. Bill nodded that he understood, and they began taking the documents out of the case one at a time.

The first document was the employment record of Agent Zhōu, the Washington, D.C. F.B.I. Office head Chinese linguist. The Congressman informs Bill that he had spoken with Agent Zhōu before on the telephone but had never met him personally. Bill asks, "I wonder why his folder is in here?" The Congressman looks at the photo attached in the top corner of the folder and replies, "Maybe someone wants us to know he is a good contact or source of information. He did not appear to be that old from the photo and was already the head of the Washington D.C. office of the F.B.I., impressive.

The following folder contained reports and photos of the Baltimore Bridge, which had been destroyed weeks prior by the undetermined actions of someone. Bill thumbs through the folder and says, "This must be the stuff my contacts at Homeland Security told me about concerning the Bridge incident."

The following folder, taken from the briefcase, contained photos and reports on the Wuham Lab in China. The reports appeared to be from several sources from organizations worldwide and referenced the COVID-19 virus. Bill noticed that one document was a handwritten note by a scientist who had since disappeared deep into China. Bill addressed the Congressman, "Sir, this note looks like the original, not a copy. Wherever these came from, the person was well connected."

Another set of documents clipped together appeared to be personal information about South American leaders. Congressman Harris sifted through and responded,

"Look here, Bill, the file contains the banking records of each of these leaders. Swiss bank accounts, Crypto funds, everything. Where did they get all this information?"

The following folder contained reports and documents about a pipeline shutdown in the eastern United States. It included a report listing the hacker code used to turn off the pipeline system and the possible source of the code.

The subsequent two folders contained reports of power outages in India and Mexico. Bill asks the Congressman, "Why are they two combined into a set of folders this way, Sir?" The Congressman answers, "I don't know why, but someone wanted them combined to alert us they belong together for a reason. Someone wanted us to know they are somehow linked together and wanted us to treat them as one item.

A thick folder contained information on several Chinese operators working inside the United States. Bill asks, "I wonder who all of these people are?" The Congressman scans the folder and replies, "If I were to venture a guess, I think these are the Chinese enforcers working in the U.S. We have been shutting down Chinese police operations within the United States over the past few years. This list is probably a list of the people operating those illegal police stations."

The final folder contained files on known Mexican Cartels, the leader names, and family members, and included their last locations in Mexico. Included in the folder was a listing of almost two hundred of Cartel's control centers located in the United States that had been destroyed by Federal Agents weeks before. The Congressman looks at Bill and says, "This Bill was to prove that everything in this briefcase is real. Only a few high-ranking officials know about these raids on the Cartel control centers, and I am one of them."

The Congressman and Bill sifted through the folders, looking for anything that would yield a clue as to what they had to do with these documents. After two hours, they packed the briefcase and placed it in the office safe. The only document the Congressman did not pack into the case was the F.B.I.'s Agent Zhōu file. He kept that out in case he needed to contact Agent Zhōu for advice on Chinese matters or other questions. He considered that file to be benign and placed it into his briefcase.

The Congressman sits back in his desk chair and says, "Let's call it a day, Bill. We are both tired and overwhelmed at this point. Tomorrow, I will make some calls and try to figure out what this all means, and the following day, I need to go to Miami to see a friend who may be able to shed some light on this problem. You must stay here, take care of things, and guard this office."

Bill looks at the Congressman and replies, "You can count on me, Sir. Everything will be safe while I am on guard here. And Sir." The Congressman interrupts, "No Bill, no damn gun!"

CHAPTER THREE

The Betrayal

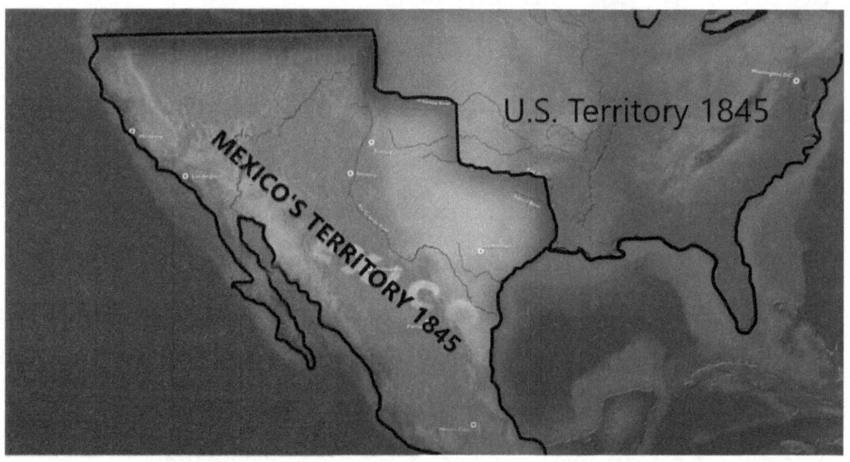

Congressman Harris had remained in Washington to work on other leads found in the materials in the President's briefcase. Still, tomorrow, he needed to return to Miami to re-interview Renel Destina, the informant from Haiti. Harris sat in his office, wondering if Renel could pick out the Chinese hacker he saw at the meeting in Mexico earlier from the twenty-four photos of the captured hackers. It would be great to know who the

'Big Guy' was working directly with the Chinese Ambassador to take down the United States at the meeting.

He remembered what Professor Norris had said about the Chinese; they would rather die than lose their honor and use it against them. Before using anything against anyone, I need to know which of the twenty-four hackers was with the Ambassador. He turned to his computer and reads the long list of e-mails he had not answered. My God, he thought, there was so much to accomplish and so little time. The only people with time were the Chinese, as they had all the time in the world.

Ten a.m. the following morning, Congressman Harris was on a southbound plane to Miami. His destination was F.D.C. Miami, a Federal Detention Center, to meet with Renel Destina, the unwilling informant from Haiti. As the plane touched down in Miami, F.D.C. Miami staff was waiting to transport the Congressman to the detention facility. The Congressman slid into the rear seat of a Ford Explorer without speaking and, twenty minutes later, arrived at the facility. As the Explorer pulled up to the facility's front entrance, the Congressman slowly exited the vehicle, reaching back in to grab his briefcase. Turning away from the car, he walked to the large glass-enclosed entrance. Upon entering the building, the Congressman was confronted by a large metal detector blocking entry. As he began to place his belongings into a basket, he heard a friendly voice echoing in the distance proclaiming, "Sir, no need to go through there," a door off to the right opened, allowing passage. The Warden stood on the other side of the door, hand extended, saying, "Good to see you again, Sir. I hope you had a good trip down from Washington." The Congressman replies, "The trip was perfect. How is my friend Mr. Destina doing?"

As the Warden and Congressman made their way to the Warden's office, he briefed the Congressman on Mr. Destina's upgraded living conditions and special privileges. "Mr. Destina is receiving excellent care here at my facility." Said the Warden. "We are still feeding him food from the staff kitchen, and he has been allowed to use the exercise area without restriction." The Congressman says, "I want to be sure he is kept in good spirits as I will need him in Washington before the intelligence committee." "I understand, Sir." Answered the Warden.

They reached the Warden's office, where the Warden unlocked the thick wooden door. The Warden pushed open the door, and the two men entered the room. Laying his briefcase on a chair, the Congressman begins, "Warden, I will need the same room as before. Everything must be videotaped and recorded. I will also need one of your senior staff members as a witness and beverages in the room." The Warden replies, "Congressman, I have had everything arranged, and I will have Mr. Destina moved into the room at your pleasure." The Congressman walks toward the Warden's private bathroom, saying, "Give me ten minutes, and I will be in the interview room and ready to start."

Mr. Destina and the Senior staff member were seated when the Congressman entered the interview room. And as per regulations, a guard stood by the door as a deterrent for trouble. The Congressman wasted no time and started the conversation, "Mr. Destina, I understand you have been treated fairly here at this facility." Mr. Destina, nodding his head, replies, "Not bad. I still wish there was take-out or delivery here." The Congressman looks to the Senior staff member and asks, "Can Mr. Destina receive a food delivery here at this facility?" The Senior staff member replies, "I looked into that, Sir, but regulations have prevented food delivery for security reasons. I will try again, but I am unsure I can do it."

The Congressman opened his briefcase, removed some photos of the captured hackers and other documents, placed them on the table, and said, "Mr. Destina, we believe you have been accommodating, and as promised, I will continue to work toward securing your safety. I have talked with the Federal Prosecutor in Florida, and he still believes you may be eligible for the witness protection program offered by the Federal Government. I must again clarify that you may lose your protection if you contact any of your relatives while in the program. Also, if you violate any laws, you can and will be deported back to Haiti. Do you understand what I just told you, Mr.

Destina?" Destina nodded his head, showing he understood. The Congressman continues, "We still need you to testify before a Congressional committee at some point; is that also agreed upon?" Destina nods his head again in acceptance.

Congressman Harris slides the photos to Mr. Destina to review before speaking, "Please look at these photos and see if you can identify the Chinese guy you saw in Mexico using the computer while holding the kid's book. Please take your time." Destina looked at each photo and shook his head one at a time, indicating he was not the one.

Congressman Harris asks, "Are you sure you have not seen him yet?" Destina looks up to reply to the Congressman, "Hey, many Chinese guys all look alike. Give me a little time to check these." "Sorry." Replied the Congressman.

Destina continues through the photos, restacks them, and starts over to ensure he does not miss anyone. Finally looking up, he shakes his head, indicating the guy was not in the stack of photos. Destina stood up slightly to slide the images back to the Congressman, stopped, stared momentarily, and said, "That's the guy!" Harris shows his excitement and says, "Which one of them?" Destina pushes the images to the side and points to a file with a photo attached in the top corner, sitting in front of the Congressman. "He is the guy, and he is the one with the kid's book who got mad when I looked at it. He's the guy." Destina replied.

Congressman Harris sat back in his chair before speaking, "Are you sure this is a photo of the guy you saw at the Mexico meeting with the Chinese Ambassador, who had the kid's book and was using the computer?" Destina gives the Congressman a look that could kill before replying, "I am sure that is the guy at the damn meeting using the computer with the kid's book. When he grabbed the book from me, I noticed a small scar on the left side of his head shaped like a half-moon and looked like a little smile."

Congressman Harris stood, slid back his chair from the table, and spoke, "Warden, do you have a secure telephone in your office? I forgot to make an important telephone call this morning, and I should do it right now to avoid a problem." The Warden says, "I have a secure line, and you are welcome to use it." Congressman Harris turns to leave the room, looks back, and says, "Why don't we get Mr. Destina something to eat and drink while I make the call." The Warden nods to the staff at the door to comply with the Congressman's request for lunch for Mr. Destina as Harris left the room. As the Congressman walks down the hall, he hears the Warden's voice, "Right behind you, Sir, to let you in my office." Reaching the office door, the Warden unlocked the heavy door, allowing entry. "The phone on the right side is the secure one."

Said the Warden. "Thank you, and I will need some privacy for this call." Replied the Congressman. The Warden closed the door as he left the office.

Congressman Harris sat in the Warden's chair and momentarily closed his eyes, deciding what to do. He reached over, picked up the telephone, and dialed the Washington D.C. office of the F.B.I. A soft voice answered, "F.B.I. D.C. office, how can I help you?" Congressman Harris replies, "This is Congressman Harris. May I speak with Agent Zhōu, please?" The voice at the other end of the phone replies, "I am sorry, Agent Zhōu is out of the office today. Can I take a message for him when he returns tomorrow?" Congressman Harris lays out his words carefully as he speaks, "No, it is not important. Hey, the last time Agent Zhōu and I were together, I could not help but notice a small scar on the left side of his head. I was wondering how it happened?" A small giggle followed with, "We call that scar his little smile, and it happened when he was a child on a swing where he fell off and struck a rock. It never healed totally, and he was left with an area without hair, giving the image of a smile." Congressman Harris replies, "Thank you and have a good day," before hanging up the telephone.

The Congressman looked at the ceiling, trying to precisely recall what Agent Zhōu told him about the book, "We Are the Dragons," in a previous conversation weeks before. Agent Zhōu advised me the book was "a sort of children's book by all appearances. Strangely, it is written in two different Chinese Dialects. And he could not relate it to any Chinese celebration or anything like that. He stated, frankly, the book is poorly written at best, and he would be surprised if it sold a single copy." If Agent Zhōu was at the conspiracy meeting in Mexico, the entire story was a ruse to mislead me. It would also mean that he is directly involved with the hackers' attempted attacks on the United States. For all I know, he could be the guy that wrote the damn book 'We Are the Dragons." I will need a lot more information about Agent Zhōu, and I think I know the guy who can get it without creating a problem.

Again, picking up the telephone, he called his office in Washington, D.C.. Bill's voice on the other end answered, "Hello, Congressman Harris' Office. How can I assist you today?" The Congressman replies, "Bill, it's me, Harris. I need to get in touch with Ken, the crackpot computer guy. See if you can set up an appointment for tomorrow after-noon sometime." Bill replies, "Is there something wrong, Sir." Congressman Harris says, "I think I can sum it up with a few famous words. 'Houston, we have a problem!'" The Congressman hung up the telephone and turned the chair to his left. Congressman Harris stood, left the Warden's office, and strolled down the lonely hall back to the interview room. Entering the room, he sat back in his chair across the table from Mr. Destina. "Well, Mr. Destina." Said the Congressman, "I thank you for your help here today, and I must again tell you not to speak with anyone about what you are telling me. Your safety is in your hands, and I do not want to see anything happen to you." Destina nods his head in agreement with the Congressman. The Congressman continues, "I will keep you in this fine facility to keep people away from you. The Warden will see you have everything you need to make you comfortable, but I will take my time in this matter for your safety. Be patient, as I do not want anything to happen to you."

The Congressman stood from his chair and walked to the door to leave the room. Congressman Harris left the room with his briefcase held tightly in his hand. On his way back to the Warden's office, he kept thinking about Destina's claim about who the Chinese guy was in Mexico on the computer. How would Destina know about a scar not visible in the photo he identified? Someone at the D.C. F.B.I. office verified the scar today. How would Destina know unless Destina was correct in the identification? Destina has recognized the head Chinese linguist at the Washington D.C. F.B.I.'s office as the person at the conspiracy meeting in Mexico using a computer and the book "We Are the Dragons." It is all beginning to make sense now. F.B.I. Agent Zhōu is the twenty-fifth Chinese hacker or maybe even the creator of the book "We Are the Dragons" himself. That is why he 'downplayed' the book when he reported his findings. The head Chinese linguist at the

F.B.I. in Washington, D.C., was a Chinese spy! The bigger question is why the President included Agent Zhōu's folder in the documents given to the Congressman. Does the President know or even suspect Agent Zhōu is a spy? The President gave me those documents for a reason, and maybe this is just the beginning as to their true meaning.

Along the walk back, the Congressman stopped dead as he returned to the Warden's office. His thoughts returned to the number of copies of 'We Are the Dragons' sold. Only twenty-four of them, and we have in custody twenty-four hackers. Amazon removed the books from their site, which are now no longer available to the hackers. It was at that moment the Congressman had a terrifying thought. What if Agent Zhōu was also a hacker and did not need Amazon because he already had both books? Agent Zhōu could be the only 'Manchurian Candidate' remaining in the hacker attack and hiding in plain sight in the upper echelon of the Washington D.C. F.B.I.

Reaching the Warden's office, he requested a ride back to the airport to Washington. His flight was still over three hours away, but something about the soothing noise of an airport allowed him to place his thoughts into a logical order. Besides, who would want to sit around a prison?

CHAPTER FOUR

Help Arrives

When sitting in an airport, your best friend is usually the person sitting next to you. The Miami International Airport is no exception to the rule. Conversations generally turn quickly to the last or current vacation or trip home to visit the family. As the Congressman sat on the hard plastic chair waiting for his flight, today's intercourse would be no exception.

Surrounded by a family returning from the Dominican Republic, he was privileged to hear about their excellent time together the previous week. His thoughts about clearing his head to think things out were long gone, and the images of palm trees swaying in the wind along a sandy beach replaced his problems at hand. The younger girl with the family reminded him of his daughter years before. Her parents protect and shield her total innocence of what is happening in the world around her, giving her the freedom to be a child.

Memories can be wonderful or harsh. The Congressman takes a moment to drift back to almost twenty years before when his family sat in this airport after returning from a trip to the Bahamas'. His little girl greeted everyone to show the sea shells she had gathered along the white beach, telling a story of how they belonged to a mermaid and were now hers. He closed his eyes, and his memories moved into the last year's events. His daughter was leaving for college to become a woman of the world and was still carrying the small bag of sea shells gathered years before, the same bag of shells that now lay on the mantle in his dining room. He looked back at the young girl of his newly found friends and promised himself that fate would not be hers.

His daydreaming was interrupted by a voice over the airport intercom, "Miami to Washington now boarding on gate thirty-two." As he stood out of the chair, he remembered what he had told Bill in his office, "We are going to stop a nuclear war with pens and pencils." He looked at the young girl as he walked toward the boarding gate and thought, 'But if I need a damn gun, I will use it too.'

The flight back to Washington was troubling. Destina had identified the F.B.I.'s head Chinese linguist, Agent Zhōu, as the person who attended the meeting in Mexico to destroy the United States. It was Agent Zhōu, according to Destina, who was on the computer using the kid's book 'We Are the Dragons.' The Congressman relied on Agent Zhōu to verify what the book was about. Agent Zhōu downplayed the book as a poorly written children's book. Agent Zhōu scanned the book with Criptor Seven, version nine, to find the addresses of the Cartel control centers to locate and remove them. Agent Zhōu, everything comes back to Agent Zhōu.

The Congressman had nothing else to link Agent Zhōu to anything besides Destina's identification. Agent Zhōu's employment record looked stellar on its face. Agent Zhōu had awards and accommodations threaded throughout the file. What could I do? Call up the F.B.I. Director and say, "Excuse me, Sir. I hate to bring this up. But you have a Chinese spy at the head of your Washington D.C. office." He closes his eyes and reviews another story to tell the Director, "Good morning, Sir. I have the Lockness monster at my home in a fish bowl." For some reason, both versions of the story had the same credibility. If

Agent Zhōu were a Chinese agent, he would need more evidence to expose it.

Sitting deep into the seat aboard the aircraft, he looked deep into the overhead console above his head. He could see the single reading light glowing deep inside the plastic housing. He smiled while moving his head from side to side. Damn, he thought, I am going to need to rely on Ken, the crackpot computer guy, to help me with this. I can not trust the Washington F.B.I. office for help because others may be embedded there. We will need to work on this from the outside without supporting help from law enforcement. The deeper I get into this mess, the more plausible the 'Deep Throat' story seems.

The Congressman reclined back in the seat and drifted off into a light sleep. There would be nothing to do until he arrived at his office in Washington. Worrying about what had occurred would not change anything, and over-thinking it would only lead to specters in the night. A friendly voice over the aircraft intercom alerts him of a landing in twenty minutes. Finally, he thought, just in time to go home and try to get some sleep for a long day tomorrow.

As he de-planed, his only thoughts returned to Agent Zhōu. The one person he believed he could trust was Agent Zhōu. The one person the F.B.I. and the United States trusted seemed to be Agent Zhōu. And the one person he may need to take down could be Agent Zhōu.

As he arrived home and unlocked the front door, he thought he could hear his wife's movements inside the home. But as always, he heard only the movement of a fan he had forgotten to turn off, stirring the air in the kitchen. Bill was right; when you are tired, your mind will play such beautiful tricks.

The Congressman was surprised at how well he slept that night, maybe because he believed the first step in solving the enigma of the briefcase had been solved or perhaps because he was just exhausted by thinking about it. Whatever the reason, he needed to get to the office and speak with Bill about what had happened in Miami the day before.

Arriving shortly after nine a.m. because of traffic delays, he opens the front door of his office. He enters to find Bill seated at his desk and across from Bill, his first surprise of the day. Addressing the person who was now standing, he greeted him, "Agent Anderson, I believe?" The agent replies, "That is correct, Sir. Secret Service Agent Anderson here at your service." The Congressman, surprised, replies, "But you are assigned to the White House and the President." Anderson interrupts, "Not now, Sir. The President had me assigned to your office. Probably to punish me for the mistake I made about the briefcase from the other day when you were in the White House." Bill sat at his desk without expression and just listened to the conversation. Anderson continues, "The President told me it was not punishment, but he felt I would be more needed here with you for a while. I assure you, Sir, I will do whatever is needed here and hope to return to the White House after this; whatever it is, we will complete it."

The Congressman paused before replying, "Agent Anderson, I assure you it is not punishment. Please do not take offense. I need a man of your expertise here with me at this time. I will explain it in the next day or two, and I believe you will understand why the President sent you here." Agent Anderson, expressionless, replies, "Thank you, Sir, for that."

Congressman Harris heads for his private office and summons Bill to follow. As they pass through the door and Bill closes it, he speaks, "Son of Deep Throat, uh, Sir." The Congressman does not answer. "Why did you not tell me the President gave the briefcase to you?" Bill asks. The Congressman replies, "Bill, the President gave me the briefcase in trust. I did not have the right to divulge where it came from. Please understand. To everyone outside this room, it came from 'Deep Throat,' and that must be the only answer to its origin." Bill nodded in agreement, saying, "Deep Throat it is."

The Congressman motions for Bill to sit alongside his desk before speaking, "Do you have an update on the meeting with Ken? Will he make it here today?" Bill replies, "I spoke with Ken shortly after your call yesterday from

Miami, and he is scheduled here around noon today." "Great." Replied the Congressman. Ensure you inform Agent Anderson that a visitor named Ken is coming so he does not get shot at our door." Bill smiles and answers, "I will tell Anderson that Ken will be here, and by the way, did you see the size of Anderson's gun under his coat?" The Congressman interrupts, "No Bill, no Damn gun."

Bill frowned and left the office to tell Agent Anderson not to shoot Ken when he arrived. The Congressman turned to his computer to review the long list of e-mails. Shaking his head from side to side, he reasons why the Post Office is going broke. E-mail killed the Post Office. It was E-mail that killed paper letters. I wonder if I could introduce a law to charge a penny for each e-mail sent. After all, the computer marks it as mail, and the law says the only entity authorized to transport mail is the Post Office. After thinking about that idea for a moment, he could envision his home being fire-bombed should he do that, and he continued reading the e-mails.

Ken arrived at the Congressman's office just after noon for the meeting. After entering the office, the front door was locked, and Agent Anderson resumed his position in the central office waiting area. Bill and Ken moved into the private office of Congressman Harris and closed the door. As Bill and Ken each sat down, the first words spoken came for Ken. "Twenty-seven and almost twenty-eight," Ken said. The Congressman replies, "What is twenty-seven or twenty-eight?" Ken, looking confused, answers, "Twenty-seven miles per gallon, what else? The car, the car." "Oh," said the Congressman, "We are talking about the car I purchased for you." Ken replies, "Of course; what else am I here to discuss?" The Congressman says, "I am glad you enjoy your car, Ken. But today, I have something else I need you to help me with."

The Congressman slides the folder with Agent Zhōu's photo from his briefcase and pushes it over to Ken. As Ken picks up the folder, the Congressman asks, "Do you know this person?" Ken looks over the folder and replies, "I know of him. I have never met him. He works for the Feds in Washington. Some supposed big wig." The Congressman continues, "Can you tell me anything about who he is or what he does from those documents?" Ken looks at the Congressman, "Not really from this stuff. This stuff is an employment record only. I would need more than this to give you a good feel about who or what he is." The Congressman sits back and says, "That's too bad. I need to know more about this guy. It is important, but I can't call the F.B.I. and ask any questions."

Ken looks up again, puzzled, before speaking, "Then don't call them. I was hoping you could hire me to find out what you want to know. Is there a gas card in it? If so, I will find out what you need to know about this guy." The Congressman glances back toward Ken and says, "But that is all I have, and it appears to be his complete record of who and what he is." Ken starts to laugh before replying, "Are you kidding me? I work with these people and their other similar agencies. They complete a ton of daily paperwork about everything they are working on. Who they speak with. Whatever tools or references they use to come to their conclusions. They document everything in form after form. You have heard of the 1023 form the Senate demanded for evidence for a hearing. That is only one of an assortment of forms filed daily with each report. This guy must have filled out many forms for everything he has worked on over the years." The Congressman looks down and replies, "But if the Senate could not access these forms, how would I get to look at them?"

Ken reaches under his chair, removes his laptop from a case, and says, "Why bring Mohammad to the mountain when the mountain can be transmitted directly to Mohammad." As Ken plugged in the computer, the Congressman asked the likely question, "Ken, do you happen to have a valid security clearance?" Ken looks back at the Congressman, "Sir, with all due respect, no one has a security clearance to hack into and download documents from the F.B.I. Central office." Not knowing what to say, the Congressman motions for Ken to continue whatever he was about to do to get the needed information, all while thinking in the back of his mind, U.S.P. Leavenworth, here we come.

Ken watched the computer screen and occasionally pressed a key or two on the keyboard while rocking his chair. The Congressman and Bill watched and waited, unsure if they should want to see anything going on as a witness to whatever Ken was doing. Finally, Ken removed a thumb drive memory stick from his pocket, pushed it into the laptop computer, and copied some large files onto it. Ken removed the thumb drive and handed it to the Congressman, saying, "There you go, Sir. Here is the information you requested concerning Agent Zhōu's work history with all reports and filed documents."

The Congressman took the thumb drive and placed it on the desk next to him before asking, "Ken, why didn't you help out the Senate Committee when they needed stuff like this?" Ken replied, placing his laptop back into the case, "That's easy. They never asked me to get that stuff for them. Most of those meetings are just shows for the public."

The Congressman sits momentarily before speaking, "Again, Ken, do you have a security clearance?" Ken replies, "Sir, I work with Homeland Security, The C.I.A., The F.B.I., and Interpol on hacker and terrorist threats worldwide. I have a security clearance to do almost any-thing that needs to be done. The only difference is that I need to go outside the restrictions placed on government agencies to achieve the undoable. For that, these agen-cies have looked the other way. I can tell from that file on Agent Zhōu's that you are in deep trouble with something, and I hope I have helped you with your problem. Be safe, Congressman. You may be in dark waters with whatever you are doing. By the way, can you get me a five hundred dollar gas card for my work here today?"

Congressman looked over to Bill and said, "You go out and purchase a one thousand dollar gift card for gas for Ken right now and make sure he has it when he leaves." Ken replies, "That is more than generous, Sir. Thank you."

Bill leaves the office to purchase the gas card, and the Congressman continues with Ken, "Since you have a security clearance, I can relate some things to you. I will need help decoding and working through a large amount of documents. I am unsure of what they could be or what they mean. That is why I need you. I can pay you with money and not just with gas cards. Can I put you on board this project?"

Ken pauses before answering, "Congressman, I know you have lost your family because of the actions or, should I say, inactions going on in this country. I have heard rumors about some of the things you have done and are doing, and I believe you are trying to make things better for the United States and maybe even the world as a whole. If you need my help, Bill has my direct cell number, and I will make myself available. It is strange, Sir, in what I do, people think we are all bad. That is not the case at all. Sometimes, you must go directly to the source and take things out by the roots to make things right. Trying to manipulate your way through a legal system set up to roadblock progress is often too time-consuming. That is where I come in. Count me in as long as it is for the country's or the people's good."

Bill returned holding a new gas card for one thousand dollars worth of liquid gold and handed it to Ken. On the way out of the center of the office, Bill introduced Ken to Agent Anderson and informed Agent Anderson that Ken would always be welcomed into the Congressman's office. Then, for reasons that escaped me, Bill informed Agent Anderson not to shoot Ken if he should arrive at the front door.

The Congressman sat in his office chair, eyes closed, pretending that Bill did not just say that. He thought, 'That is why you will never carry a gun, Bill, that is why.'

At least he had another person on the team to ferret out whatever he was looking for. Crackpot or not, Ken would be a significant player in this project. The Congressman sat deep into his chair and began to laugh. The crackpot Ken might be the only one with a clear vision of what would be needed to finish this ordeal.

CHAPTER FIVE

Building the Team

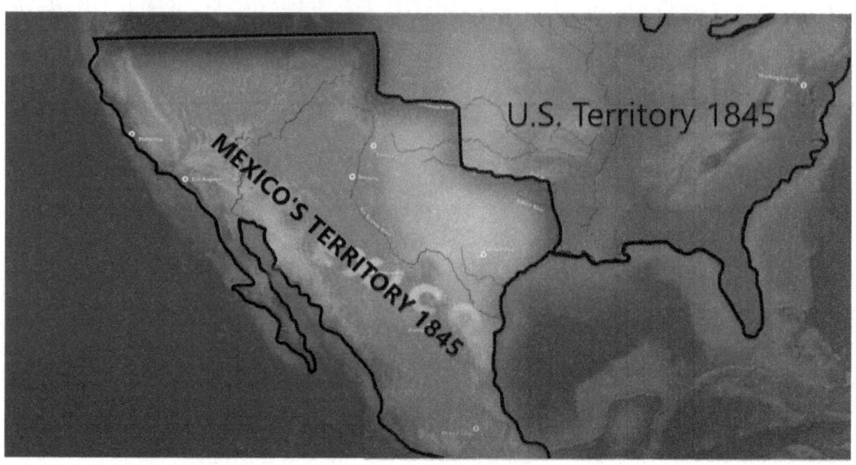

Bill peeks into the Congressman's private office and says, "What is next, Sir?" The Congressman looks up from his computer and replies, "Please have Agent Anderson come into my office so I may speak with him." Agent Anderson walked into Congressman Harris's private office a few moments later, closing the door behind him. Agent Anderson begins the conversation, "Sir, I know Bill was kidding, and I am not going to shoot anybody."

The Congressman, moving his head side to side, replies, "I know you are not going to shoot anyone, and I know Bill was kidding. That is not why I called you in here. I have something important to go over with you. The President sent you here for a reason. The President is not punishing you for missing the briefcase I was carrying. Do you have a current security clearance?"

Agent Anderson looks confused when asking, "Yes, Sir, I have a Top Secret Clearance with the addition of carrying classified documents between facilities if necessary." The Congressman continues, "As far as carrying your firearm, are there any limitations on its use?" Anderson responds, "Well, obviously, I can not fire on an innocent bystander or protestor. But if I sense a clear and present danger, I am authorized to use deadly force to protect the subject I am there to protect."

The Congressman sits back in his chair before speaking, "Agent Anderson, I believe I am speaking for the President right now. He sent you here because he thinks you are the best person to assist me. I will tell you something now, and it is not to leave this room. The President turned that briefcase over to me to perform a mission outside the reach of his administration. The President sent you here, Agent Anderson, to ensure the mission succeeds, and I must assume from that action that a life-threatening issue is attached to the mission." The Congressman could hear Agent Anderson mumble under his breath, 'I knew you did not have that damn case with you when you came in.'

The Congressman pauses and continues, "I am sorry we needed to place you in that position, but whatever this mission is, it must be at the level of national security. You should feel honored that the President of the United States selected you to head up security on a mission of that importance. I need to ask if I can count on you to be part of this mission. I need to be honest with you. I do not know the scope of the mission at this time, but I can tell you from what I have discovered so far that it is of major national importance." Agent Anderson nods while speaking, "Sir, if the President of the United States thinks I should be here with you, then I am here with you until the end."

Congressman Harris replies, "I was hoping you would forgive the President and me for using you that way, but we had no other way to move the briefcase without your help. I will need you to ensure no unauthorized person can enter this office, even after hours. I will require you to help us review the documents and other items as we discover them. Anything discussed in this office must remain in this office, and even other law enforcement agencies are not to be advised as to what we are doing or what we have discovered. Is that clear, Agent Anderson?" Anderson responds, "Sir, my father was military police for over thirty years. My brother died in Afghanistan because of a soldier who could not keep his mouth shut. I have learned the hard way about people who talk too much. Sir, I am like a table, with legs, no eyes, no ears, and no mouth."

Congressman Harris reaches across the desk to shake a man's hand and welcome him as number three on the team. The Congressman presses the button on the office intercom and summons Bill into the private office. Upon entering, the Congressman says, "Bill, Agent Anderson is going to assist in the project concerning the briefcase. There will be no secrets between Ken, Agent Anderson, you, and myself while within this office concerning what is in the briefcase. Whatever this involves is too essential to play games with, and we can not fail. One last thing, Agent Anderson, please do not let Bill handle your gun."

Finally, everyone in attendance had something to laugh about.

The Congressman interrupted the laughter, saying, "We have much to review tomorrow to try and get our hands around this thing. Be prepared to do a lot of reading and making notes to lay out wherever this takes us. Nothing in written form can leave this office and must be secured in my office safe every night. After we understand what we have, we will call Ken back to get more information to review. Agent Anderson, I would appreciate it if you would personally pick the night security people to protect this office. You know who you can and can not trust. After that, let's go home and get a good night's sleep. Okay, let's finish here for tonight and get out of here."

Bill returned to his desk in the central office to finish up for the day, while Agent Anderson called security and requested two agents he felt he could trust to guard the office overnight. Congressman Harris secured the thumb drive Ken gave him in the safe and continued reading his e-mails.

Finally, each team member finished their daily house-keeping, and after the night security officers arrived, they left the office for the evening.

As the Congressman drove home, he felt satisfied he had accomplished something that day. Things were still a long way off into the future, but at least he was beginning to assemble a team of trusted people to help him.

Tomorrow, he planned to tackle the information on the thumb drive recorded by Ken with the help of Bill and Agent Anderson. Tonight, he was going home and spending the night with the memories of his wife and daughter.

Chapter Six

An Old Friend

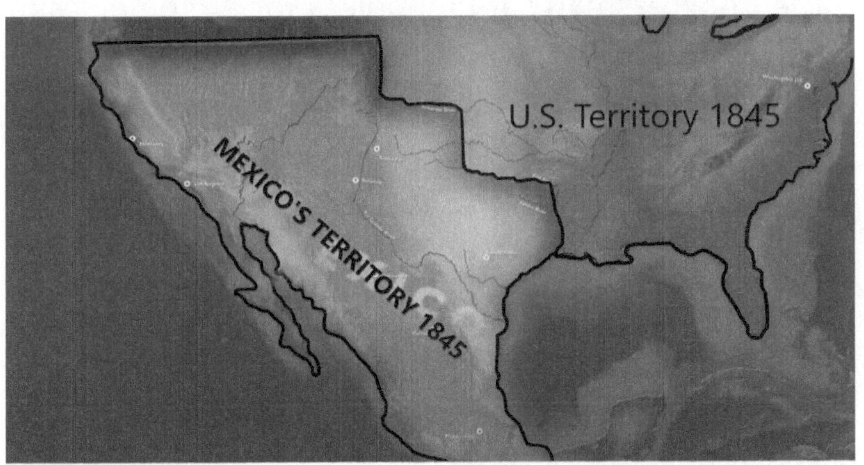

The seven a.m. alarm alerted the Congressman that it was time to begin his day. He slowly opened his eyes and looked out the bedroom window and realized the bright morning sunshine had been replaced with the sound of raindrops striking the window.

To his surprise, he could see the wings of three bright red cardinals perched on the window sill, trying to stay out of the rain. All three were standing side by side, heads moving quickly back and forth as if looking to see if he had awakened. The Congressman paused before speaking, "Good morning, girls. I see you brought a friend along with you today. And just as the day before, as the Congressman finished the sentence, the three cardinals looked directly at him, turned, and flew away.

The Congressman sat motionless for a moment and thought to himself he was letting his mind run away with him. They are just red birds sitting on his window sill and nothing more; that is where he would need to leave it. But whatever the meaning or non-meaning, he needed to get ready to go to work for a big day in the office.

As he drove through the streets of Washington, he realized that even a rain shower in the city could cause delays. Sitting in traffic, he thought, what the hell was the person who designed this city thinking, laying out streets that all lead to a single point in the city's center? He remembers the original person who laid out the town of Washington, D.C. It was Pierre L'Enfant in around 1790 when Congress authorized a federal district along the Potomac River to allow easy access to the city. I needed to cut him a little slack, as he did not know that the metal monsters would replace horses and buggies. Had he known this would happen, he would have built this city elsewhere.

Finally arriving at the office, he entered through the main door to find Bill, sporting a big smile and waiting. "You have a visitor, Sir," Bill begins. The Congressman stops before speaking, "Visitor? Who would come here at this hour in the morning?" The Congressman looked over to where Agent Anderson was seated, and Anderson looked down at the floor. Bill continues, "It's a lady, Sir, and she says she is an old friend of yours." The Congressman shakes his head and walks through his private office door. Sitting in a chair in front of his desk, back turned toward the door, was a woman with short blonde hair in a military uniform. His movement alerted her to his presence, and she turned to face the Congressman. "Julie" flowed over the Congressman's lips before he could compose himself. Julie stood from the chair and hugged the Congressman, saying, "It has been a long time, Kevin. I'll bet over twenty years. Remember the night of the prom." Her words carried the Congressman back to when he was a young man and a warm spring night at the high school prom. His only response was, "I remember. Let me close the door so we may talk."

The Congressman closes the door and moves closer to Julie. "How could I forget the night of the prom?" He begins. "You told me while we were dancing you wanted to get high, do you remember?" Julie replies, "Of course I remember. And you don't know what you missed out on that night." Followed by a small laugh. The Congressman looks down at the floor and says, "I am sure."

The conversation became more serious when the Congressman said, "I was sorry to hear about your husband,

Jeff. A terrible accident. Are you okay?" Julie's face loses the smile when she answers, "I am fine. Jeff, being a test pilot, always understood the risk and accepted it. The Osprey that took his life was not ready to fly, and I think he understood that. But his mission was to prove or, in this case, disprove its safety. Comes with the job. Three years ago, it still seems like it happened just yesterday." The Congressman replies, "I am very sorry it happened. Jeff was a great guy." Julie responds, "Thank you. But you have also had a bad time the last year or so." The Congressman speaks slowly, "We all have our crosses to bear. I have learned over the last year that it is not how you handle the good things in life but how you handle the bad. I pray to God that I am handling it well. But what about you? You graduated from the Air Force Academy and were flying F-16 fighters." Julie smiles and says, "I told you I wanted to get high, and I did. That's all. I just needed a little more power to get there."

Congressman Harris laughs, saying, "I should have taken you up on that prom night. But why are you in Washington today?" Julie smiles and says, "Today, I am going to fly a bunch of investigators over the Patapsco River area, the site of the Baltimore Bridge, in a helicopter, of all things. And I am running late right now to pick up my bird and get over there. Good to see you again, Kevin. Please keep in touch. Maybe a drink or lunch. My telephone number is on the desk. I need to go. See you later." And Julie left the private office.

The Congressman watched as she strolled out the front door of his office. And just like all memories, she walked away into a place we call the past.

As the Congressman moved into the center office area, Bill gave him a look. "Old friend, uh, Sir?" Said Bill. The Congressman responds, "Yeah, Bill, just an old long-time friend." Bill responds, "She is quite a looker, Sir." The Congressman looks at Bill before speaking, "Watch it, Bill. She has her own private F-16 fighter and knows how to use it. Agent Anderson, please lock the front door. We need to get started with the information we now have. Is there a pot of coffee in the office? We will probably need it." Bill replies, "Coming up, Sir."

Five minutes later, three men on a mission were standing over a flat table, spreading the documents from the briefcase nearly out for review. The Congressman inserts the thumb drive into his computer and downloads its information. He sat deep into his chair before beginning and thought, 'Now, Agent Zhōu, who the hell are you really?'

The printer on the desk of the Congressman came to life and started spitting out paper after paper of documents from the downloaded file. It would be a long day based on the number of printed pages. The Congressman felt sure someone had disguised the answer to Agent

Zhōu's true identity deep within this pile of paper, and he and his team of Bill and Anderson would learn the truth. The only question remaining was how long it would take and whether they had enough time before the next attack on the United States.

How do you tackle the problem of attacks on the United States when the head F.B.I. investigator is involved? The better question is, why is he involved?

CHAPTER SEVEN

The Secret Haystack

The printer continued to spew out the documents. Page after page filled the printer's exit bin. It became apparent Agent Zhōu had been busy over his many-year career with the F.B.I. The only question in the Congressman's mind was who he was working for.

Agent Anderson suggested we arrange the papers into case or project numbers as the printed documents laid on the long flat table. He identified the location of each number on the page and circled it to make it easier to find. Agent Anderson noticed either Agent Zhōu's handwriting was terrible or inconsistent or someone else had signed the forms. The single forms alone would not make this evident, but when Bill placed them side by side to review, it was apparent the handwriting was not the same. Bill comments, "Not only can this guy speak different languages, but he can also disguise his handwriting and signature."

As we worked, sorted pile after sorted pile began to form on the table. Hours slipped by, and the printer continued to fill its exit bin only to be emptied and fresh paper refilled by Bill or the Congressman. Finally, cases we could recognize began to come off of the printer. Most notable was the COVID-19 investigation he worked on in years past. The Congressman said, "This file, Agent Anderson, would be a good base point to start with as it was well known to each of us and recent enough." Agent Anderson left the private office to get another table to work on the COVID-19 case isolated from the other documents.

Included in the COVID-19 documents were photos of the Lab in Wuhan, China. From the image, you can see the large size of one of the leading lab buildings and, in the background, the hills and sprawling power line towers used to feed the electricity to the Lab. The Lab appears surrounded by a wire fence to keep unwanted stray people away, but it is not much of a barrier to protect someone from a deadly virus. Also visible are other buildings of some purpose, unknown and unidentified in the photo.

Wuhan Lab China

Strangely, within Agent Zhōu's file concerning the Lab in Wuhan was another report from another agent, unsigned and undated, that follows:

"The idea that the coronavirus leaked from a lab in Wuhan, China — instead of jumping from animals to humans — was dismissed as a conspiracy theory by many scientists a year ago. That has changed now. As President Biden's chief medical adviser, Dr. Anthony Fauci, told a Senate Appropriations subcommittee: The historical basis for pandemics evolving naturally from an animal reservoir is extremely strong. And it's for that reason that we felt that something similar like this has a much higher likelihood than the virus artificially made in a lab and released by accident."

The author added another sentence at the bottom of the page that someone particularly blacked out. It read: "No one knows, not even I, 100% at this point, which is the reason why we are in favor of further investigation." This one sentence was placed in the file to be unnoticed or overlooked by an average person reading the report.

Someone had altered an essential part of the document to remove or limit the visibility of the part about further investigation into the Lab at Wuhan, China.

The most disturbing part of the Lab at Wuhan file was why Agent Zhōu was involved. Agent Zhōu's background was not in chemistry or viral engineering; what was his involvement? The various investigators produced every report page in English, not Chinese. So what did they need Agent Zhōu to do with it? The three men continued to sift slowly through the pages relating to COVID-19, and a pattern began to form. The COVID-19 file was not a report or investigation performed by Agent Zhōu. Agent Zhōu edited other investigators' reports and other documents and 'adjusted' them to steer the talking points away from the lab leak theory. Agent Zhōu had edited numerous areas of the reports, altering them, leading anyone to believe the lab leak theory was the most unlikely source of a virus that killed millions of people around the world.

The remaining question was how Agent Zhōu got assigned to such a critical investigation. We were sure in the F.B.I. that you do not raise your hand and volunteer for an inquiry. How did Agent Zhōu get assigned? That was the answer we spent the next hour searching for. The answer was as strange as the source of the virus itself. It came in a simple note from an Asian doctor practicing in D.C., and it read: "If the virus is of Chinese origin, I, Dr. Jhusa, would highly recommend people of Asian heritage investigate to add a possible layer of resistance of being infected should they come in contact with the virus." This doctor's recommendation got Agent Zhōu assigned to assist in the critical investigation ahead of more qualified investigators.

The Congressman took the doctor's note to his desk and picked up the phone. Dialing information, he requested the number of Washington, D.C. American Medical Association. He dials the phone number, and after a voice answers, he introduces himself and requests to speak with a representative. "Yes," The Congressman begins, "I am trying to locate a Doctor Jhusa who practices in Washington, D.C." He waits for an answer. The voice returns and answers, "Yes, Sir, he did practice here briefly but decided to return to China to continue his practice. I hope this information helps you." The Congressman replies, "Thank you very much. It helps more than you could know." And the Congressman hung up the telephone.

The Congressman looks up to Bill and Agent Anderson and says, "Agent Zhōu was a plant on this investigation by the Chinese. This so-called doctor who created this note returned to China after he had done the job the Chinese had sent him to do. Since no one knew what the COVID-19 virus was, it was easy to deceive F.B.I. staff. Everybody was afraid, and this note was enough to push Agent Zhōu on to the inquiry.

Agent Zhōu reviewed the entire thing and adjusted documents and reports to push the natural origin of the virus. He alone blocked the truth from coming out. Agent Zhōu may be responsible for the death of hundreds of thousands of people because of his actions. It will be a long night, so let's keep going. There must be a lot more stuff here. What's next?"

Bill looks up quickly, "Hey, what is this? It looks like a person's name and pictures. Let's see here it said 'Huang Yanling.' I wonder who that is?" Agent Anderson tips back his head, trying to remember the name, and says, "That's the person believed to be 'patient zero' at the Wuhan Lab. She disappeared from the Wuhan Institute early in 2020 and is believed to be dead, and all records of her existence disappeared also. From what I recall, the Chinese government stated she never existed and was a conspiracy theory to pin the virus on China. The photos of her on the Internet were a ruse to move the conspiracy theory forward and are not real."

Bill hands the document to the Congressman and says, "Well, here is the person who does not exist with her photos of her working in the Lab. What I find strange is the document has been stamped with, 'Do not remove from this file or distribute' and signed by Agent Zhōu."

Huang Yanling Photo

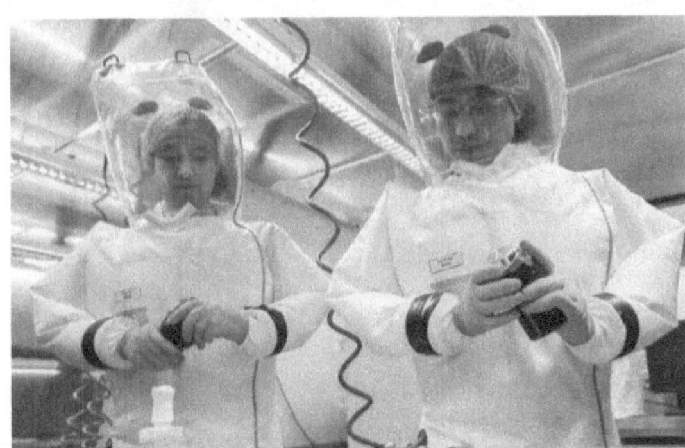

Huang Yanling at work in the Wuhan Lab in China

The Congressman responds, "It is starting to make sense now. The Chinese needed to stall the investigation and used their inside guy, Agent Zhōu, to put the brakes on it. No one would question his judgment, and he was the one person who could make it all go away. These official photos would have supported what was on the Internet, and the Chinese could not afford that to happen. What else can we find here tonight? See if you can find anything on the Baltimore Bridge in all this stuff."

The three men sifted through the piles of documents, searching for a mention of the Baltimore Bridge incident. They found nothing in the piles of documents on the table. Bill looks at the Congressman and asks, "Well, what does that mean if we can not find anything about the Bridge?"

The Congressman bites his lip and says, "I had advised Agent Zhōu that the Chinese were likely involved with the Baltimore Bridge incident. I know that because I pointed it out to Agent Zhōu when Ken discovered it in the book, 'We Are the Dragons.' I did not tell Agent Zhōu where the information came from, only that it was in the book—knowing that Agent Zhōu should have documented it somewhere. Yet, we do not see a mention of the bridge or Chinese connection anywhere here. That would have derailed the Chinese hackers and limited their ability to execute the plans to destroy the U.S. infrastructure.

Ultimately, Agent Zhōu was buying time for the other hackers to complete their missions. Ken figured out there were twenty-four Chinese hackers, enabling us to round them up before they could do the deed. Now we need to look through this stuff and find notes where Agent Zhōu used Ken's program Criptor Seven Version Nine to locate the Cartel control centers in the United States."

Two more hours of sifting through documents came up without information about 'We Are the Dragons' or the 'Criptor Seven' software. Agent Anderson speaks up, "Sir, how did Agent Zhōu give up the addresses of the Cartel control centers if he did not scan the book 'We Are the Dragons' and get them?"

The Congressman takes a moment before speaking, "Agent Anderson, Agent Zhōu did not need to scan the book to get the addresses because he already had the list of the Cartel control centers. He is the son-of-a-bitch who wrote the book! There is no other way Agent Zhōu could have gotten the information. He needed to use the Criptor Seven to scan the book, or Agent Zhōu had his own list because he created the book. That means Agent Zhōu had copies of both books and all the codes required to destroy the United States Infrastructure, and I have the only other set of books to defend the infrastructure. If there is such a thing, the good news is that Agent Zhōu does not know we are aware of who he is. The bad news is Agent Zhōu may find a way to redistribute the 'We Are the Dragon' books and import additional hackers."

Bill asks, "Can we just call the Director of the F.B.I. and inform them of what we have found?" The Congressman replies slowly, "Bill, if I told you a story like this, you would think I was reading it out of a conspiracy novel. The Director would laugh at me and send me for evaluation at the local V.A. Hospital."

"But, Sir," Bill responds, "I did not see anything in these files stating Agent Zhōu has any computer training. Where did he get the training to perform this hacking?" The Congressman says, "I don't know for sure, but I think our man Ken can find out if anyone can."

Agent Anderson says, "Sir, we are making many as-sumptions here so far. We have no direct proof that Agent Zhōu is a Chinese spy, hacker, or anything else. These documents can all be explained away as mistakes, omis-sions, or outright errors." The Congressman goes to his briefcase on his desk and removes another folder before speaking, "As I told both of you when we started this, there would be no secrets between us while within this room. I traveled to Miami to interview a detainee who attended a meeting to take down the United States. I have verified every part of his story, which checks out precisely as he described it. This includes the people in attendance, the plan, and everything. He identified Agent Zhōu as a person at the meeting with a Chinese ambassador using

a computer and referencing the book 'We Are the Dragons while doing it. I verified Agent Zhōu's identification
before making any accusations against him. Agent Zhōu
was at the meeting in Mexico, and Agent Zhōu was the
man operating the laptop computer; Agent Zhōu is the
twenty-fifth hacker we will need to take down."

Bill replies, "Are you sure, Sir? The head man at the
F.B.I. will be a problem to attack. They will cover their
own up to the very end. They may even come after us for
suggesting they have a spy onboard."

The Congressman replies, "We do not plan to attack
Agent Zhōu directly through the F.B.I. We have some
leverage right now. Agent Zhōu is not aware we are onto
him. He and I have both books, 'We Are the Dragon'. And
we have a secret weapon unavailable to him. We have
Ken the crackpot on our side."

The Congressman looks around the office at the piles
of classified documents. "Bill," he says, "We will need a
large safe for this office tonight." Bill responds, "Tonight,
Sir?" The Congressman replies, "Tonight, Bill, get on the
phone and get the safe company here tonight." Bill looks
at Agent Anderson for support before speaking, "Well, I
don't know if I can get them here tonight with a safe."
Agent Anderson responds, "Of course, we can get one
here tonight. Let's tell them the President's Head Secret
Service Agent requests an emergency delivery of one
large safe to this address within the hour." Bill gives Agent

Anderson a look that would kill before speaking, "It is five o'clock, and I have a dinner date with a hot blonde at six thirty downtown. A safe delivery will take some time to arrive and install." Agent Anderson replies, "I will be here with you. Call the blonde and tell her something came up that is a national security issue. Women like that kind of stuff. I use it all the time, and it works great."

Bill picks up the phone, calls the hot blonde date, and pitches the national security line to her. He was surprised at how well she accepted it and would be happy to reschedule the date if Bill told her how he was saving the world. Shaking his head, Bill agreed to give up the world's secrets at the following date.

"All right, that's done." Said Bill, "Now I will call the safe company and get them here to install a safe tonight. After that, Agent Anderson and I will secure these documents and lock this place down. Is that agreeable, Sir?" The Congressman replies, "That is more than agreeable, Bill. Just get it done and make everything here secure."

The Congressman picks up his briefcase and starts toward the door, and behind him, he hears Bill ask Agent Anderson if he would show him his gun. The Congressman yells as he opens the front door, "No gun, Bill, you do not need a gun." And the Congressman left the office for the evening.

CHAPTER EIGHT

A Day at the Office

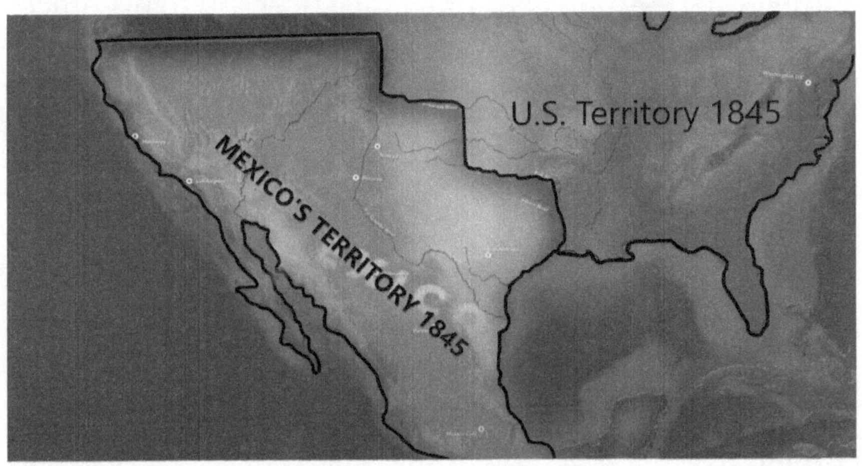

As Congressman Harris entered the office the following morning, he could see Bill and Agent Anderson looking tired after a long night, waiting for the safe to be installed and securing all the documents before going home.

Bill speaks first, "All set, Sir. Capital Safe Company installed a new high-security safe in your private office, and everything was secured inside as you requested. Oh, one other thing. I needed to dip into the petty cash fund and tip the three workers a hundred bucks each." Congressman Harris stops and looks at Bill before replying, "Everybody in Washington has their hand out for something, and cash is king. For another hundred, they would have probably left the delivery truck here."

The Congressman continues the short trip to his office. Opening the door, he sees a shiny silver safe in the corner of his private office, almost six feet tall and three feet wide. He estimated it weighed about two thousand pounds and carefully looked at the bottom of the safe to view its wheels. The Congressman turns to Bill and Agent Anderson, saying, "I don't see any wheels on the safe. How did they move this thing in here?" Bill looks at Agent Anderson for the answer but finds no details coming forth. It was now up to Bill to describe how the safe got into the office in all the gory details.

The detailed installation of the safe spewed from Bill's mouth, "Sir, this is going to sound much worse than it was. Due to the weight of the safe and its physical size, the workers needed to cut the carpeting and remove it from the center of your office. Once they rolled the safe in on a dolly, they drilled into the cement floor under the carpeting and bolted the safe to the floor using large anchor bolts to secure it. And the damage to the door frame I will have repaired next week after everything settles down." The Congressman interrupts, "You mean we can not move this safe or relocate it somewhere else in this office?" Bill replies, "Exactly, Sir. It can not go anywhere. It does not get any more secure than that." Congressman Harris responds, "Yeah, that's what I thought. By the way, the pattern on the carpet does not seem to line up correctly anymore." Agent Anderson says, "Well, Sir, that is the best the workers could do after they cut it all out. It was tough to get it that good. By the way, I took the liberty of installing a one-way film on the window glass later today so we can see out, but no one can see in. Security will install the window film within the hour."

The Congressman moves over to his desk chair, sits, and looks at Bill and Agent Anderson before speaking, "If I ever need a tomb built, you are the two I would call. Bill, before we begin sorting through the documents in the safe, is there anything else I need to do."

Bill walked over to the Congressman's desk and handed him two large keys for the safe. "These," Bill said, "must be inserted into the tumbler dial before you enter the combination, or the safe will not open."

Bill and Agent Anderson left the private office and closed the door. The Congressman sat staring at a monster silver thing in the corner of his once beautiful office. The beast taunted him as it sat there with a blank face of defiance as if screaming, 'Come on, try and open me.'

A knock on the door alerted the Congressman his day was still just beginning. Bill opened the door and peeked in through the crack, "I have something else here, Sir, that needs to be in your office." Congressman Harris sits expressionless, wondering what other surprises await. Bill opens the door wide, and two workmen roll in a medium-sized computer desk and place it in the only remaining corner of the room. The Congressman speaks softly, "And what is that desk for?" Bill replies, "Why Ken will need a workplace." Then, Bill closed the door to the private office, leaving Congressmen Harris to enjoy the privilege of his position.

There was a knock on the door just after eleven a.m., and Bill handed Congressman Harris the latest report on The Republic of Sanctuary, which contained notes on the newly formed Republic's progress.

It had been over four months since Congressman Harris received his first report from the Border Agents on the Republic of Sanctuary wall. The first report detailed daily activities and logged issues encountered, including under the heading 'high priority issues,' he found the details of three bodies recovered. The Congressman hoped this report would be more positive.

He could almost feel the blood pumping in his fingers as he opened the sealed document case and slowly withdrew the pages containing the report. Placing the report on his desk, he begins to read: "Over the last four months, Border Agents have not recovered any deceased citizens of Sanctuary." The Congressman paused for a moment to thank God they had stopped killing each other.

The following paragraph of the report totaled the number of arrivals in the Republic by the week since it was last reported. A quick look at the numbers showed over Thirty-five hundred more guests have arrived in less than seven months since the first arrivals. It appears the black ice agents are doing their job of getting these violent people out of the States, and all with the help of the sanctuary cities. By all appearances, these cities finally realized that they could not support crime in their streets and needed to do something.

The following page detailed the food, material supplies, and fuel delivered to the Republic under foreign aid. A footnote detailed how Border Agents calculated the amount of each commodity needed by the number of citizens in the Republic. Inventory completed at the time of delivery showed the calculations to be correct, and agents will repeat them once per month.

Then, the third page of the report caught the Congressman's attention with the heading in large print, "Encounters and Escapes." The Congressman sat deep into his chair and began to read the latest tale of escape from the island:

"As of this writing, there have been no escapes from the Republic of Sanctuary. We have experienced several encounters along the divider wall, and a warning repelled the intruders."

The Congressman smiled while thinking, 'So far so good.'

The report continued: 'This time, there was another challenge for the security Buoys with what appears to be a modified EV car."

The Congressman places his hand on his forehead and rubs it gently, thinking, 'I can't wait to read about this. A car that can drive on water.'

He continues to read the report: 'At some point over the last few months, some of the Citizens of Sanctuary modified one of the EV cars into an electric powered boat. From images captured on surveillance cameras, it appears the citizens modified the bottom and sides of the EV car, enclosed in a wooden tub resembling a large rowboat. It also appears the Citizens removed the wheels from the EV car, and makeshift paddle wheels were mounted to the drive wheel assemblies to propel the car/boat through the water. Surveillance cameras captured several passes back and forth along the beach to test the vehicle they created. After what they believed to be a successful set of test runs, the car/boat was launched by several Citizens just after midnight on the 12th of this month. Surveillance cameras captured approximately two hundred Citizens along the beach area to witness the test escape in the car/boat. The first warning laser locked onto the craft as the car/boat approached Buoy number eighty-nine. Twenty-two seconds later, Buoy number eighty-eight locked a warning laser onto the craft. At that time, warning alarms sounded, declaring imminent danger to the craft and the two Citizens believed to be in the car/boat. The craft steered directly between the two Buoys, and warning shots were then fired by the Buoys to warn off the craft. The craft continued its direct course between the Buoys, and the Buoys fired approximately fifty twenty-caliber tracer rounds at the car/boat to deactivate it. Unfortunately, the tracer rounds ignited the car/boat's batteries, and a massive explosion and fire ensued. The Navy Base on the island's Eastern side was then on high alert as they believed the base might be under attack because of the bright red and yellow fire from the burning of the EV car batteries that lighted the sky. Three Navy helicopter gunships were dispatched by Navy Command to evaluate the situation from the air over the island's Western shore.

Border Patrol immediately informed Navy Command on the island that there was an electrical fire on the Western side, and the Commander called off the alert. According to the Navy Commander, the recording equipment on each of the three Navy helicopters malfunctioned, and no video evidence of the electrical fire exists for some unknown reason.

At this time, we have not recovered the remains of anyone believed to be in the car/boat and, frankly, do not believe we will recover the remains of anyone in the car/boat.

The Republic will need a replacement EV car sometime in the future, and I will advise when that becomes necessary."

The Congressman sat back in his deep chair, thinking, 'They must have thought the buoys were a bluff. And then his thoughts turned to the fact that a twenty-caliber gun is the same as one used on fighter jets to shoot down aircraft, and a twenty-caliber firing tracer is even worse. Tracer rounds are on fire as they travel through the air. I wonder how fast these people thought that car/boat would go?'

The Senior Border Agent signed the report detailing the Republic of Sanctuary, dated the day before yesterday.

The Congressman picked up his secure telephone and directly dialed the island's Head Border Agent, Mr. Fuller. The Agent answered, and the Congressman introduced himself. The voice on the other end of the line echoed, "Good to hear from you, Congressman. What can I do for you?" The Congressman replies, "I have received and read your report covering the last few months. We must acquire signs and post them along the beach area on the island's West side." The Agent interrupts and suggests what the signs should say, "How about? Maybe, No Swimming?" The Congressman pauses and then speaks, "No, this is important. They must clearly state the Buoys are equipped with live torpedoes. Do not use any submerged vehicles in these waters. Make the letters large and in several languages so there can be no mistake."

The Border Agent questions the Congressman, "Sir, do they actually have torpedoes on the Buoys." Congressman Harris replies, "Take my word for it; they are there and very lethal. Get the signs made and post the signs immediately before they try to build a submarine to escape and find out for themselves they are real. Have a good day." And the Congressman hung up the phone.

Congressman Harris leans back in his chair, thinking, 'Well, I guess when you live by the sword, you die by the sword; only this time, they were killed by a Buoy. I can not imagine how that EV car lit the sky over the island. It must have been like the 4th of July on steroids.

The Congressman presses down the intercom to summon Bill. The private door opens, slamming into the monster safe, and Bill looks in. "Do you need something, Sir?" Bill asks. "Bill sent a note to the committee reviewing those EV cars and their batteries for safety. Inform them I have an unpublished report that the batteries can catch fire on impact. Leave it there; they can call me for more information." Bill responds, " Sir, can EV cars actually catch fire and explode? Is that a fact or a scare tactic against the manufacture of EV cars?" Congressman Harris replies,

"An EV car may catch fire and explode when struck by a foreign object. A lot depends on the object that hits the car."

Bill could tell the Congressman was not telling him the entire story about the EV car-catching file problem but did not question the answer given. On the other hand, Congressman Harris did not want to tell Bill that the EV car was fired at by a security buoy on The Republic of Sanctuary either.

As Bill closed the door, the Congressman thought, 'Now, I need to return to work on these other projects while there is still time. That monster safe in the corner must be full of information, and we must find it.'

CHAPTER NINE

Destiny Takes a Hand

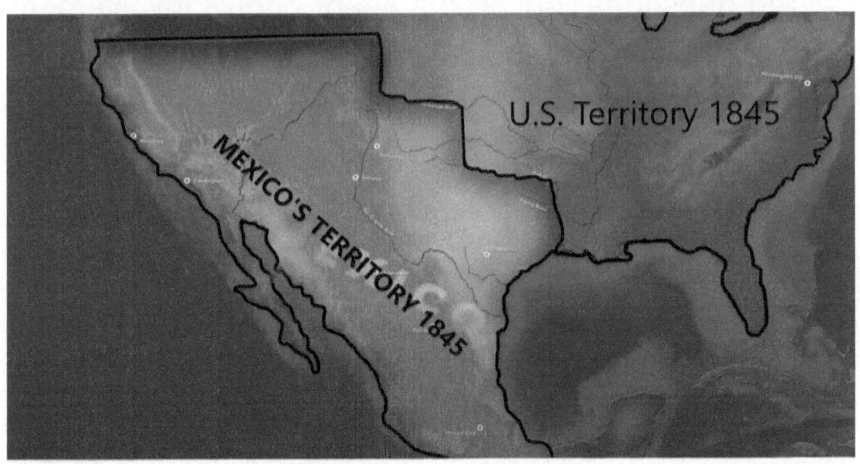

There never seems to be a shortage of things to do when you are a Congressman. John Lennon said it best, "Life is what happens to you while you're busy making other plans." Today, we planned to tackle the documents secured within that monster safe again, and life was adding detour after detour to those plans. The Congressman swore he could hear the documents calling; I'm in here, come and get me. Unfortunately, the documents needed to wait between the telephone, reports, and other paperwork.

He turned and pressed the intercom button to call Bill, his secretary. Bill answered with the familiar, "Yes, Sir, do you need assistance?" The Congressman says, "See when we can get Ken back here. We have too many unanswered questions concerning Agent Zhōu's involvement with this. Maybe he can figure some of this out?" "Got it," Bill replies and hangs up the intercom.

Another hour passes, entertaining the grand opening of a major store chain downtown. The Congressman declined the invitation as politely as possible, stating that he had a prior engagement. Of course, the preceding engagement may prevent a nuclear war, but he did not feel the invitee needed that information.

The one thing becoming apparent today was that it would not yield insight into what was in the silver monster. The Congressman looked around his beautiful office and saw chairs piled on each other. A safe large enough to be in a small bank. An armed security agent is stationed directly by the President sitting outside his office. A computer desk shoved into the only remaining corner of the private office and a window resembling a 'line-up' viewing window in a jail. He could see out, but no one could see in. The only thing not present was a character from the movie 'Star Wars,' but the day was not over, and he figured that character would show up sooner or later.

It was becoming evident they would need a better plan to move forward with the investigation as to what was in the safe. The plan came into being just before five p.m. that day with a call from Julie, the old friend and F-16 pilot from years before.

The buzzer of the intercom sounded, "Congressman," Bill says, "Someone on the telephone for you." Congressman Harris responds, "Who is it? I don't want to speak with anyone right now. Take a message and tell them I will call them tomorrow or the next day." Bill replies, "Okay, Sir, I will tell Julie you are very busy and that you will call her back when you get a chance. Is that okay?" The Congressman pauses and answers, "It is at this very moment, Bill, I realize what a jackass you can be. What line is Julie on?" Bill answers, "Line three, but if you are busy, I will tell her so." The intercom went dead, and Bill could see line three light as the Congressman took the call. Bill sat back in his chair and thought, 'Well, I guess he was not as busy as he believed.'

Congressman Harris starts the conversation, "I did not expect to hear from you so soon Julie." Julie replies, "The fly over the accident site the other day did not take very long, and the next day nothing was scheduled. I am currently stationed in the Washington D.C. area at Bolling Air Force Base." The Congressman responds, "I have never been there; what is it like?" Julie replies, "Small, actually very small. The Navy and the Air Force share the facility. The Air Force part of the base features a nine hundred square meters helipad. That is where I flew out of the other day. The rest consists of civilian families and other military personnel housing. A little city of military people waiting for reassignment somewhere else." The Congressman laughs and says, "Sounds exciting." Julie responds, "Trust me, exciting is not the term one would use for Bolling AFB."

The Congressman asks, "Well, where are you now?" Julie replies, "Standing in a library about to close, trying to find something to read tonight. I find it amazing that I can stand surrounded by all these books and can't even find a good conspiracy novel to read." Congressman Harris responds, "Maybe you should write a book. I am sure your experiences as a fighter pilot should provide a wealth of things to write about." Julie answers, "I can't write anything anyone would want to read or even believe. If I were to put my experiences in the Air Force as a pilot on paper, people would think I made them all up. Strangely, I fly an aircraft worth tens of millions of dollars, yet no one would believe me if I told a story about my experiences." The Congressman interrupts, "Dinner tonight?" Julie replies, "I thought you would never ask. Text me from your cell to this number, and I'll text you the address where I am. I will see you shortly." Julie hung up her cell phone and waited for the text message from the Congressman, and she replied with the library's address.

A half-hour later, Congressman Harris arrived at the library, and Julie and the Congressman headed to a nearby restaurant for dinner. "Table for two." Said the Congressman. Julie and the Congressman were seated in a booth at the rear of the restaurant within five minutes under low lights and soft music playing in the background.

Julie said, "You seemed to be under a lot of stress, Kevin. What is wrong?" The Congressman replied nothing and everything, I guess. It comes with the job; things are all going right, and things are all going wrong, and many times both on the same day. How about you? What is going on with you?" Julie looks down while speaking, "I am in a position of, well, between jobs, let us say. Nothing is going on for a female F-16 pilot. Female F-16 pilots become window-dressing to highlight diversity in the military. Sure, we fly missions in combat, but the hazardous stuff is still reserved for the male pilots. Politically, a female pilot captured behind enemy lines is still unthinkable for apparent reasons. It is just part of the way things are in the military. Hurray for the women as long as they know their place."

The Congressman pauses, speaking slowly, "Well, what do you do all day at Bolling Air Force Base?" Julie replies, "I call the Officer on Duty every morning to see if I am needed, and frankly, hang around the base most days." The Congressman asks, "Julie, do you still have a security clearance, and if you do, what level is it at?" Looking unsure what Kevin was asking, Julie replies, "Well, all fighter pilots have a 'Top Secret' security clearance. For the second part of your question, flying any military aircraft, fighter jet, or helicopter must be current. Why?" The Congressman looks directly at Julie, "Because I need someone with a security clearance, someone I can trust, and someone I can rely on. Does that answer your question?" Julie replies, "But Kevin, I am in the Air Force and do not work for the Federal Government. How could I possibly help you?" The Congressman hands Julie a napkin and says, "I want you to write the name of your commanding officer on this napkin, and from there, I will handle it." "What is on your mind Kevin?" Asked Julie.

The Congressman sat back in his chair, repeating, "Wonderful things, Julie, wonderful things."

The Congressman drove Julie back to Bolling Air Force Base and escorted her to her living quarters. As Julie exited the Congressman's car and walked to her door, she heard Kevin yell, "My secretary Bill will call you tomorrow. Don't miss the call, and good night, Julie, and don't let the bed bugs bite."

CHAPTER TEN

A Day at the Office

Congressman Harris had a restful night's sleep for the first time in many months. In the short time he had spent with Julie, he had replaced the nightmares that waited around every turn for him, slowly replacing them with dreams of better things to come.

His conversation with Julie had breathed new life into the Congressman the evening before. As he readies for work, his thoughts return to a story that Julie had related to him last evening. The story concerned the events on the morning of Sept. 11, 2001, the day the United States came under a direct attack from al-Qaeda terrorists. While Julie stared into a blank space on the restaurant wall, she detailed the action of Major Heather Penney, one of the first fighter pilots in the air over Washington, D.C. It was that morning she was to intercept the hijacked United Airlines Flight 93 that was heading to the capital. In the scramble, she and Col. Marc Sasseville had to launch without live ammunition or missiles and were prepared to ram the Boeing 757 at the likely cost of their own lives and those of everyone on board the airliner.

While the story's details overpowered the Congressman with the sheer details of bravery, the only way to take down the Boeing 757 would be to use the F-16 as a ramming device like a kamikaze pilot. Julie continued. Penney's mother later revealed that we were thankful that Heather could put her emotions aside and not even consider her father might be the pilot of Flight 93.

The Congressman interrupts, "Are you telling me Penny's father was the pilot of United Flight 93? Julie paused, "As it turned out, John Penney was not, but John Penney was a captain for United Airlines at the time and flew 757s along the East Coast for months before, and Heather would not have known if her dad was or was not the captain of United 93. She would have taken the plane down, killing herself and everyone on board if necessary to protect the United States.

*Heather Penney -- The F-16 Pilot
Who Was Ready to Use Her Jet as a
Missile on 9/11*

As the Congressman brushes his teeth, his thoughts again wander to how difficult it is to get a signature on a good piece of legislation by many of his Congressional friends without making deal after deal to move things forward. There are not enough Heather Penneys in the world, he thought, not enough Heather Penneys.

When Congressman Harris entered his office the following morning, he handed Bill a napkin with a single name and phone number written on it. The Congressman instructed Bill to call the person on the napkin and work with him to have Julie assigned to work with Congressman Harris on a new recruitment project for the Air Force. Bill looks up before dialing the telephone and says, "Sir, are we going to have time to start a new recruitment project with all that is currently happening?" The Congressman pauses before replying, "Bill, please just make the call, and everything will work itself out in time." Bill says, "Well, yes, Sir, but what if he refuses to assign Julie? What should I do?" The Congressman stops in the doorway of the private office. He says, "Bill, ask the Colonel what he believes would be an improvement at his facility and link that improvement to the Colonel transferring Julie to us for the project." Bill answers, "But Sir, that sounds like a 'quid pro quo' deal, which is frowned upon." The Congressman fires back, "Bill, that is exactly a 'quid pro quo' deal, and right now, I am frowning on you for not making it happen. Welcome to the real way business in Washington is done. Welcome to the real world of politics."

As the Congressman continued to push open the door to the private office, he could hear the loud thump as the door slammed into the silver monster safe sitting behind the door. He thought, 'Two inches more, just two more inches, and the door would have cleared that damn safe.'

Bill calls the Air Force Colonel and promises to upgrade the recreation area at the base to get Julie assigned to the Congressman's staff for a recruitment project. Bill struck a deal with the Air Force Colonel, trading a new recreation center for Julie. Bill pressed the button on the intercom to inform Congressman Harris that they had struck a deal with the Colonel and that Julie would be made available for as long as needed. The Congressman replies, "Now see, Bill, that is how business is done in Washington. You scratch my back, and I will scratch yours. Bill, by the way, did you get hold of Ken, and if so, when can he come in and help us with all these documents?" Bill responds, "He is already on his way here. Another hour or so before he arrives. Should I go out and get him another gas card?" Congressman Harris replies, "I don't think a gas card will do it anymore. We need a complete review of the book 'We Are the Dragons' to see what Agent Zhōu omitted from his reports." Bill asks, "Then how should I plan to compensate Ken for his efforts?" Congressman Harris takes a moment before responding, "I guess we will need to give Ken cash or maybe gold bars like everyone else gets in the swamp."

Julie arrived at the office an hour later, and Bill directed her to go into the Congressman's private office. When Julie opened the office door, it crashed into the silver monster safe behind it. Julie looked at the Congressman and asked why he would put the safe there instead of out of the way of the door opening. The Congressman replied, "Part of our new security system is to keep un-wanted people out, and Bill and Anderson thought that would be a great alarm."

Two and a half hours later, Ken, Julie, Agent Anderson, and Bill stood in the center of the Congressman's private office. With all the key players present, the Congressman laid down the ground rules to avoid future problems with this project. Congressman Harris begins: "First, if anything goes wrong, I alone am responsible for every-thing here. Second, none of you have ever viewed the documents here or know of their existence. Everything you know about anything came from my mouth, period. Third, nothing can be copied or may leave this office area. Trust no one. The people we are investigating have little, if any, care for a life. Fourth, I do not know how far or who this involves. As bad as we believe this whole thing is, it may be far worse, so be alert and ready for anything."

Julie interrupts, "Kevin, I am the newcomer here, and I am not sure what this is about yet." The Congressman replies, "Be patient, Julie. By the end of today, you will understand."

Bill points to the corner of the room and tells Ken to set up his computer there. "I got this desk for you," Says Bill. Agent Anderson moves the two flat tables into the center of the office while Congressman Harris opens the monster safe for the first time. Julie looks in as the door swings open and responds, "What the hell did you guys do? Did you rob a stationary store of all their paper?" The Congressman replies to Julie, "I know there is a lot of paper in there, but it all means something, and that is why we are here to figure it all out.

Congressman Harris removes the hardcover book 'We Are the Dragons' and hands it to Ken. As he passes the book by Julie, you can see that she does not know what to make of the book with all of the brightly colored pictures on the cover. He advises Ken that a copy of the electronic version of the book is on a thumb drive in the safe." Ken replies, "Great, I need both to complete the scan and comparison. What do you think I should be looking for?" The Congressman responds, "I am not sure what to look for. Maybe I am just skeptical, but something doesn't seem right. There must be more to the books than we realize. We must check everything in them and break them down in every detail." "On it," Ken replies.

During this conversation, Julie stood off to the side, and from the expression on her face, she had no clue what was going on. The Congressman removed the paper documents from the safe and placed them on the flat tables. The large print "Top Secret" on the papers surprised Julie. She says, "Kevin, these should only be handled in a SCIF or secure facility." The Congressman replies, "Julie, I know precisely how they should be handled and what they are. These documents were provided to me by the highest authority to find out what they all mean and do what needs to be done. If you find this too uncomfortable to handle, I understand, and I will hold no hard feelings if you want out." Julie looks directly at Kevin before asking, "Is it that important to jeopardize your entire career and possibly end up going to prison?"

The Congressman did not answer and found himself without proper words to answer for the first time. Possessing these documents could mean going to prison, and no one would believe the source of their origins. Agent Anderson sees the Congressman searching for words to reply and steps in to assist. Agent Anderson speaks slowly and directly to Julie, "Julie, I was the Head Secret Service Agent for the President less than ten days ago. The President of the United States transferred me here to assist Congressman Harris in whatever this is. It is crucial, and I also stand to lose everything, but here I am. Sometimes, we need to step outside the usual way of doing things, and I believe this is one of those times.

While discussing the 'Top Secret' documents with Julie, Ken says, "This is strange. The book also references other places around the world. I see India and Mexico, and there is a reference to a pipeline on the United States East Coast."

Julie interrupts, "What the hell is that book about? All I see is a bunch of pictures." The Congressman softly replies to Julie, "The book is the road map full of hidden code to destroy most Western infrastructure in the United States. The stuff hidden in the book, 'We Are the Dragons,' was already used to take down the Baltimore Bridge and possibly other structures we have not yet discovered. We are all here to stop the people behind this plot. Julie, I need to know if you are in or out." Julie steps back and answers, "Are you kidding me? This is my chance to get back at these bastards that are attacking my country. I'm in. Where do you want me to start?"

Agent Anderson begins briefing Julie on how and why the documents were arranged by case or project number in the safe. He advised her they believed an F.B.I. head agent may be involved, and Ken was working to determine the extent of his involvement. After a very short time, it was apparent that Julie could pick out details that went together over different documents. Her Air Force training taught her to identify things and place them logically.

Ken tells the Congressman, "I see so many things hidden in this book. But I need someone to understand why they are here and what they mean." The Congressman asks, "Someone like who?" Ken replies, "The book is referencing places all over the world as, I think, targets. But there must be a reason for selecting these places and not others. Why pick a spot in India and not Russia or Germany? What is the significance of these places compared to, say, London."

Bill says, "The only person I can think of with a good background in world history is Professor Norris, but he does not have a security clearance to view this stuff. Congressman, maybe you can speak with him in a hypothetical mode and get the information from him that way."

The Congressman remembers the last time he used Professor Norris for information, which led to the F.B.I. raiding the Professor's home because he knew too much. He would hate to put the Professor and his family through that ordeal again. Reluctantly, the Congressman says to Bill, "See if you can arrange a dinner date with the Professor, and I will try and keep it as general and low-key as possible. The same restaurant in New York City as before would be great."

Bill left the room to call the Professor while the others continued to sift through the piles of materials. The Congressman stood staring at the piles of papers as the others reviewed each document. He thought one break, just one break, and this entire puzzle would begin to collapse. But if the one break were in the pile, it would be buried deep.

Julie sputtered, "Wait a minute, here is something about a power outage in India. Is that what Ken was talking about?" She handed the paper to Ken to review. Ken compares the paper to what he found in the book 'We Are the Dragons.' Ken responds, "Now that makes some sense. The book points to power generation stations in India. I will need to download and look at the hacker code, but this is likely what they were after."

Julie sputtered again, "Wait, here in Mexico, countries in South America, Taiwan, the Philippines, and others." The Congressman calls Bill in the other office, "Bill, I need a meeting. Get me a meeting with the Professor." Bill's voice echoed back, "I am trying, Sir. Please give me a little time."

The one thing that had become obvious was the extent of the operation, which used countries worldwide. The Chinese did not simply want to attack the United States; they were preparing to take down anyone who stood in their way of world domination. The Mexican government, in their short-sighted blindness, believed that once they recovered the territory loss in the 1848 Cession to the United States, China would leave them alone. The book 'We Are the Dragon' painted a far different picture of what would come. After China weakened the United States, other countries worldwide would fall prey to China, one at a time. There would be no one left to defend them from the cyber attacks launched by China. The adage, 'Divide and Conquer,' was the game plan, and the only thing standing in the way was a children's book named 'We Are the Dragons' and a handful of people crazy enough to take on the Chinese.

The Congressman then realized his crucial witness, Renel Destina, the Haitian informant, needed to remain in custody at the Miami Detention Center. Bringing him to Washington to testify before the Intelligence Committee would likely get him killed. Congressman Harris knows that Renel Destina is the only person who could or would positively identify Agent Zhōu as the person who was at the meeting in Mexico where discussions of destroying the United States took place. Destina also recognized Agent Zhōu as the person who was using the book 'We Are the Dragons' while using a laptop computer while at the meeting. The same book Agent Zhōu identified as nothing more than a poorly written children's book when questioned by Congressman Harris.

CHAPTER ELEVEN

It's All in the Details

What became evident was that the briefcase con-tained many fragmented incidents from around the world. The Congressman now understood why the President handed the briefcase over to him and did not handle the information it contained himself. The President of the United States had access to the world's most significant resources, but using those would lead to a direct offense to the Chinese. The documents and the evidence and claims presented within the documents would undoubtedly have led to conflict between China and the United States. With supporting evidence, it was clear that China had initiated one or more attacks on the United States and other countries. The giant balloon flying over the United States months ago was China's way of intimidating the President himself. It was a slap in the face of the most powerful man in the world for all to see.

It was also apparent that the President was well aware of what Congressman Harris had accomplished with the 'Black Ops' funding and approved of the Congressman's actions while still maintaining a 'plausible denial' stance. The most powerful man in the world, the President of the United States, was stuck between doing nothing and a possible nuclear war with China. A situation China was well aware of and would exploit as long as they could.

As Ken tapped on his computer keys, the other staff members read the documents as they were removed from the safe by the Congressman. Bill ordered a lunch delivery, and after a short break to eat the pile of foot-long submarines, the staff continued to dig through the mountain of papers. Julie tries to break the moment's seriousness by commenting about the takeout lunch Ken ordered. Julie says, "I noticed the pile of banana peppers you ordered on those subs. I should have known better than to eat those peppers. Those peppers and grapes, they are the ones that will kill me later." Ken replies,

"Don't worry, we will not dock you for bathroom breaks." And the staff began to laugh. Not wanting to be outdone, Agent Anderson replies, "I like grapes. Maybe I should bring some in tomorrow." Julie says, "You bring in grapes, and I will shoot you with your own damn gun." Congressman Harris smiles and says, "Okay, guys, no more grape jokes. Find me the key to all of this mess."

After what seemed to take forever, the Congressman's staff had sorted the documents into piles, aligning them in an order, trying to make sense of the papers. They grouped the location, type of incident, and period of each event. Everything was coming together except for a single sheet of paper that contained the name of a Senator without further information. Bill says, "Maybe that sheet of paper got into the briefcase by mistake?" Congressman Harris replies, "No, everything in the case is connected somehow to something. The Senator's name on the paper means something. Ken, could you take a moment to learn something about the Senator with your magic computer?" Ken looks up from his computer screen and says, "Right now, Sir?" Congressman Harris responds, "Sorry, Ken, but we need it now. This single page may be the missing link we have searched for."

Ken flips the computer display onto another screen and searches for information about the Senator. "Let's see here," Ken says aloud as he types. "Senator Jo Kim is forty-six years old, of Asian heritage, and has lived in the

United States all his life. Born in California, his mother is." Ken stops, "Give me a moment while I check something." Ken switches the computer display again and continues to read. After reading for a few minutes, Ken looks up at the Congressman and says, "Sir, it appears that Senator Jo Kim and Agent Zhōu are blood relatives. They are brothers by different fathers, and their mother and grandmother live in China. For some unknown reason, they both left the United States three years ago after the husband died in a hit-and-run accident. I have a report here by investigators that the hit and run was a targeted assassination, but they could not prove it. Someone, for some reason, moved the women to China shortly after the accident."

The Congressman stands in the middle of the staff before speaking, "Finally, this is all starting to make sense. China has two people inside to protect them from problems. A Senator and the Head F.B.I. Chinese investigator. That explains how Agent Zhōu moved so quickly to the top of the Washington D.C. office. With different last names, no one would link the two together as a family. And the Chinese sent a message by killing her husband that her entire family was within their reach as a target if they did not go along. Moving the mother and grandmother back to China places the Senator and Agent Zhōu into a vise to be squeezed by the Chinese whenever necessary. Can you determine if the mother and grandmother are U.S. Citizens?"

Ken switches the computer display to another screen before replying, "Yes, they are, Sir. Both were naturalized twelve years ago and still maintain United States Citizenships." The Congressman asks, "Ken, can you find out where they are in China?" Ken pauses before answering, "Sir, China is a closed society, and China highly restricts the Internet to the outside world. I can't just connect to China and say excuse me, can you give me the address of Mr. Smith. That does not work that way."

Congressman Harris replies, "Ken, don't bullshit me. I need to know where they are now, and I know you can get the required information." Ken responds, "But Sir, it would mean I need to make a connection to someone in China and use their computer connection by way of a satellite to work within China to find out the location of these people. And even if I could find them, what would we do? Knock on China's door and say open up and hand them over." The Congressman says, "Ken, I need the information about where these two people are in China. They are the wedge that is holding the entire scheme together. Without them, the Senator and Agent Zhōu would not be held hostage. Find them and figure out under what circumstances China is holding them."

Agent Anderson speaks, "Sir, do you think the President knew they were related and their mother and grandmother were taken back to China as leverage?" The Congressman takes a moment before answering, "That document got into the briefcase somehow, Agent Anderson. The President has some of the best intelligence people in the world. The problem with politics is nothing can be addressed directly by those in power. A good example would be if Iran wanted to remove the Iranian President. They would not force him to resign or even vote him out. He would perish in an accident and make him a dead martyr. Martyrs are forgotten quickly and leave little or no stain on the remaining people in power."

Congressman Harris calls over to Ken, "How is it going?" Ken stops typing momentarily, "Sir, I am doing my best. First of all, it is twelve hours later in China than here. Second, everything is in Chinese, and the computer must translate what I am reading. I have learned when and where they arrived in China and am now trying to track them from that location. I need a little more time and will have your answer."

Another hour passed before Ken answered, "Okay, the mother and grandmother are currently housed in. Are you kidding me? They are living in an apartment building in Wuhan, China. The Chinese have housed them a few miles from the Wuhan Lab."

The Congressman says, "That makes perfect sense. Should they need to pressure either of the brothers, they could remind them of the terrible things that could happen at the Wuhan Lab. Ken, is there a U.S. Embassy near Wuhan?" Ken begins to search again on the computer. "The U.S. Consulate General Wuhan, Room 4701, Jianghan District, Wuhan, in the New World International Trade Tower on Jianshe Avenue, less than five miles away," Ken replies.

The Congressman asks Ken, "Can the Chinese identify that your communications come from outside China?" Ken replies, "No, I am uplinking to a Starlink satellite, and it appears to China that my communications are coming from within China. It is a spoofing protocol hackers use to appear to be someone else." "And right now, who do they think you are?" The Congressman asks, "I am 'spoofing' and using one of the Beijing police computers as my connection point so that it would appear to them that I am Chinese law enforcement making inquiries." Replies Ken.

The Congressman continues, "How about the Wuhan Lab facility itself? Is there access to it from the Starlink satellite?" Ken sits back before answering, "Probably not directly through one of the computers in the Lab, but give me a few minutes here, and I will come up with something to open up the Lab like a can of sardines."

Ken opens a digital manual on his laptop and scans for the item he is searching for. "This is what I need," says Ken. The computer screen reads.

A.R.P. stands for "Address Resolution Protocol," a protocol for mapping an I.P. address to a physical M.A.C. address on a local area network.

A.R.P. is a program used by a computer system to find another computer's M.A.C. address based on its I.P. address. Once you have the M.A.C. address, any local communications will use the M.A.C. address and not the I.P. address, removing the security on electronic devices while communicating with another without questioning what or who is operating the device.

Agent Anderson asks Ken if he can see what he is reading, and Ken hands Agent Anderson a printout of this hacker command for review. Agent Anderson questions Ken, "You mean to tell me once you can connect to any device within the Wuhan Lab, and I mean any device, you can interrogate the entire Lab network?" Ken replies, "Well, it is not quite that easy. Reviewing the A.R.P. report and seeing what I want to work on will take me a few minutes. I don't want to view the contents of a printer or light fixture."

Agent Anderson moves close to the Congressman and speaks softly, "Are you sure he is on our side? This guy is scary at best." The Congressman responds, "He is our guy, Anderson, he is our guy."

Ken sits in front of his laptop computer and plays the keyboard like a piano, creating only music the computer can understand and searching for an unsecured device at the Wuhan Lab to allow access to all the other devices on the network. Finally, after over an hour of scanning, a device shows as active on the unsecured A.R.P. table at the Lab. It appeared to be a blood analyzer, and a test was being performed on a sample as he watched in real-time.

Ken looks to the Congressman and says, "That's what I have been waiting for, and I'm in." Ken begins to log that device's M.A.C. address and a list of others associated with that network at the Lab. It took time, but Ken finally completed the hard part and created a 'back door' into the Wuhan Lab to access anything that needed to be achieved. While Ken scanned the Lab's computer network, he located a server labeled, 'Employee Archive Records.' Wow, he thought, imagine what kinds of stuff you could find on this thing. And, of course, Ken, being the hacker he was, plugged in a large thumb drive and downloaded the entire employee file of the Wuhan Lab from the archive records server while searching for other systems on the network for information.

While Ken scanned the network at the Wuhan Lab, he noticed several disabled devices that were not reporting any activity. His review of the devices told Ken the disabled systems were mainly related to safety controls and warning devices. Ken sat thinking that if a required exhaust fan failed, the system would not report the failure for inspection and repair. Another atmospheric control that reported a positive pressure in the Lab indicating an imminent leak to the outside world, was not operational. Ken sat back in his chair, thinking, 'No wonder this place is such a disaster; things going wrong are not being recorded for repair by the safety devices.'

Ken secured his 'back door' access to the Wuhan Lab network and began to scan outside the Lab, searching for other devices of interest. He noticed device after device that the I.T. staff in Wuhan did not appropriately secure. He thought this place was a hacker's dream to troll for information.

The Congressman asks Ken, "Can we return to the lab to search for additional information later?" Ken replies, "I am leaving ports open as I go in case one or more of them are discovered by the Chinese I.T. staff. I am making it look consistent in the code as if the Chinese I.T. staff failed to correctly set it up during the initial installation, unlike someone who hacked into the system and altered the settings. I want to take a little time and see the location where they are housing the mother and grandmother of the Senator and Agent Zhōu. There must be something special or unique about where they are keeping them. I will link to the satellite and try to get an overview of the area around the Lab area."

Agent Anderson comments, "With all the problems and questions about the origins of COVID-19, you would think our intelligent people would know every inch of the area around the Wuhan Lab."

The Congressman speaks; someone on the inside must have been running interference for the Chinese. Someone more than Agent Zhōu and the Senator. I reviewed the findings of the Congressional committees and found inconsistent testimony throughout. If I were a betting man, following the money trail would lead to who is responsible for creating the COVID-19 virus and who blocked the world from discovering who financed it. I would not be surprised if the United States paid Wuhan to develop it, and when China got caught, it pressured the people who got the financing to keep quiet. Hopefully, it will all come out someday, and we can take down the people responsible."

Ken looks up from his computer screen and says, "I think we need to get out of the system for today. I am spending too much time in the Chinese system, which may raise suspicion to an alert I.T. guy. Tomorrow, I will go back and continue searching for more holes." Ken presses a few keys on the computer and unlinks from the satellite for the evening. "Besides," Ken says, "I have a full thumb drive from the Wuhan Lab I can scan through tonight to see what is on it."

Bill looks over at Ken before speaking, "How will you look through a thumb drive of information probably written in Chinese?" Ken replies, "The computer does not know the Chinese language. The laptop only sees 'zeros and ones' when it scans through it. I will take a list of topics, say names or places, and let the computer scan through the data on the drive and see if there is a match. If it finds a match, it will flag it with a short phrase before and after the 'hit' for reference. We can then read the short phrase and decide if we should be looking deeper into it." Bill replies, "Sorry, I questioned you on such a simple issue because that is what I was thinking of doing to scan the drive."

Ken laughs before speaking, "I am sure that is how you thought about doing it. Let me show you how easy it is. Let's search for 'Huang Yanling,' the first known person believed to have contracted COVID-19, the person zero who disappeared from the Wuhan Lab never to be seen again." Ken enters her name, presses the enter key, and waits for a response. After a few moments, he reads the screen and says, "The data on the drive tells me ...." Ken stops and stares at the computer screen without speaking. Bill says, "Well, what did the computer tell you?"

Ken turns his head slowly and addresses the group before speaking, "According to this archive file, 'Huang Yanling is still alive and being held in Wuhan!"

The Congressman interrupts, "Now that makes sense. She became infected and spread COVID-19 outside of the Wuhan Lab. When the Chinese figured it out, they 'disappeared her' and all of her records. She could tell the world the story of the origin of COVID-19, and they are hiding her so she can not talk. Bingo, we have a first-hand witness to who created the virus and why."

Agent Anderson speaks, "Well, Sir, we now know we have a witness, but may I point out she is Chinese in China, and they are not likely to hand her over for questioning. They went to a great extent to remove all traces of her existence. Why would they turn her over to the United States?"

The Congressman replies, "That is what I hate about the Secret Service, always telling me what I can not do. Don't tell me what I can not do. Tell me how we are going to do it."

Agent Anderson responds, "I just wanted to point out, Sir, that China is not open to giving up anything. Especially after they have spent a long time lying about it."

The Congressman sits in his office chair before speaking, "I don't plan to ask China to give up Huang Yanling or the Senator's mother and grandmother. We will put together a plan to go in and take them."

Agent Anderson shakes his head and responds, "Sir, With all due respect, China will not let anybody get anywhere near Huang Yanling. I believe, like many others, our government had something to do with the creation of the COVID-19 virus. I suspect the story of financing and a cover-up will become known in a few years. Probably just after the statute of limitations runs out, everybody will walk away."

The Congressman replies, "How tall are you, Agent Anderson?" Agent Anderson responds, "Sir, I am six foot one inch tall, African American, and weigh two hundred and eighteen pounds. May I ask why, Sir?" The Congressman looks at the ceiling before speaking, "You may be the tallest and darkest Chinaman in existence."

The Congressman spoke as the others in the room all looked at each other for an answer to that last statement, "Let's get this stuff back into the safe and call it a night. I want every one of you to think of a way to get someone out of China tonight, and we will discuss it tomorrow." With that said, the Congressman left the private office, leaving the group to deal with the papers and other documents.

As the group loaded the documents into the safe, Julie spoke, "Kevin has been under a lot of stress. Is it possible he is losing his mind?" Bill says, "There have been rumors the Congressman created an entire country within the last year. If those rumors are true, getting a few people out of China should be easy." Agent Anderson interrupts, "You people are all crazy. China would treat something like that as an act of war." Ken sat listening before speaking, "It would be an act of war if China knew who took them out of China. What if they got mixed in with the others migrating to the United States because of a mixup in paperwork or something? China could not blame the United States as we have told them not to come. But once they are here, they are fair game." Agent Anderson replies, "But how would the paperwork get mixed up in the first place?" Ken slides his laptop into his bag and says, "Passport documents are all electronic. I know a hacker who can take care of our problem. Why don't we all go home and think about it like the Congressman asks? Tomorrow is another day."

CHAPTER TWELVE

The Ground Work

The drive home from the Congressman's office gave him time to reflect on the day's events. It was now evident why the President presented him with the briefcase full of documents. The President of the United States could not assign staff to dive into what the papers indicated was happening without creating, at the very least, an international incident or, worse, a war with a significant world power.

He lost track of where he was along the way home, and his thoughts moved to what his wife and daughter would think he should do. Even in death, they were a driving force in his life. My God, he thought, I am standing in a position of creating a possible war, doing nothing, or risking more people's lives to do what is right. The President of the United States, the most powerful man in the world, transferred the task to him, and he was alone to do whatever was needed. He remembered what a staff member had said about something above his pay grade. What is the pay grade for something like this? At that time, he realized he needed help, not with the plan or project but with finding the strength to do what was required.

A short detour and three and a half miles later, Congressman Harris was where he needed to be. A place for those lost and seeking knowledge and wisdom. A place he knew he could trust. Sitting alone on a hard wooden bench, the Congressman listened for the echoes of the voices of those who had passed. It was here, in his church, that he believed he would find the guidance.

He thought that over many years of his life, he did not consider himself a hardcore believer in much of anything, including God. After the untimely death of his wife and daughter, he believed even less in a supreme being. But, spending time at the grave site of his wife and daughter, something changed. He honestly thought they were there and speaking with him.

While he sat silently alone in the shadows, he became aware of someone else very close. As he turned to his right, Reverend Richie came into view. The Reverend spoke softly, "Good to see you again, Kevin." "And it is good to see you again, Reverend." The Congressman responded. The Reverend sat alongside the Congressman for a short time without speaking. Finally, the Reverend said, "It is apparent you have something troubling on your mind." The Congressman begins to speak, and the Reverend stops him, "No, I do not need to know what the issue is you are trying to work out. My opinion or input on your line of work with the government would not be of much value. You only need to consider that what you are about to do is right and for the right reasons. Once you have aligned yourself on the side of what is right, everything else will fall into place."

The Congressman closed his eyes and lowered his head to digest what the good Reverend had just told him. When he re-opened his eyes to thank the Reverend, he realized he was alone again. Alone again but armed with the answer, he came to this place to find.

As he stood and left the church, he felt relief and almost satisfaction with himself. The Reverend's words kept repeating in his head, "What you are about to do is right and for the right reasons." Tonight, the Congressman would sleep well; tomorrow, his staff and he would design and lay the plan he knew was "right and for the right reasons."

During the trip to the office the following morning, the Congressman filled his head with questions and ideas but was void of answers. He reviewed the staff he already had on board and considered others to fill in the staff short-comings. As he drove his car, he defined the roles of each staff member. His secretary, Bill, was the backend per-son who contacted people and made sure office projects continued to get done. Agent Anderson was the first line of protection and had extensive military training. Military training would be helpful when planning an operation inside of China. Julie, someone the group could trust, was a pilot of the F-16, helicopters, and other aircraft and military training. Then we have Ken, the hacker program-mer. The Congressman saw Ken as the critical player in any plan to extract the people from China. They would need Ken for Wuhan's remote intelligence and to locate where the people they planned to extract were located at any given time. Also, Ken was required to re-evaluate the book 'We Are the Dragons' to see what details were not divulged by F.B.I. Agent Zhōu to conceal the book's true meaning.

What was missing was the group did not have someone with a historical background to provide insight into how people in different countries think and react. The group did not have a person to take custody of the people after a successful extraction for their protection. The group did not have a place to house the people for safety. The group did not have any method to transport anyone safely. They would also need assets from China and other locations to support operations. The Congressman was pulling into his parking place when he realized he did not know where the money was coming from to finance the operation.

My God, the Congressman thought, I haven't even arrived at the office, and my list of things we do not have is staggering.

As the Congressman enters through his office's main door, he is greeted by the staff in the central office area. To his surprise, they were all smiling and seemed excited about something. He paused and looked around the office for some indication of why everyone was excited, but he found nothing. "Okay," the Congressman begins, "Why are we so happy today?" Julie answers for the staff, "We talked after you left yesterday, and we concluded that you must be crazy to think we can go into China and rescue those people. Then we talked about the millions of people around the world the Chinese killed with the COVID-19 virus they created. It was then we realized you are not crazy. You are seeking justice for the people who can no longer seek justice for themselves. We are behind you and will do whatever it takes to make it happen."

Congressman Harris was without words for the first time in his life. He stood momentarily before speaking, "I have also given this idea much thought. I planned to walk in here today and offer to release anyone uncomfortable with this idea. Looks like you guys beat me to the punch. Thank you for your confidence and support."

The Congressman walks toward the private office door, stops, and says, "I hope we got coffee. I forgot to stop for some this morning. Five minutes, and we can get started. We have a lot to go over and think about. And today, you will hear the entire story of everything that has been done to date to help make the country safer."

With everybody on board, the adventure of a lifetime was about to begin in a small Congressional office in Washington, D.C.

CHAPTER THIRTEEN

The Plan Details

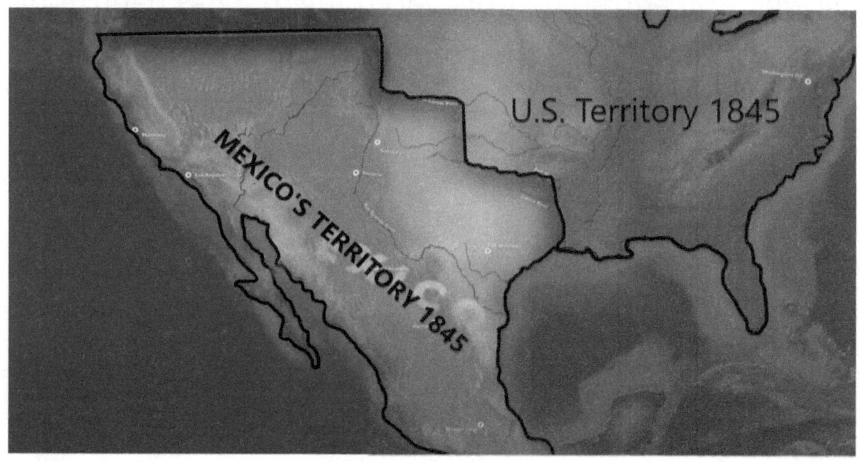

The staff gathered in the private office for the organizational meeting, with Congressman Harris sitting behind his desk. The Congressman begins the meeting by saying, "Before we move into this endeavor, I feel obligated to ensure we all know and understand what has been accomplished this year. If something I am about to say needs more detail, please stop me, and I will fill in anything I may have missed."

The Congressman pauses for a moment for questions before saying, "Earlier this year, I formed a small committee, and we created a new republic on an island sixty miles off the coast of California. The Republic's name is 'The Republic of Sanctuary' and is supported by a foreign aid commitment by the United States. The Republic shares the island with a United States naval base, secured by a border wall and ringed with security buoys." Agent Anderson interrupts, "Sir, what is the Republic used for?" The Congressman responds, "When an illegal immigrant commits violent crimes, and the country of origin will not allow the United States to repatriate them, they are removed and become a citizen of The Republic of Sanctuary. Periodically, I receive a report on what is happening at the Republic from the border patrol, and you are welcome to read them should you choose to do so."

Bill speaks, "So the rumors of you creating a new country are true." Julie asks, "And what about the sanctuary cities? How are you getting the problematic illegals out of those areas?" Congressman Harris responds, "Well, the sanctuary cities charters state they will not turn over immigrants to I.C.E. for deportation. So we created a new enforcement organization called 'Black I.C.E.,' and these cities are happy to turn these dangerous troublemakers over to them. We have created a 'Black I.C.E.' detention center and have our transportation system in place. The troublemakers become citizens of The Republic of Sanctuary and can make and live by the laws they create and enforce. Like any other country, the United States does not have jurisdiction in the Republic of Sanctuary and does not intervene."

Agent Anderson speaks, "Perfect, these people now live in a place where they can be violent to each other or learn to live together like civilized people."

The Congressman continues, "We have also learned of a plan by Mexico to take back the lands Ceded by them back in 1848." The group began to laugh. The Congressman says, "I know how that sounds, but it is true. Mexico had put together a plan to flood the United States with illegals and force the United States to surrender the land back to them. We learned of a meeting between Mexico, the Mexican Cartels, Chinese drugs distributed by the Cartels, groups of terrorists sneaking in to attack the U.S. from within, South American countries dumping their unwanted into the U.S., and the Chinese connection with all of it." The staff looked at each other for a moment, almost with a look of disbelief. Congressman Harris continues, "As hard to believe as this may be, you can't make this stuff up."

The Congressman paused while the group took some time to absorb everything he had just presented. Congressman Harris begins again, "That is an overview of what has happened and what we are dealing with. Now we have discovered China is holding two American Citizens and the likely first person to contract COVID-19. This is another piece of the puzzle we need to unravel in this tangled mess of a world. I think that brings everyone up to date. Do you have any questions?"

Again, the Congressman pauses for questions and continues, "So where are we today? Normally, I would consider creating a committee of congressmen for this mission. After due consideration, I realized it would be too risky for their careers, and the other side would be that it would make the operation appear to be being done by the U.S. government, which could lead to a war with China. A group of people must do this operation with a plausible denial of ownership by the United States. We are going to be that group of people. I have thought about who we have on our staff, and I can see we will need a few others to round out our group. Should something go wrong, the United States government will disavow any knowledge of our existence, and we could be considered outlaws outside the United States. One last time, are you still in, or would any of you like to pass on this one? No one here would blame you for leaving."

The entire group sat and waited for the Congressman to speak the following words. "It looks like we are all going to make this happen. Now it is time to get down to who we need to help us and how we intend to extract these people from China."

Congressman Harris says, "My thoughts this morning on who we may need to help is someone with a historical background to provide insight into how people in different countries think and react. A person to take custody of the people after a successful extraction for their protection. A place to house the people for safety after the extraction. Safe methods of transportation once these people are in our control. We will need assets within China and other locations to support this operation, and I need to secure the money to make it all happen. While I go to the other office to grab coffee, think about what I said and tell me what I forgot to consider." The Congressman stood and walked into the outer office to get a coffee, and the staff talked about what they had heard.

When the Congressman returned to the private office, he opened the discussion by saying, "Any questions or suggestions?" Bill was the first to speak, "When it comes to historical background and customs of foreign countries, the only choice would be Professor Norris." The Congressman looks at Bill and nods his head in agreement.

Agent Anderson was next to speak, "Sir, while I know it would not be ideal, you mentioned you have a facility you created for the 'Black I.C.E.' detention. I am sure they could convert part of it to good living quarters and what could be safer for the people we extract. I am sure they would understand, and it would likely be better than where they live in China."

Julie said, "Regarding transportation, I am qualified to fly most aircraft, including twin-engine jet transports. Besides, I have access to a SyberJet SJ30 private jet owned by a friend of my husband's. It has a top speed of Mach 0.83 and a range of almost twenty-eight hundred miles before refueling. It would make a great 'get away quick' aircraft to find friendly skies. Or, maybe with your help, we could get the Air Force to lend us their long-range V.I.P. transport jet. That jet can fly almost eight thousand miles between fuelings.

Congressman Harris responds, "We are doing great, but we will need Chinese assistance in Wuhan to make anything work. Bill looks down at the floor before speaking, "I have a contact in the C.I.A. and an old friend who can help with assets in China." Congressman Harris replies, "Are you sure he will work with us to get us access to C.I.A. assets in China?" Bill responds, "I am sure because he owes me a favor from a long time ago. He will get us the assets we need in China and elsewhere."

Congressman Harris says, "The only thing left is money, and I know exactly where to get the funding for the project." Ken speaks for the first time, "It will cost a lot of money to pull this thing off. Are you sure they have that kind of money?" The Congressman looks at Ken before answering, "The people I am talking about have budgets of a small country at their disposal. I will get the funding."

Congressman Harris addresses the group, "Agent Anderson, no unauthorized person comes into this office. Bill, contact Professor Norris and arrange a meeting with me at his earliest convenience. Also, contact your friend in the C.I.A., and let's make the China assets they have available to us. Julie, you should contact your friend with the jet and ensure it can be ready quickly. Ken, I saved you for last. We need you to map out every electronic device in the Wuhan Lab and the entire city of Wuhan. I want every traffic light, emergency warning system, computer network, and anything you can control from here. We need a map of where they are and what they do." Ken looks toward the Congressman before speaking, "Sir, that could be a major undertaking to map every electronic device in an entire city and the Wuhan Lab. May I ask why you want me to do it?"

Congressman Harris replies to Ken, "To extract three people who are likely being watched very closely from Wuhan, China, will require a disaster. And Ken, if anyone can create a 'virtual disaster,' you are the man to do it." Ken replies, "I am not sure what you mean, Sir?"

The Congressman looks at Ken and speaks, "China failed to warn its people and the world when the Wuhan Lab released the COVID-19 virus. I am sure they live on pins and needles today and are watching for another lab failure around the clock. Ken, when the time is right, we will test their Wuhan Lab protective systems and ensure everyone is safe. We will simultaneously set off all the warning alarms in Wuhan." Ken responds, "But Sir, that will cause chaos throughout Wuhan. The city will be out of control for hours before authorities can restore order." The Congressman sits straight in his desk chair and says, "That is what I am counting on. Enough chaos to confuse the entire city so our assets in Wuhan can sneak off with the three people we need to extract and get them out of China. Now it is time to get started, and I need to find us some money to make all this happen."

CHAPTER FOURTEEN

Professor Norris Joins the Group

Some sixteen hundred years ago, the Greek philosopher Sextus Empiricus wrote: 'The mills of the Gods grind slowly, but they grind small.' Sixteen hundred years later, Washington continues this process, slowly and small. Delay is a part of everyday life in Washington, D.C., and this project was to be no exception, no matter how important.

Ten days had passed since the first meeting of the group Congressman Harris formed to decipher the documents in the briefcase. During this time, Congressman Harris arranged the financing through the black ops program for the funds the group needed for the operation.

Bill's friend at the C.I.A. agreed to connect the group with the C.I.A. assets in China and the surrounding area. The only remaining issue was a completed plan before the C.I.A. would assign assets to the project.

Agent Anderson helped wherever he could to speed things up and did his job of making sure no one interrupted the staff in the office. It became apparent why the President transferred Agent Anderson to the Congressman as he was the best of the best in security and took his job seriously.

If there were an upside to the last ten days, it would be that Ken had enlisted Bill's help to map all the electronic devices in the Wuhan Lab and the city of Wuhan on a spreadsheet. They had broken down each device by type, location, function, and access method. Ken felt confident he could control the Wuhan Lab networks and warning devices, the warning devices in the city of Wuhan, and the traffic control signals. With this information collected and detailed on the spreadsheet, Ken could control the operation from the private office half a world away.

With the Congressman's help, Julie made arrangements to access the Air Force V.I.P. jet, which the group would need to transport the extracted people, and the Air Force would make available on a twenty-four-hour notice. Earlier today, Bill arranged a dinner meeting with Professor Norris, Julie, and the Congressman at a Washington Restaurant, and she was en route with the plane to Albany International Airport to pick up Professor Norris for dinner tonight in Washington with Congressman Harris and her.

Air Force V.I.P. Jet Loaned To Congressman Harris

The Congressman reviewed the group's progress daily and met every afternoon to discuss where they were with the project. It was made clear by the Congressman that if something was not going to work or could cause a problem, the group would find another way to move forward. The group brainstormed daily at these meetings, searching for issues and answers.

What this small group was about to do had never been done before, and they would get only one shot at it. Failure would not be an option as people's lives depended on completion and success.

Shortly after noon, Julie called the Congressman from Albany, New York, to report that the Professor had boarded the plane and they were about to take off. The three hundred and seventy-five-mile flight back to Washington should give them an arrival time of around two p.m. at Bolling Air Force Base, where the jet was to be stored. Congressman Harris advised Julie to get the Professor a hotel room and transport him to the hotel to freshen up for dinner later that evening. He also told her to offer a rental car to the Professor should he care to have one.

As the Congressman left his private office to get a cup of coffee, Agent Anderson stopped him. "Sir," Agent Anderson begins, "We will need a makeup artist, like the ones used for the movies." The Congressman replies, "Do you think a makeup artist can make you look like a six-foot-one-inch Chinaman Agent Anderson? They would need to remove your knees." Anderson replies, "No, not for me, Sir. If we are going to take three Chinese females out of China, they will need to appear to be American women when they are in public." Congressman Harris thinks about that momentarily before responding, "That is a good point. Sometimes, these women will be in plain sight of others in Wuhan and must appear American. Great thinking, Anderson."

The Congressman walks over to Bill's desk and advises that they need a trustworthy makeup artist. Bill responds, "Sir, Julie looks great the way she is, and I think a makeup artist would be overkill." The Congressman replies, "No, Bill, not for Julie. Please find me a trustworthy makeup artist willing to travel." The Congressman fills a coffee cup and returns to his office, shaking his head.

As the Congressman sat behind his desk, he felt relief for the first time in days. Agent Anderson's suggestion proved that the group was taking this mission seriously and trying to ensure no stone would be unturned. As he sat there, he realized how correct Agent Anderson was. Three American-looking women boarding a United States plane to leave China would attract little or no attention, and three Chinese women would raise a red flag.

After four p.m., Julie called and informed the Congressman they had landed at Bolling Air Force Base, and Professor Norris was staying in a local hotel. She was going home to shower and would pick up Professor Norris at his hotel around five-thirty. Then, she and the Professor would meet the Congressman at the restaurant. The Congressman replies, "That's great. If it would not be too much trouble, could you figure out how we will present all of this information to the Professor without breaking federal secrecy laws? I knew I could count on you." And the Congressman hung up the phone quickly before Julie could respond.

At six p.m., Professor Norris and Julie arrived at the restaurant, where Congressman Harris greeted them. The Congressman had already reserved a booth in the rear of the restaurant where it would be more private. The waitress escorted them to the booth and requested a drink order. The Congressman ordered a bottle of wine to start the evening and asked the waitress for a bit of time before they ordered the appetizers. The waitress left and returned with a bottle of wine and glasses for the guest.

The Professor starts the conversation, "Good to see you again, Congressman, but I am sure you did not fly me to Washington to see my pretty face." The Congressman responds, "That is exactly why I had you come down, to see your pretty face." Julie says, "The Congressman and others have spoken highly of you, Professor. We rely on people like you to help us with information and guidance. Working within the government, we become isolated from people of different cultures, and there is nothing worse than insulting someone's culture." Congressman Harris sat with his mouth partially open as Julie spoke. Julie had surpassed his wildest dream of justifying this meeting with the Professor. The Congressman sat back in his seat, waiting for Julie's following words to flow from her lips for the reason of the meeting.

Julie asked the Congressman, "Kevin, would you like to add anything to the reason for this meeting?" The Congressman shakes his head and replies, "No, you seem to be covering it very well, so why don't you continue." Julie replies, "Thank you, Kevin. Professor, we have several hypothetical things to run past you and could use your advice on handling them." Professor Norris says, "I will be more than happy to give both of you anything I have. I hope I will not let you down." Julie smiles before speaking, "Don't worry, Professor, tonight, I am sure you will not be the person to let me down." Julie looks over to the Congressman with a smile as she finishes speaking.

Professor Norris says, "Well, I am glad you think I am the right person for whatever you need me to do. But would it be too much for you to give me an idea of these hypotheticals you need information about?" Julie struggles to find the right words to continue, "Well, you see, we need." Julie passes the football to Kevin, "Tell him what we need, Kevin." The Congressman says, "We have a group of people who need an education in the ways and customs of the Chinese." Professor Norris replies, "Could you give me a better definition of what you need? That seems to be a little vague." Congressman Harris says, "Well, some of the group is going to China, and they want to blend in with the locals there." The Professor asks, "And where are these people going? It makes a difference as China is so large, and dialects and customs differ." Congressman

Harris pauses before answering, "The group is going to Wuhan to visit the U.S. Embassy and on a tourist trip."

Professor Norris leans back in his chair before replying, "Well, I can tell you a little about Wuhan. Wuhan is famous for being a central transportation hub in China, often called 'the Chicago of China' due to its extensive railways, roads, and expressways connecting to other major cities. Additionally, Wuhan is known for its historical significance, having briefly served as China's capital city in 1927 and 1937. Wuhan is the capital of Hubei Province in the People's Republic of China. With a population of over eleven million, it is the most populous city in Hubei and the ninth-most-populous city in China. Then, of course, the Wuhan Lab is also there and the subject of many international investigations." The Congressman interrupts, "Okay, I believe you have the information we need."

Julie asks, "Professor, have you ever visited Wuhan, China?" The Professor replies, "No, on my salary, I could not afford to travel anywhere like that. I can only dream of going to somewhere like that one day." Congressman Harris smiles and says, "Professor Norris, today may be your lucky day. We require education, and you would like to travel. We can come to an agreement that will benefit both of us. And the best part is the government will pick up the tab for everything. Are you interested, Professor? The government will pay all your expenses while you are in Washington, D.C., working to educate my group. When it comes time for the group to go to China, you will be with it. And to complete it, the government will pay your full salary while you are involved with the group."

The Professor sits quietly before answering, "Of course, I have my wife to consider. Staying in Washington briefly is one thing, but going to China without her is another." Julie says, "Well, maybe it could be arranged when the group goes to China. Your wife could go with you. Now, wouldn't that be a good idea, Kevin?" Congressman Harris looks at Julie before speaking, "Yeah, that is what I was thinking. The Professor should take his wife with him to China."

The Professor smiles and says, "Well, this is my lucky day. I will need to let my wife know when we are going so she can take time off from work. A few day's notice is all we will need." The Congressman asks, "By the way, what does your wife do?" The Professor replies, "My wife teaches cosmetology and specializes in hair color, skin and facial makeup, nails, and many other things. One year, for Halloween, she turned me into a green monster. It was so real it fooled everyone." Congressman Harris interrupts, "Professor, I can't think of anyone better to bring along than your wife. Now let's order a good dinner to celebrate a good deal for everyone."

The Professor excused himself as dinner ended and went to the men's room. Julie had been waiting to speak with Kevin alone, "Why were you so happy to bring his wife to China?" The Congressman replies, "Because we discovered today we must disguise the three women to move them out of Wuhan. The Professor's wife can change their appearance to make extraction easier. We can make them up to look like American women."

The Professor returns and sits when Julie says, "I was thinking, Professor, we should also pay your wife's salary. There is no reason for her not to be paid." The Congressman lifts his hand to his head and says, "That's a great idea, Julie. Can you think of anything else you want my office to pay?"

The Professor and Julie left the restaurant to return the Professor to his hotel, and she went home for the night. Congressman Harris sat by himself briefly, thinking about how he would write up his expenses for this project. The Congressman stood and left the restaurant, walking to his parked car. As he slid into the driver's seat, his thoughts reviewed how well Julie carried the evening. Julie's actions tonight reminded him of his deceased wife, who he lost in a car crash.

Sometimes, things take a woman's touch, and a woman's touch got the job done tonight.

Chapter Fifteen

Devil In the Details

The group worked on the plan for days before Congressman Harris finalized anything. And as with anything, the Devil is always in the details.

The group had the use of a C-37B Air Force V.I.P. configured jet. The plane is a modified Gulfstream G550 designed to transport nineteen passengers with a range of seventy-seven hundred miles at a cruising speed of five hundred and twenty-eight miles per hour. Julie calculated that since the aircraft could not fly directly from Washington, D.C., to Tokyo, Japan, the trip from Washington, D.C., to Tokyo must be broken into shorter trips.

Julie decided to fly the Gulfstream from Washington, D.C., to Los Angeles International Airport, and the group would stay overnight in Los Angeles. After refueling, the C-37B aircraft could travel from Los Angeles International to Tokyo, Japan, where the group would spend the night in Tokyo. The flight from Tokyo to Wuhan, China, was about sixteen hundred miles or three and a half hours of flight time, which the group would make the following day. The Congressman decided to refuel the Gulfstream in Wuhan and leave the aircraft at the Wuhan Airport until the group was ready to depart.

The return trip would reverse the first, except for a final trip to Florida after a stop in Washington, D.C., for the people we extracted. The group would house the extracted people in a modified detention center for their isolation and protection.

The group sat in the Congressman's private office and reviewed the transportation plan several times before approving it. Julie had worked out the transportation part of the project, and the group could move on to the more complex issues they needed to deal with. The group knew that anything going wrong inside China could have drastic consequences.

Ken proved to be invaluable when it came to information concerning the group's electronics. He informed the group it's important to remember that the Great Firewall of China is very real: Websites like Google (including Gmail), YouTube, Facebook, and others are all blocked in China. The Chinese block or ban anything, especially touching sensitive subjects. Ken would need to load a VPN (a virtual private network) on all of the group's devices before entering China, allowing the group to use the Internet as usual freely without things blocked by China's firewall. The sensitive cell phones used by the Congressman and staff would be encrypted to add an extra layer of security. He also acquired a dozen satellite tracking devices that would work in China. Should a group member or person we were extracting become 'lost,' we could find them quickly with these devices.

The Congressman's secretary, Bill, worked on the travel details for the non-governmental people in the group. Each person must have a current U.S. passport, and for U.S. citizens, the cost of a tourist visa for travel to China is $140, whether for single-use or multi-entry use. Bill remarked that he feels like a travel agent, and the Congressman responded, "You have completed one of the most important parts of this Mission. The last thing we need is to get tied up in technical travel issues."

Agent Anderson laid out the fourteen-and-a-half-mile trip from Wuhan Airport to Wuhan City. He spent hours reviewing maps of the Wuhan area to ensure safety and no other issues would arise. He would be the only security person with the group and would be unarmed while in China. Agent Anderson needed to ensure the group would not attract unnecessary attention during the trip. His job was to make it appear that the Congressman and staff were visiting the U.S. Embassy in Wuhan for an inspection, and the group would spend the remaining time touring the city of Wuhan. Agent Anderson still needed to figure out how the group gained three extra people when leaving, but he was still working on ideas to accomplish the gain in people.

While sitting in a meeting, Agent Anderson raised the problem of getting the three women out of Wuhan. Ken stopped typing on his computer to answer, "All we need to do is get a 'Special issuance passport' for travel when the bearer is on official business for the U.S. government." Congressman Harris replies, "But we will need pictures to go with the passport to make them look official." Ken replies, "I know we have pictures of the women as they already have passports, and we have a picture of the lab worker in our file." Agent Anderson says, "What good will those pictures do us if the women are disguised as Americans to get them out of China?" Ken begins to laugh before speaking, "Are you kidding me? With my new 'A.I.' image software, I will convert those photos into a road map for your makeup person to follow. They will look so real no one will question them."

Agent Anderson stands up and walks toward the private office door while saying, "He is the scariest son-of-a-bitch I have ever met." The Congressman, overhearing Anderson's words, replies, "But he is our son-of-a-bitch, he's our guy." And the entire group laughed.

When Agent Anderson returned to the private office, he marked the location of the United States Diplomatic Mission on a map of Wuhan. Agent Anderson says, "The Mission is at 396 Xinhua Road, Wuhan Minsheng Bank Building, Jiang'an District, Wuhan 430015. The Mission will be ground zero for our base of operations. When we locate the three women, we must get them to the Mission for the makeup person to work on them. We will need a woman to pick out American clothing in several sizes to dress the women in and pay special attention to the shoes. Ken will locate the targets, and C.I.A. assets will monitor their daily habits and who, if anyone, is guarding them. I believe the best way to account for the three women leaving with us is to take three women in with us and claim it is a change of staffing at the Mission. Three staff in and three staff out."

Congressman Harris comments, "That is a great idea. No one would question a staff change." The Congressman continues, "We are left with locating the women, finding out how they are being watched, determining their daily movements, and coordinating seizing them and moving them to the Mission. A lot of that information will come from the C.I.A. assets in Wuhan. It would be best if the C.I.A. assets make the first contact with the three women, as the assets will likely be Chinese. The trip's timing will depend on the information the assets will provide. Bill, I think we have enough to give to your C.I.A. contact and get this thing started. I will need two days to notify Professor Norris so his wife can take some time off work. We will need three female Embassy staff members willing to spend a short time in China. And let us bring five additional staff to make the visit look official. Bill and Ken will remain in Washington to monitor and control the operation remotely. Ken, do you have ideas for a distraction so we can get the three women to the U.S. Mission undetected?"

Ken turns from his computer and says, "I think the distraction should start at the Wuhan Lab. I am sure they are always on high alert after the last incident with COVID-19. I will create a false leak warning in the main building. I will monitor the Chinese response to the alarm and set other alarms to confuse the Lab staff. I have access to the Wuhan City warning system and will set off that system shortly after the Lab leak warning alarm. These alarms should begin to cause chaos in the city regarding what is going on, especially after the virus leaked a few years ago from the lab. I can monitor traffic flow using the highway and road camera systems and cause traffic jams at critical locations in the city. Ensure you all have your tracking devices so I can direct the traffic control signals to allow you the fastest way back to the airport to get out of there. If I see any police or other security following you, I can cause a major traffic jam to stop them while clearing the way for you to keep moving."

Congressman Harris leans back and says, "I think we have a plan. It will be up to the C.I.A. assets to get us the information we need. Bill, give your contact the plan, and for now, we need to focus on our normal work in this office for a couple of days. Let's make this happen."

CHAPTER SIXTEEN

No Loose Ends

Two weeks passed without hearing anything from Bill's C.I.A. contact concerning the assets in Wuhan, China. The Congressman's secretary, Bill, had spoken with his contact at the C.I.A. three times in the last two weeks. The report was the same all three times: "No feedback at this time." It was Wednesday of the third week when Bill finally heard from his contact at the C.I.A. The report was promising concerning the three women the group was targeting to remove from China. The C.I.A. assets confirmed that all three women were detained and housed in Wuhan. The assets also reported that police or other security did not guard them. The C.I.A. assets reasoned that being in Wuhan, China, there was nowhere to go and no need to guard the women.

The report read the missing Wuhan Lab Scientist, Huan Yanling, left her living quarters at one p.m. each day and walked the local park paths for about two hours per day. From her daily walk, she usually went shopping for food that evening before returning home. The C.I.A. assets reported they saw no issue intercepting her during her daily walk.

Agent Zhōu's mother and grandmother were housed by the Chinese government less than a mile from Huan Yanling's residence. Just as in the case of Huan Yanling, the mother and grandmother were not guarded during the day. They also left their living quarters to walk daily in the afternoon. The only issue the asset reported was the grandmother was in a wheelchair and pushed by her daughter. Intercepting them would not be an issue, but the grandmother in a wheelchair needed to be addressed by the group in the plan.

In the report from the C.I.A., the assets recorded the addresses of all targets and a recommended time for the interception. The only thing the assets believed could cause an issue was if it were raining on the day of the interception. The Congressman sat and thought about how the group had worked so hard to allow for all issues, and the entire project could be foiled by a rainstorm. The Congressman noted, 'Must do the extraction on a sunny day,' and pressed the intercom button to speak with his secretary, Bill. "Bill," The Congressman begins, "We need to know if there is a rainy season in Wuhan, China, and if so, what are the likely times during the day for rain." Bill replies, "On it, Sir." And Bill disconnects the intercom.

The time for the execution of the plan was approaching, and the Congressman was not going to let a rainstorm spoil the mission. As Congressman Harris sat in his private office, he estimated the plan would be ready for the following week. The group meeting scheduled for later today was going to finalize everything. Once set into motion, the plan needs to move forward.

His next thought was about the reason for one of his female staff members being in a wheelchair as she came off the plane at the Wuhan Airport. We needed a female in a wheelchair to move the grandmother, who needed a wheelchair, back onto the plane as we left Wuhan. We will make her an older staff member, and I will say she tripped as she was climbing the aircraft's stairs and needed a wheelchair due to a leg injury. I've seen it happen many times, so it would be believable.

An hour later, Bill handed the Congressman what he had discovered about the weather patterns in Wuhan.

The report reads:

"Rainfall phenomena play a significant role in shaping Wuhan's climate patterns. While drizzles are a common sight throughout the year, the range of average monthly rainfall jumps from 1.02" in the colder season to a notably high 8.86" during the summer months. Considering all weather dynamics, the optimum period for visiting would likely be late spring and early autumn. During these times, temperatures remain pleasant, and rainfall levels drop significantly while maintaining comfortable humidity."

Bill says, "Sir, if rain is an issue, the group must go within the next two weeks to minimize the chance of a rainy day during the mission. Can everything be ready in that time frame?" The Congressman answers, "We will be ready to go next week. That should place us in Wuhan at the lowest chance of rain on any given day. Have we put together the extra staff members and the needed paperwork?" Bill replies, "I have all the special passports for the staff, and Ken has created the photos for the three women we are removing from China. I must admit they do look like American women in the photos. These photos are in the special passports and ready to go with you to Wuhan."

The Congressman says, "The oldest of the staff women is going to be in a wheelchair from a trip and fall accident on the airplane during the flight. The wheelchair will allow the group to move the grandmother from the U.S. Mission to the Wuhan Airport without raising red flags. I want to start today's meeting within the next hour to put this project into a go mode. Can you notify the staff?" Bill replies, "One hour, Sir, and we will all be here in your office." Bill turns and leaves the private office to advise the staff of the time for the meeting.

The meeting started with the Congressman thanking everyone for working through the problems over the last few weeks. "It has been a long and bumpy road to make what we are about to undertake a successful mission," He said. He continues, "We are all here today to put the finishing touches on the details. Bill, I want U.S. diplomatic staff labels on all luggage, and we will need them on the wheelchair so they can be seen clearly by the Chinese officials. Bill, do you have everything you need to do complete?" Bill nodded his head to acknowledge his part was ready.

The Congressman looks toward Julie before speaking, "Is the plane ready to make this long trip to China?" Julie replies, "The aircraft had complete maintenance a short time ago and sits fueled and ready to fly with an hour's notice." The Congressman turns to Agent Anderson, saying, "You are the only security person making the trip with us. Is there anything else you need or anything we did not think about? Now is the time to bring it up." Agent Anderson responds, "Do we know how long we will be in Wuhan? The longer we are there, the more chance of something going wrong." Congressman Harris replies, "We are only going to be in Wuhan long enough to collect the three women, make them up to look like an American, and get out of there. It could be one day or three days. We will need to play it by ear with our C.I.A. assets."

The Congressman looks back at Bill, "Do we have our eight Diplomatic staff replacements ready?" Bill responds, "They are here in Washington, D.C., and are ready to go on short notice. Another thing is I may need access to the safe and the documents in case some information is needed when you are in China." The Congressman replies, "I will make sure you have access to the document safe before we leave. And we must be aware that the eight diplomatic staff members do not have enough security clearance to learn about the documents in the safe. We must be careful when speaking about what they contain around everyone. So, the plan will work by taking all eight staff members we bring with us to the U.S. Mission, including the staff member acting injured on the flight into Wuhan. Five existing staff members and the three women we will extract will leave the U.S. Mission with us. That will give the appearance of a staffing change, making the total number of people eight. It will appear that eight staff members went in and eight members came out. As for the person in the wheelchair injured on the aircraft stairway on the flight in, she decided not to stay due to the injury and will be returning with us. Of course, that will actually be the grandmother in the wheelchair. I believe this to be a sound plan to move the women." The Congressman turns to Ken and speaks, "Ken, I saved you for last because of the amount of things we have asked you to do. Where are you as of today?" Ken speaks slowly, "Well, as far as mapping everything in Wuhan, I believe that is complete. I am working on a failsafe backup plan that will include a second laptop computer loaded with all the software and ready in case of a computer failure. I am installing backup power supplies for the equipment this weekend to prevent a power failure. In addition to the office's Internet connection, I am installing a satellite uplink as a backup connection to the Internet. I am not taking any chances with a loss of Internet during this mission. Bill and I have been preparing for weeks for this, and we will not disappoint you."

The Congressman replies, "I think I can speak for the group; we feel confident with your and Bill's efforts and the preparation you two have put into this. I will inform Professor Norris and his wife tonight that we are leaving next Wednesday. Does anyone here have a problem with that date, or maybe something I have overlooked?" The staff stood silent, nodding their heads, indicating they were ready.

The Congressman confirms everything by saying, "Then it is set for next Wednesday, and may luck be with us. Thank you again, and let's call it an early day."

Ken looks around the room before speaking, "You guys all get to leave, but I have much to do here to prepare. Just get out of my way. I don't need you guys anyway." "See you in the morning, Ken," the group said as they left the private office.

Ken turned to his computer to ensure every tiny detail was attended to. The lives of the staff would be on his and Bill's shoulders starting next Wednesday, and Ken was determined not to fail his friends. As Ken stared at the computer screen, he thought, 'Now, what could go wrong?' as he checked each program he would need to make the mission a success.

CHAPTER SEVENTEEN

Creating New Images

The telephone rang shortly after eleven p.m., and Julie answered, half asleep, "Hello." The voice on the other end of the phone identified himself, "Julie, it's Kevin." Julie replies, "I know who it is, as no other sane person would call at this hour of the night. I hope this is important." The Congressman responds, "Of course it is important, or I would not have called." "Hair color, skin makeup, the stuff we will need for Mrs. Norris to make up the women.

We need to purchase these items and take them with us." Julie pauses before answering, "Kevin, I am sure these things are also available in China. We can purchase them in Wuhan." The Congressman replies, "I know the items are available in China, but manufacturers will label things in Chinese. How will we know what we are buying? We do not read or write Chinese."

Julie took a moment to clear her head and replied, "You may be right. We have no guarantee products in China will also be labeled in English. That means we will need to take everything we may need with us to China." The Congressman says, "That was just something that crossed my mind tonight. Julie, you must know someone in the make a woman beautiful business, and they can tell us what we need to purchase. Let me know, and have a good night." The telephone disconnected. Julie slid out of bed and headed for the bathroom, thinking, 'I was having a good night until you called.' Julie returned to bed and lay there looking at the ceiling, thinking, 'Who do I know in the cosmetics business who can help me with what products we will need? And this question repeated itself until after three a.m. when Julie finally fell asleep.

The following day, in the Congressman's office, Julie advised the Congressman that selecting makeup would not be easy. She had spoken with two people with whom she was acquainted in the makeup or cosmetics business. Both informed her the products a makeup person uses are a personal preference and not a list of everyday things to use. One makeup person may use one product, and another would use something different to achieve the same result.

The Congressman presses the intercom button, and his secretary, Bill, answers, "Yes, Sir. What can I do for you?" The Congressman replies, "Bill, I need the complete education and work profile I requested you get concerning Professor Norris's wife yesterday. Could you bring it to me, please?" Bill responds, "I will bring it right in, Sir, as soon as I can get it printed." The Congressman releases the button and waits for the report outlining the Professor's wife and her skills.

Bill enters the office with the report, sits before the desk, and asks, "What qualifications are we looking for?" The Congressman looks at Bill and says, "I am not sure. Start with her education and go through the places she has worked and what she did at those places."

Bill begins to read the report, "She graduated from a two-year college in Upstate New York as a makeup artist. She worked for three years for a local television network for on-set talent makeup. Mrs. Norris worked for a year with a production company for theater shows. After that, she moved to teaching cosmetology in Upstate New York and has been teaching ever since. It appears, Sir, she possesses many art-related makeup skills." The Congressman sits in his chair and replies, "Thank you, Bill. You may have given me exactly what I need." Bill responds, "And what did I give you, Sir?" The Congressman says, "A way to make it all happen." Bill stood up and walked to the door, still unsure of what he had given to the Congressman, but whatever it was, he was happy with it, and that was all that mattered."

The Congressman now realized he had no choice but to inform Professor Norris' wife what he wanted her to do in China and have her select what products she would need to transform the Chinese women. He sat thinking about how to present it to her and attempted to lay out a script when he spoke to her. 'How are your design skills, and do you have a good eye for symmetry and angles? And when working on people's faces, do you have a steady hand? How are your artistic and creative flair and attention to detail?' My God, he thought it sounded too much like a job interview.

After an hour, he decided to take a straightforward approach to Mrs. Norris. 'Mrs. Norris, we are going to China to rescue three women, and I was hoping you could make them look as American as possible so we can remove them from the country. And, by the way, I need you to purchase everything you need while we are here, and we need to take it with us to perform your magic in China. And you may use my credit card to make all necessary purchases.'

The Congressman pressed the intercom button and said, "Bill, Mr. and Mrs. Norris will be in Washington on Monday. Please inform them Julie and I are taking them to dinner that evening. Let them know it will be casual, and if they prefer something special, let me know." He then released the button and went back to reading his emails.

The Congressman had lost so much time working on the trip to China plan that he worked the entire weekend at his office to catch things up. Ken would come into the office during the weekend, install some electronics, and leave only to repeat this event a few hours later.

While the activity with Ken coming and going all week-end, time and time again, the Congressman's thoughts turned to how he would present the makeup or disguise issue to the Professor's wife. Over and over again, the answer returned to the straightforward approach. Going with the straightforward approach also meant Professor Norris would need to know the actual mission and why they were taking him along. The Professor had proven to be a close and knowledgeable friend, and the Congress-man needed as many friends as possible for this mission.

Monday was a review of the plan details from the previous meetings. Ken came up with the idea, 'What if you need to pay someone off while in China to prevent a problem?' The group all looked directly at Ken for a moment. Bill said, "I think Ken may be right. What if you did need to make a payoff to prevent a problem?" The Congressman replies, "I have never made a payoff. If we needed to make a payoff, we would need to bring cash. How much money should we bring with us?" Agent Anderson says, "We should take around fifty thousand dollars. Ken is correct. In case of a problem, cash is king." The Congressman replies, "Bill, find some way to get fifty thousand dollars from somewhere without raising a red flag. No, wait a minute. I know where we can get our hands on some cash. Later today, I will have the cash from the same people financing everything else. Any other loose ends we missed?"

Julie left the meeting and headed for Bolling Air Force Base to borrow the V.I.P. transport jet and fly to Albany, New York, to pick up the Professor and his wife. A call from Julie two hours later confirmed she had collected the Professor, his wife, and their luggage. Julie expected to return to Washington by five p.m. and would make arrangements for the Professor and his wife in a local hotel and settle them before dinner that evening.

Congressman Harris left the office at four thirty to go home and prepare for dinner with Julie and Mr. and Mrs. Norris. As he drove, he practiced his pitch repeatedly to the Professor's wife. If she accepted the plea for help, she would only have one day to gather the necessary things for the disguises. On Tuesday, Mrs. Norris would need

Julie to chauffeur her around to purchase the items for the disguises and pack them in a luggage case.

At six p.m., Professor Norris, his wife, and Julie arrived at the restaurant, where Congressman Harris greeted them. The Congressman had already reserved a booth in the rear of the restaurant where it would be more private. The waitress escorted them to the booth, requested a drink order, and read off the day's specials. The Congressman ordered a bottle of wine to start the evening and asked the waitress for a bit of time before they ordered the appetizers. The waitress left and returned with a bottle of wine and glasses for the four guests.

The Professor starts the conversation, "Good to see you again, Congressman. Are we all ready for the big trip?" The Congressman responds, "Everything is ready, and I just wanted to speak with you and your lovely wife before we leave on Wednesday. Frankly, I need help from you and your wife to make this trip successful. The trip to China has several layers to it. We are going to inspect the U.S. Mission in Wuhan, we are going to tour Wuhan, and..." The Congressman pauses before continuing, "We are going to, well, rescue three women being illegally held by China and smuggle them out of the country."

The Congressman waits for a response from the Professor and his wife for several moments. The Professor looks at his wife before speaking, "This is unbelievable. We are going on a secret mission to China. Oh great, what do you need us to do?" Congressman Harris looks toward Julie before speaking, "Professor, I will need you to educate our group on Chinese customs and what we should expect when dealing with them. Mrs. Norris, I understand you teach cosmetology, but you attended a school for makeup artists. May I ask why you are teaching and not performing makeup work?" Mrs. Norris smiles before answering, "Frankly, I did makeup work for a few years and learned fast only a very few makeup people make good money. You work ten and twelve-hour days to make thirty to forty thousand a year. Don't get me wrong, I love to create new looks for people, but the money is just not there. I moved to teaching and doubled my income with a lot fewer hours. Now, once a year, I practice on Mr. Norris on Halloween."

The Congressman says, "Mrs. Norris if I asked you to make a Chinese woman appear to be another nationality, where would you start?" Mrs. Norris thinks momentarily before saying, "Well, Chinese women, as they get older, usually cut their hair short, probably because it is very dark. So, I would first add extensions to their hair and lighten it to a lighter color. That would give them a younger look. Also, the Chinese eyes are very distinct. One way to address this is to remove and raise their eyebrows. And I think a slight skin-darkening would make the woman look interracial. Those three things would make a Chinese woman appear to be Polynesian."

Congressman Harris responds, "If I gave you some photographs of these women, could you tell me if you could make them look like the photos?" Mrs. Norris asks, "Do you have the photos with you?" The Congressman reaches into his pocket, removes the photos of the women Ken had altered with 'A.I.' software, and hands them to Mrs. Norris. She turns on the flashlight on her cell phone to view the images the Congressman handed her. "The hair is wrong in these photos. It's still too short. Eyes also need to be addressed. Who made these?"

The Congressman replies, "Ken created these using 'A .I.' software at the office. Can you assist Ken in creating better images of the women?" Mrs. Norris replies, "First of all, men only notice women from the neck down, if you know what I mean. Ken, whoever he is, is no exception. If I meet with him, we can create a more realistic image for the women. Once we have a realistic idea, I can make these women appear as anything other than Chinese. When can I meet with this Ken person?"

The Congressman looks at Julie and says, "Ken will be in my office tomorrow morning. Julie can bring you in with her, and you two can create a more non-Chinese image of these women. If you have the re-done photos, could you purchase the materials to transform the women so we can take them with us? I mean the chemicals, hair, or whatever is needed." Mrs. Norris replies, "Tomorrow, Ken and I will create images of three beautiful women, and I will make these women look just like the images we create on the computer. Then Julie and I will shop for what is needed to make it happen."

The Congressman says, "I think we have a plan. I'm sorry, Professor, it seems you have been left out of the conversation tonight." The Professor responds, "Are you kidding? We feel like we are secret agents. I am 007, and my wife is 008." Mrs. Norris interjects, "No, dear, I am 007, and you are 008." The Professor responds, "Sorry dear, what was I thinking."

Julie says, "Come on now and let's order dinner. I've been flying all day and have not eaten a thing."

The Congressman waves for the waitress, and she comes to the table to take the orders. The four eat dinner, laugh, have a toast to success, and wonder what lies ahead on the mission to China.

Only after Julie and Mr. and Mrs. Norris left the restaurant did the Congressman consider how dangerous this mission could be. China was not going to be happy with his group extracting the three women. He would need to carefully investigate the rules for diplomatic immunity with attorneys in case something serious goes wrong. Somehow, every person going on this trip was required to be covered with immunity so the Chinese government could not hold them in custody. The Congressman was unsure if there would be paperwork to sign or something

else, but before Wednesday, the legal staff would complete it.

161

Chapter Eighteen

The Last Day

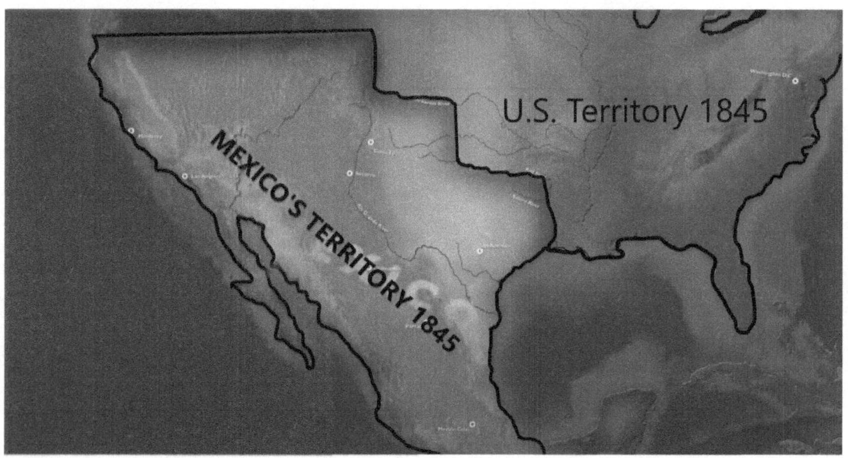

The Congressman headed first to the government legal attorney's office on Tuesday morning before going to his office. Meeting with the attorneys, he verified that all staff members, Julie and he enjoyed diplomatic immunity. The attorney instructed the Congressman to bring the information concerning the Professor and his wife to his office later that day, and he could have a temporary diplomatic visa issued for the Professor and his wife, giving them diplomatic immunity for thirty days while in China.

When the Congressman arrived at the office, he directed Bill to get information about the Professor and his wife, take it to the government legal office this morning, and not leave without the diplomatic visas.

He entered his private office and found Mrs. Norris and Ken working with the 'A.I.' software to adjust the photos for the three women's passports. Once complete, Mrs. Norris would purchase the things needed to make the three women look like the photos.

Julie periodically peeked into the private office to see if Ken and Mrs. Norris had finished adjusting the photos. In the center office, Agent Anderson was sticking labels on some of the staff's luggage that said "U.S. Diplomatic Staff" in bold letters. In a box, he had several more labels to take to Bolling Air Force Base to apply to anything not labeled. In the corner of the office sat a brand new wheelchair also marked as "U.S. Diplomatic Staff."

The Congressman heard Mrs. Norris say, "Those are perfect, Ken, I can work with those." Julie also listened to her comment and visited the private office to see the new images. Julie looked at the photos and said, "You can make the women look like those photos?" Mrs. Norris replies, "I will get them so close nobody would question the validity of the documents." Ken printed copies of the photos and presented them to Mrs. Norris. Julie says,

"Time to go, Mrs. Norris. We need to purchase the stuff for you to work some magic." Before the Congressman could say goodbye, Julie and Mrs. Norris had left the office. Everything was now in high gear. Tomorrow, the group will be on an airplane heading to Los Angeles for an overnight stay before heading to Tokyo and then on to China.

The Congressman asks Ken, "How are you doing with all of this?" Ken replies, "I will insert these new photos into their diplomatic passports. We have completed all the paperwork, and it is ready to go with you. All computer systems are prepared and tested. Bill and I will cover our end while you are in China." The Congressman responds, "Great job. May I suggest you bring a cot into the office because this may take more than a day, and you will need somewhere to rest?"

While out to shop for supplies for Mrs. Norris, they stopped at the hotel and rented Professor Norris a car so he could go to a museum downtown. Congressman Harris laughed when he heard about the Professor going to a museum. He commented to Julie, "Now I know why Mrs. Norris wanted to be known as '007' as she was the person in charge.

The Congressman sat at his desk, trying to recall if he had forgotten anything. He quickly sat straight up in his chair and grabbed his cell phone to call Bill. Bill answered, and the Congressman said, "Bill, after you finish with the government attorney and the visas, I need you to go to an address that I am going to text to you." Bill replies, "Okay, but what am I doing there?" The Congressman says, "Go to office number 2106 and ask for Mr. John Martin. They will hand you a briefcase to go to China with us." Bill replies, "Oh, that briefcase." And he disconnected the phone.

Two hours later, Bill returned to the Congressman's office, carrying the briefcase and an envelope containing the visas for Professor and Mrs. Norris. The Congressman tells Agent Anderson, "Please put a diplomatic label on that briefcase, and I will lock it in the safe for tonight. It must go with us tomorrow, so place it on your list of things to take." Bill says to the Congressman, "We almost forgot the payoff money, didn't we." The Congressman replies, "No, I just wanted to wait for the right time to pick it up."

After four p.m., Julie reported that Mrs. Norris had located and purchased the needed makeup supplies. They also bought a small suitcase to transport the purchased items and would require a diplomatic staff label for that suitcase. Bill thanked Julie for calling the office and asked her to hang on to see if the Congressman needed to speak with her.

The Congressman picked up the phone and said, "Good job Julie. You were the only person that could have done it. Go home and get a good night's sleep, as tomorrow will be a long day. See you in the office at nine, and we will go over everything for the trip." And the Congressman hung up the phone.

The Congressman looked around the office and saw Bill trying to convince Agent Anderson to show him his gun. The Congressman moved slowly to his private office door, saying, "No Bill, no gun, you do not need a gun." Agent Anderson tells Bill, "You heard the boss, Bill, no gun."

The Congressman requested that Bill and Agent Anderson come into the private office briefly. Congressman Harris says, "Bill, will the small transport bus be here by noon tomorrow? I have told the eight diplomatic staff members to be here by then with their luggage." Bill replies, "The bus will be here by eleven a.m. tomorrow, and we can begin loading it then. The Congressman continues, "Agent Anderson, you may bring your sidearm and one other defensive weapon with you, but it must remain on the airplane once we land in China. Your job as a security guard will be to interfere with Chinese security and divert them if you believe there is a problem. I don't know how you will do that, but be creative. Remember, there can be no physical contact with their security. Whatever you come up with must be verbal." Agent Anderson says, "I understand, Sir."

Congressman Harris replies, "As soon as your relief arrives to guard the office, go home and get a good night's rest. If we have missed something, we can correct it in the morning." Bill looks over to Ken, who is still typing on the computer and says, "Ken, I think it is time for you to return to your hotel too. You're the key guy in this thing, and we need you well-rested." Ken replies, "I will be out of here in less than ten minutes."

Congressman Harris looks at his staff for a brief moment, smiles, and heads to the door to leave the office. When he reaches the door, he stops, turns, and says, "I could not be prouder of you guys." He nods his head, opens the door, and leaves.

As the Congressman drives home, he looks back to the day the President of the United States entrusted him with that briefcase. The President's briefcase contained documents that may allow the Congressman and his staff to change the world forever.

Chapter Nineteen
The Trip to China

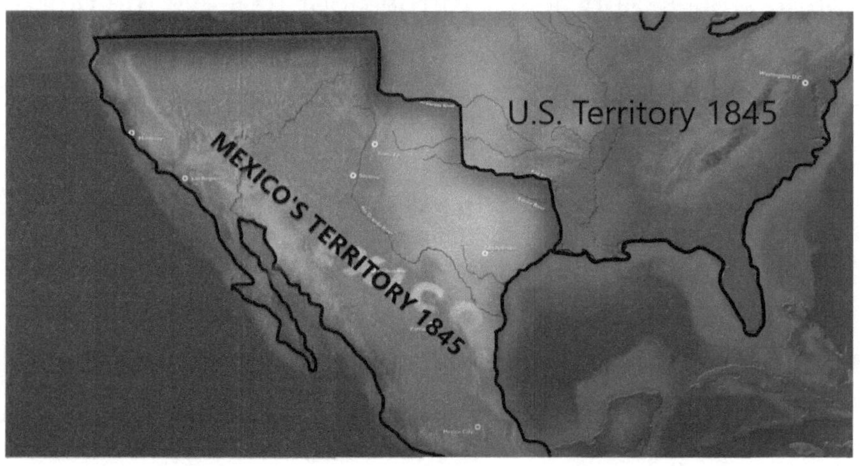

The Congressman arrived at the office shortly before nine a.m., dragging his luggage behind him. As he opened the front door and entered the office, he was surprised to find Julie, Agent Anderson, Bill, Ken, Professor Norris, and the Professor's wife waiting for him. As he passed through the center office, the staff echoed, "Good Morning, Congressman, we have been waiting for you. Did you oversleep?" Congressman Harris turns and replies, "No, I did not oversleep. I was caught in a traffic jam on my way here this morning for several hours." He pauses to give the staff time to laugh before saying to Julie, "May I see you in my office for a moment."

Julie follows the Congressman through the private office door and closes it behind her. Congressman Harris says, "Have we made a call to verify the plane is ready to fly?" Julie replies, "I made that call at seven hundred this morning, and the plane is fueled and ready to go." The Congressman continues, "Perfect. And Julie, I hate to admit this, but I never learned the Professor's wife's first name. Do you know what it is?" Julie smiles before replying, "Her name is Angel, Angel Norris." The Congressman says, "Well, that fits. Imagine spending twenty-four hours a day with Professor Norris. She must be an angel."

A knock on the private office door followed with Ken's voice, "May I come in?" The Congressman responds, "Come on in." Ken enters the office and says, "Where are they?" The Congressman, looking surprised, replies, "Where is what?" Ken responds, "The electronic locator tags we purchased. You are supposed to have one on each of you so I know where you are, remember?" The Congressman looks at the floor before replying, "Oh yeah, those things. Where are they, and who gets which one." Ken walks over to his computer desk and picks up a small package of electronic devices and a sheet of paper detailing what device belongs to who." Ken continues,

"Each person's name is next to the number on the device. That way, I can identify who is where. There are several extra devices, and if you attach one of them to something, update me with the number and what it is attached to so I can update my files and track it." The Congressman takes Ken's box of trackers and hands it to Julie. "Julie," Said the Congressman, "I think you should handle the distribution of these and update Ken with new device updates. And Julie, you're an angel." Julie smiles before speaking, "No, Kevin, I'm a pilot. Mrs. Norris is an angel. Don't get confused." Julie reaches into the box, selects tracker number one, and hands it to the Congressman. She says, "I believe number one is for you, Sir. I will distribute the other trackers to the staff as they arrive, and if I place one on an item to track, I will update Ken. Is there anything else you need me to do right now?" Congressman Harris replies, "Julie, I surrender to your trusted hands." Julie responds, "Smart move." And she leaves the private office.

The Congressman asks Ken, "Is everything ready?" Ken responds, "I have everything in place here to move forward. Please mention to Julie that the last tracker number must be attached to the jet's windshield so I can track it in the event of aircraft transponder failure. I noted it on the sheet but want to ensure it gets placed there." Congressman Harris replies, "If the tracker is on that sheet, Julie will ensure it gets placed on the airplane. She is the most detailed woman I have ever met. And Ken, you tell me you can track each device halfway worldwide?" Ken answers while typing on his computer, "Anywhere in the world. Some satellite will pick it up and give me its location within twenty-five feet of where it is."

The Congressman walked back into the center office, where everyone was working on the final preparations for the trip to China. Looking around the office, he failed to see the staff's luggage anywhere. He addresses his secretary, Bill, "Where is the staff's luggage?" Bill looks over to Agent Anderson, and Agent Anderson pulls open the door to the bathroom, now piled high with the staff's luggage and each piece labeled "U.S. Diplomatic Staff." Congressman Harris says, "Oh, great idea, but where do we go to the bathroom?" Bill responds, "Two doors down the street at the realtor's office. Got their permission to use their bathroom yesterday." Congressman Harris does not speak but turns and goes back into his office.

The eight diplomatic staff people started to arrive at eleven a.m., and their luggage was labeled and placed in the bathroom. The transport bus pulled up to the office at eleven-fifteen, and Bill and Agent Anderson began loading the bus's cargo areas with the luggage. By eleven-twenty, the last diplomatic staff had arrived, and Agent Anderson labeled and loaded her luggage into the bus.

Agent Anderson loaded the wheelchair in the bus's cargo area, securing it for the Bolling Air Force Base trip. We waited for Agent Anderson's security replacement and boarded the bus to be taken to the Air Base after he arrived. Bill, Ken, and a federal security guard would staff the Congressman's office for several days or as long as necessary.

The bus left the Congressman's office and headed to Bolling Air Force Base, about a half hour away. The bus and its passengers were all checked at the base security gate and allowed entry onto the base. As the bus driver drove the bus out to where the private jet was parked, a call from Ken verified all the tracking devices were working and displaying each of their locations. Air Force personnel loaded the plane with the luggage, paying particular attention to maintaining a balanced load on the aircraft. As each piece of luggage was loaded, Agent Anderson verified the proper labeling was attached. Agent Anderson placed a tracker on the briefcase containing the fifty thousand dollars while it was at the Congressman's office, hiding it from prying eyes. Julie was already aboard the plane, doing a pre-flight checkout and communicating with ground control before takeoff. The co-pilot assigned by the Air Force for the long flight from Washington to Wuhan was Captain Scott Crossfield, who was busy verifying the aircraft's instruments.

Congressman Harris had nothing to do as his staff had taken control. The Professor kept circling the plane slowly, admiring the artistry and paintwork. The Professor's wife, Angel, sat on the bus with the diplomatic staff of eight people and watched her husband walk around the airplane.

Julie appeared at the aircraft's door and signaled to begin boarding the plane. The diplomatic staff boarded first and moved toward the rear of the aircraft. Professor Norris and his wife boarded after the diplomatic staff, with Agent Anderson and Congressman Harris boarding last.

The door to the aircraft was secured, and the ground crew connected a pushback truck and pushed the jet clear of the hanger area. Once the ground crew was clear of the plane, Julie fired the engines and waited for them to come up to temperature. Julie's voice over the plane's intercom instructed all passengers to fasten their seat belts and prepare for takeoff. Slowly, the plane travels along the taxiway and stops, waiting for final instructions for clearance to take off. The jet turned onto the main runway a minute later, and the engines started pushing the plane forward. The passengers could hear the tires thumping on the pavement, slow at first, speed up, and as the airplane lifted off the runway, the tire noise stopped. The front of the airplane began to angle up, surprisingly steep, and the aircraft began to climb at a high rate of speed. The Congressman looks at Agent Anderson and says, "I have flown on many airplanes, but this thing seems more like a rocketship than an airplane." Agent Anderson replies, "It's not the airplane, Sir. It's the pilot. The Air Force trained Julie to fly jet fighters, and they usually climb to altitude quickly. Don't worry; the flight-management computer will take over the aircraft shortly, and the computer will correct the rate of climb." Congressman Harris replies, "How do you know something like that, Anderson?" Agent Anderson responds, "I used to date a commercial pilot, and she told me how these airplanes work. And yes, if you need to know, I am a mile-high club member." Congressman Harris replies, "That is more information than I needed, Agent Anderson, but I am glad you received an education about something somewhere."

A half-hour into the flight, the airplane was at a forty-two thousand foot cruising altitude and a speed of around five-hundred and fifty miles per hour. Julie's voice came over the intercom, "It looks like clear sailing from here into L.A.X. in California, and our flight time will be about five hours. Today, we have two choices for your entertainment. We have the world-famous Professor Norris, who may lecture on China, its history, and present-day events, or we have a movie called "Godzilla Vs the Sea Monster. It's a 1966 Syfy thriller where Godzilla must take on Ebirah, the giant crab monster. Congressman Harris will count a show of hands for Professor Norris."

The Congressman watched for a show of hands from the staff, but nothing. A voice from the plane's rear echoes, "Where is the escape door on this plane? I have heard Professor Norris's lecture before, and we may need the escape door." That answer started the staff into loud laughter, followed by a chant, "We want the Godzilla and Crab movie."

The Congressman unlatches his seat belt and stands to address the staff. "Five hours is a long flight, and I think Professor Norris, an expert on China, will be helpful as you represent the United States. The eight of you are being sent to China to rotate out the current staffing in Wuhan, and the Chinese have stringent customs that you must follow. Professor Norris will be the entertainment, at least for some of the flight, to bring you up to speed with China and its customs. Please bear with me and use this time to learn. I will now turn over the conversation to Professor Norris. And the Godzilla movie was only a prank."

The Professor unbuckles his seat belt, stands, and be-gins with, "The belief that all Chinese are short is a myth. China's northern provinces of Liaoning and Jilin are home to the tallest people in the country, on average 173.45 cm for men and 160.52 cm for women. Jiangxi, Sichuan, and Hunan inhabit the shortest people, on average, at 165.59

cm for men and 155.06 cm for women. That converts to five foot nine in the north for men and five foot four in the south. I must also note that Chinese in the northern provinces have a darker skin tone than those in the southern regions."

Agent Anderson listened to the first part of the Professor's presentation for about three minutes. He nudges the Congressman and asks, "Where is that escape door on this plane? I may need it." Congressman Harris replies, "I know, but he has much good information to share." While the Professor continued his lecture, Agent Anderson reached into his pocket, drew out an envelope, and opened it. While reading the paper, he says, "This is my 401k retirement plan. How do you figure something like this out? A series of letters must represent a company followed by numbers with plus and minus signs next to them. Nobody but an accountant could figure this thing out." Agent Anderson folds the paper and stuffs it back into his pocket. Congressman Harris smiled and laughed at Agent Anderson's remarks about the 401k report.

Over the next two hours, Professor Norris's lecture covered several regional dialects and customs. Followed by an entire "Do's and Don't" series to avoid offending the Chinese. The highlight of the lecture came when the Professor stopped and sat down in his seat. The Congressman was sure he could hear the staff again chanting, "Where is the Godzilla movie?"

Finally, Julie's voice came over the plane's intercom, "We will be landing at L.A.X. in twenty-five minutes. Please fasten your seat belts."

About thirty minutes later, the jet taxied into a government-reserved hangar area where it would spend the night. The passengers de-planed with their carry-on bags, and an airport bus shuttled to a nearby hotel for the evening. The time difference made it four-thirty p.m. in California, and the Congressman's staff decided to catch dinner before retiring. Julie, Agent Anderson, Mr. and Mrs. Norris, Captain Crossfield, and the Congressman enjoyed a steakhouse chain dinner on good old Uncle Sam. The Congressman spent the rest of the evening speaking with Bill and Ken on the phone back in Washington, D.C., and answering emails from his laptop before he retired for the night.

The eight other Diplomatic staff members traveled to a local comedy club for the evening before returning and retiring. The job they faced in Wuhan would be much easier than the one the Congressman's staff had undertaken. As far as the Diplomatic staff knew, they only went to China as part of a typical staff rotation. Had they known the actual reason for the trip, the Congressman was sure they would not have gone to a comedy club.

Congressman Harris's staff was feeling the pressure of the mission ahead and knew that the stakes were so high that failure was not an option. A mistake made in China, even with diplomatic immunity, could cause a major international event. An event even the President of the United States would not want to deal with.

As he lay in bed, his thoughts turned to the only issue still to be resolved, which was which one of the diplomatic staff members would play the part of an injured person when they de-planed in Wuhan. How would the Congressman develop a convincing story to the staff why one of them was injured and needed to be taken off the airplane in a wheelchair? As the Congressman lay in bed, he smiled. I'll let Julie figure that part out. Women trust women no matter how ridiculous a story is.

CHAPTER TWENTY

Next Stop Tokyo

Julie reviewed the flight plan with co-pilot Captain Crossfield and Congressman Harris the following morning at breakfast. Julie says, "We want to arrive in Tokyo around seven a.m. Tokyo time. Tokyo is eleven hours of flight time from L.A.X, but we also have time-lines. We should leave L.A.X. at five p.m. and arrive in Tokyo at seven a.m. We will be ahead on the calendar because of the sixteen-hour time difference. We will have an hour layover in Tokyo to refuel, and the flight to Wuhan should take under five hours with a one-hour time difference, making our arrival in Wuhan at two p.m. Wuhan local time." Congressman Harris replies, "So we will be in Wuhan, China, at two p.m., and we will need time to de-plane and move luggage. After that, everything will depend on the U.S. Mission and their staff to arrange housing and transportation for our stay." Captain Crossfield asks, "How long is our stay in Wuhan?" Congressman Harris responds, "That will depend on several unknown factors now. Please be ready to leave on short notice."

With the flight plan layout planned out, they finished breakfast and returned to their rooms to prepare for the day. Congressman Harris had asked Captain Crossfield to alert the eight Diplomatic staff members to be at L.A.X. at four p.m. to make the long flight to Tokyo. The Congressman would notify Agent Anderson and Mr. and Mrs. Norris of the plans and time frame for the flight.

With the group notified of the departure time, the Congressman sat in his room, deciding what he needed to complete before they left for Tokyo. A knock on the hotel room door alerted the Congressman that someone needed to speak with him. When he opened the door, he found Julie standing in the hallway waiting for him to answer. Without hesitation, Julie says, "We need to call Bill to have him contact the C.I.A. agents to track down the women in Wuhan before we leave L.A.X. That will give us time to finalize our plans with the C.I.A. agents. When we land in Tokyo to refuel and fly to Wuhan, the C.I.A. agents should have enough time to locate the three women and decide how they will extract them and move them to the U.S. Mission in Wuhan." Congressman Harris replies, "I was thinking the same thing, and I was about to call Bill back in Washington in a few minutes."

Julie continues, "Once in Tokyo, we need to rent the ramp for the wheelchair to get the injured passenger on and off the private jet. The cover story will be about renting it in Tokyo after the Diplomatic staff member tripped and injured her leg. We need the receipt to convince the Chinese agents when we land and take back off the reason for the ramp. It will be stored in the rear of the jet by Agent Anderson, and after the other passengers de-plane, Agent Anderson will put the ramp in place and roll the wheelchair down the ramp while the Chinese security agents are watching in full view. The more visually and open everything appears the less chance there is of someone investigating further into what we are doing. The main thing to remember is the jet is United States' sovereign territory, and the Chinese can not board the aircraft for any reason once everyone is aboard. But they could detain the entire plane with everyone on it, and that would cause a diplomatic incident. Getting past the Chinese airport security and on the plane must go smoothly and quickly."

Congressman Harris sat on the bed and just listened as she spoke. When Julie finished, the Congressman thought, "She is the most detailed woman I have ever met."

The Congressman picked up his cell phone and called his secretary Bill back in Washington. When the phone answered, he said, "Bill, Harris here, it is time to contact your C.I.A. guy and move this operation forward. We will be in Wuhan in less than thirty-six hours. After we contact the U.S. Mission staff, I will contact you with the details of how the C.I.A. guys can contact me to exchange the three women." Bill replies, "The C.I.A. agents are already waiting for you and your staff. They already know when you will be arriving in Tokyo and Wuhan. Did you think Captain Crossfield's assignment was by chance? Somehow, Captain Crossfield is connected to an intelligence agency. My contact at the C.I.A. knew Captain Crossfield would be assigned before Julie knew who the co-pilot would be." Congressman Harris responds, "It seems nobody is who they say they are in Washington." Bill says, "The agents in Wuhan will contact you shortly after you arrive. They will say, 'Are you American where there is no rain.' That is how you will know who they are. After that, things that happened will be between you and the agents. No one can assist you while you are in Wuhan."

Congressman Harris hangs up the telephone, turns to Julie, and says, "Please brief Agent Anderson about the flight plan and renting a ramp while in Tokyo. Give him all the details so he understands the importance of ramp rental in Tokyo. He must realize the ramp is all show but needs to be very convincing to avoid problems. I will go to Mr. and Mrs. Norris's room and explain everything they need to know. Being a little early at the airport would be a good idea for our group. We need to review everything and ensure this ruse will convince Chinese security. I am very uncomfortable with the U.S. Mission in Wuhan. They know we are coming for an inspection and to rotate staff, but we will need them to give us a place to work within the Mission so Mrs. Norris can do her magic on the three women. We will need to get the women to the Mission and into a secure area without raising many questions by Mission staff." The Congressman looks at Julie before continuing, "Julie, I think you need a hair trim. Is that grey I see coming through?" Julie reaches for her purse, takes out a small mirror, and looks at her hair. "I don't see any grey," Julie replies.

Congressman Harris begins to laugh while saying, "Of course not. We will claim you are over-sensitive about your hair as an excuse to set up a room at the Mission to do the work on the three women. And you may as well take advantage and have your hair done as part of the show." Julie replies, "The staff at the Mission are going to think I am vain." Congressman Harris responds, "Julie, I don't care what they think as long as they don't think something strange is happening at the Mission. I am going to Mr. and Mrs. Norris now, and you can take care of your loose ends. See what shuttle bus we must take back to L.A.X. to be there around four p.m. and let our group know." Julie smiles and says, "The shuttle bus leaves at three-thirty p.m. at the main entrance and will have us at the airport twenty minutes later. And before you ask, I will advise the rest of our group to be on the shuttle. That will leave Captain Crossfield to arrive with the eight Diplomatic staff members before flight time, which he is aware of said time."

The Congressman walks to the room door, opens it, and enters the hall. Walking down the hall, he thought, 'She is the most detailed woman I have ever met.'

At three-thirty, the group stood before the central hotel door, waiting for the shuttle. And just as Julie stated, the shuttle pulled up, and the group boarded with their carry-on luggage. Congressman Harris looked down and checked his watch as the shuttle stopped at the airport entrance. Three-forty-eight, eighteen minutes from pick up at the hotel to arrival at the airport. The Congressman smiles while thinking, 'Julie was wrong about the trip from the hotel to the airport by two minutes. So she is not perfect after all.'

The group went through the airport to the govern-ment-reserved hangar area, where the jet spent the night under military security. Julie boarded the aircraft and began the standard flight checklist before co-pilot Captain Crossfield arrived. Agent Anderson boarded and visually inspected the plane's interior as required by regulations. Mr. and Mrs. Norris found two comfortable chairs along the hangar wall and sat to watch the others work.

Congressman Harris called his office in Washington and checked in with his secretary, Bill, and computer guy, Ken. He updated them about the departure time and estimated arrival time in Tokyo. "One other question I have for Ken, Bill." Said the Congressman. "Will my encrypted cell phone work over the Pacific Ocean?" Bill hands the telephone to Ken to answer, "Congressman, the aircraft you are flying on is equipped with a satellite phone system. It ensures communication in emergencies with no dropped calls and is one reason satellite phones should be on all aircraft. The telephone I set up for you, which you are currently speaking on, will use the aircraft satellite system and work over the Pacific. Does that address your question, Sir?" Congressman Harris replies, "That answers my question, Ken. Thank you."

Congressman Harris disconnected his cell phone and walked toward where Mr. and Mrs. Norris were sitting. Standing before them, he says, "There will be some things in Wuhan that are outside our control. The U.S. Mission staff will be unaware of our actual purpose for being there. Please speak with no one at the Mission or elsewhere. As far as anyone knows, you came along to educate the new staff and as a visitor to Wuhan. Somehow, I will arrange for a room for Mrs. Norris to work within the Mission under the idea that Julie wants her hair done. It will be there; Mrs. Norris will transform the three women so we can extract them from China. A Diplomatic Visa covers you both, and you are not required to answer any questions about your visit. The best thing to do is play dumb if someone asks questions about your work in Wuhan. Please take all directions from one of our group members, and things will work out great." Mr. and Mrs. Norris nod in agreement, and the Congressman walks back toward the aircraft.

As he approached the plane, he saw off to his right Captain Crossfield and the eight Diplomatic staff people entering the hangar. The Congressman waved his hand, recognizing their arrival, and said, "We are glad you could all make it today." Captain Crossfield smiled as he walked past, climbed the stairs to enter the plane, and joined Julie for a final checkout. The Congressman checked his watch and realized it was time for everyone to board to make the five p.m. flight time. He waved to Mr. and Mrs. Norris and informed the staff it was time to board the plane. As one of the Diplomatic staff passed, she told the Congressman, "I hope you have the Godzilla movie for this long flight to Tokyo." The Congressman replied, "Better yet, each of you will have a satellite control so you can listen or view anything you want." The staff member replied, "Thank you. I have had nightmares all night concerning another Professor Norris lecture."

The Congressman waited until everyone boarded the aircraft before he climbed the stairs to enter the plane. Captain Crossfield and the ground crew secured the stairs and door before a push truck moved the jet from within the hangar. Once outside the hangar and clear of all personnel, Julie fired the plane's engines, and the jet was underway under its power. A slow taxi down an accessway took several minutes, and the aircraft stopped waiting for clearance to enter the main runway and take off. Julie's voice came over the plane's intercom, informing everyone to be ready for takeoff. The aircraft moved forward and turned on the main runway. Within a second, we could hear the roar of the jet engines with the pressure of acceleration pressing the passengers into the seats. Once the plane lifted off the runway, it began to climb into California's blue sky, although it was less steep than the previous takeoff.

Agent Anderson looks at the Congressman and says, "Julie's learning to fly a more commercial airplane." Congressman Harris responds, "Thank God. Last time we took off, I thought we were sitting atop a rocket." And the Congressman and Agent Anderson both began to laugh. As they enjoyed their short burst of humor, the jet turned West and started the eleven-hour flight to Tokyo.

Everyone on board had a source of entertainment for the flight. Congressman Harris decided to fill the time reliving the memories of his wife and daughter. He tipped his head back and looked at the ceiling of the jet, and the dreams of a better time overtook the problems of this trip. As the plane flew into the future, Congressman Harris drifted into the past, searching for all the things taken from him. The smiles and laughter of his wife and daughter would fill eleven hours of flight over the Pacific Ocean. Sitting in his seat, he realized there would come a time in everyone's life when the only things left were memories of what had passed. Unfortunately, his memories were cut so short by the actions of others, and he felt cheated by the very people the United States was attempting to help. Human nature made him think of anger, but his belief in God overcame the anger, and he tried so hard to understand the loss of his family. The loss of the two most precious people in his life were now gone and only lived on in his memories. But, for the next eleven hours, they were alive and with him.

CHAPTER TWENTY-ONE
No Turning Back

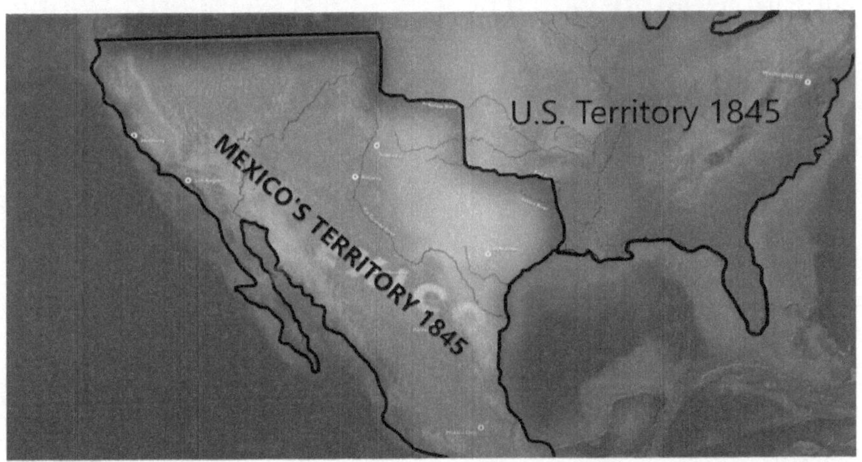

A male voice over the airplane's intercom awakened Congressman Harris from the dreams of the family he once had. Startled at first, he recognized the voice was Captain Crossfield, the plane's co-pilot. Captain Crossfield announced they would be landing in Tokyo in approximately twenty-five minutes and the passengers should prepare for the landing.

Congressman Harris looked over to where Agent Anderson was sitting and watched as Agent Anderson awakened from an in-flight sleep. He then turned, looked out over the dark blue ocean, and thought how peaceful this part of the world was. The only thing that brought discourse to the world seemed to be the human race, and without it, nature would be a far better shepherd of world events.

He gazed out the airplane's window as the puffs of white clouds passed over the jet's wings and disappeared into nothingness, following the plane and into the past, not unlike most people's lives gone without a trace. As he watched, the clouds disappeared, and island land masses rose from the ocean. On one of these islands, the plane would land in Tokyo to refuel before continuing to Wuhan.

Julie's voice announced over the plane's intercom touchdown would be in five minutes and the expected refueling time less than one hour. Congressman Harris turned to Agent Anderson and said, "Damn, I should have made arrangements for airport staff to bring food to the plane during our refueling stop. We could have gotten a bite to eat while the plane was on the ground." Agent Anderson replies, "Julie already made arrangements for sandwiches to be ready when we land. She ordered an assortment so everyone could select whatever they liked." Congressman Harris sat back in his seat, and his only thoughts were about how detailed Julie was about every-thing.

The Congressman could hear the sound of the plane's landing gear deploying above the now whispering sound of the jet's engines. The aircraft quickly turned to the left, and within a minute, the thumping of the wheels rolling down the runway overshadowed everything else. The plane taxied slowly along an access ramp and stopped at a reserved hangar for refueling. The powerful sound of jet engines was replaced with the noise of external ven-tilation fans to keep the plane cool until departure. The ground crew opened the plane's main door, and Julie and Captain Crossfield exited the plane for a visual inspection. As promised, airport staff carried trays of sandwiches up the stairs to the aircraft and placed them in the forward aisle so the passengers could select food and drinks. The Congressman could see from the window that Julie was overseeing the refueling operation of the plane with Cap-tain Crossfield standing behind her. If there were ever a doubt about who was in charge, this image would remove it forever.

Congressman Harris picked up his cell phone and called the U.S. Mission in Wuhan to verify all arrangements made by his secretary from Washington the week before were ready. After a short time on the phone with the U.S. Mission, he scratched a few notes on a sheet of paper and hung up. During the refueling, Agent Anderson rented a folding ramp from the Tokyo airport services center and stored it in the plane's rear section. They would use the rental equipment to disguise the disabled Chinese grandmother and mislead Chinese security when leaving Wuhan.

One loose end remained as Congressman Harris needed to convince a 'volunteer' from the Diplomatic staff to play the part of the injured staff member when exiting the plane. He considered several approaches to the question of who wants to play injured and ride in a wheelchair and settled on the most likely to succeed. Walking down the aircraft aisle to where the Diplomatic staff sat, he said, "Who would like to make a hundred bucks to ride in a wheelchair when exiting the plane?" The Congressman smiled when all eight staff members raised their hands. "I only need one." He said. He then selected the oldest diplomatic staff person for the injured party. The Congressman moved her to the front of the aircraft and explained her role after the plane landed in Wuhan. Congressman Harris informed her, "Should anyone question you about the wheelchair, you are to tell them that when we were in the Tokyo airport, you tripped and injured your leg and required a wheelchair. That is all you are to say to anyone about what the wheelchair is about. Will you have any trouble repeating what I have just told you?" The staff member replied, "For a hundred bucks, I will tell them I made the wheelchair myself to get around if you like." Congressman Harris smiles and says, "No, only repeat what I have told you. Nothing more." The staff member got up and returned to her original seat, one hundred dollars richer, limping as she went.

Agent Anderson watched the entire staff member recruitment and commented to the Congressman, "I think you found the right person to play the part of the injured staff member. She even walked injured when she returned to her seat." Congressman Harris replies to Agent Anderson, "It wasn't the hundred bucks I gave her. It was my smile that convinced her to play the part." Agent Anderson responds, "Give me a hundred bucks, and I will limp with both legs while taking her off the plane." Congressman Harris did not reply but just laughed at the comment.

The airport staff returned and gathered all the serving trays and other utensils used for the onboard lunch. A short time later, Congressman Harris saw the refueling truck pull away from the jet. Within moments, Captain Crossfield and Julie re-entered the aircraft, and Captain Crossfield secured the plane's access door. Julie approached the Congressman and advised him there would be a fifteen-minute delay before takeoff from the airport. Congressman Harris replied, "That will work, as I need to meet with the group briefly. Julie, could you tell Mr. and Mrs. Norris to come to the front of the plane for a quick meeting." Without speaking, Julie walked toward where Mr. and Mrs. Norris were sitting and requested they follow her to the front of the aircraft.

Congressman Harris addressed the group as they huddled around him, "I have spoken to the U.S. Mission staff in Wuhan and finalized our housing accommodations. Julie and Captain Crossfield will stay at the Jinjiang Inn Select Wuhan Tianhe Airport Branch, five and a half miles from the Wuhan Tianhe International Airport. The Professor and Mrs. Norris will remain near the U.S. Mission at the Wuhan Marriott Hotel Hankou. They will have two rooms at the Marriott Hotel."

The Professor interrupted Congressman Harris, "Sir, My wife and I still share a common bed, and we will only need one room at the Marriott Hotel." The Congressman replies, "I understand you and your wife will share a single room. Mrs. Norris will perform her magic on the three women in the second room. Another thing: Mrs. Norris will be in the wheelchair when you check in to the hotel to get the wheelchair up to the second room without making the wheelchair seem out of place or odd."

Julie asks, "Why don't we use the private office at the Mission for Mrs. Norris to work with the women?" Congressman Harris responds, "The security of all foreign embassies on their soil is the responsibility of the host government. So, nearly all are guarded by either local police or military forces. These forces are posted immediately outside the U.S. Mission's grounds. Security forces responsible for allowing visitors to enter are employed by the U.S. Mission and are usually local citizens. Either way, we have no way of sneaking the three women past these guards.

The Wuhan Missions also has a contingent of US Marines responsible for the security of controlled and classified items (which, fortunately, include the U.S. citizen employees who staff the place, and usually local office employees). These are the people we will rotate as a cover for the removal of the three women. So, if you approach the U.S. Mission in China, the first line of defense that you will see are Chinese police or military.

The U.S. Mission will house the eight Diplomatic staff in facilities attached to the U.S. Mission. Agent Anderson and I will be housed in staff facilities at the U.S. Mission for the entire stay in Wuhan. They have also agreed to give us a private office at the Mission, and we can use it as our base of operations."

Julie interrupts, "Sir, what about the aircraft? Who will be watching it? The Chinese are famous for bugging things, and this plane would be a prime spy target." Congressman Harris replies, "The airplane will be placed in a hangar at the airport and guarded by U.S. Mission staff representing themselves as maintenance around the clock. No one will be permitted to access the aircraft in Wuhan.

Furthermore, as soon as we land in Wuhan, I will call Bill and Ken to verify everything is ready on their end. Are there any more questions or things I have missed?" The Congressman waited momentarily for questions or comments. "One more thing," said the Congressman. "Ken gave me these for each of you once we were in Tokyo." The Congressman reached into his briefcase and removed a cell phone for each group member. Congressman Harris continued, "Ken programmed these, and he has encrypted them. They all have a speed dial and will display the name of the person you call. They are also trackable and unaffected by the Great China Firewall. Keep them safe, as we may need them. I think that will end this meeting." With that said, everyone dispersed from the meeting area.

Five minutes later, Captain Crossfield announced over the intercom that they were preparing for takeoff and that passengers should return to their seats and put on their seat belts. The last two Diplomatic staff members took seats and secured their seat belts. As they finished buckling the seat belts, the passengers felt the tug on the plane's front wheels, and the aircraft was turned around and made ready for departure. As before, once all the ground crew was clear, Julie fired the jet's engines and waited for them to warm up before preparing to take off. The plane remained at the terminal building long enough for the engines to reach temperature and then slowly began to move under its power down the taxiway.

The Congressman could hear Julie communicating with the control tower, requesting permission to access the main runway. Julie then told Captain Crossfield to reset the aircraft's routing system to avoid a thunderstorm between Tokyo and the Chinese mainland. Finally, the plane turned ninety degrees to the left, and the engines began accelerating the jet. And within forty-five seconds, the air under the plane's wings gently lifted the aircraft.

The Congressman sat back in his seat and believed Agent Anderson was correct when he said Julie was learning to fly a commercial aircraft as the ascend was gradual and pleasant this time. What a great job when she retires from the military as a female commercial airline pilot. It will be great to fly the friendly skies and not have anyone shooting at you. The only thing between Julie's Air Force retirement and life as a commercial pilot was this trip to China. The task was to extract three women and remove them from the country without getting caught and killed by the Chinese. What could be easier than that?

Congressman Harris closed his eyes and thought about his wife and daughter. "Hey, guys. If you are listening, we need all the help you can give us to make this happen. If you see anything going wrong, I would appreciate a little heads-up. I'd give you my cell number, but I don't think you have a phone, so yell if you need to speak with me."

The Congressman was unsure if his departed wife and daughter could hear him, but it made him feel better to reach out to the two people he could trust to bail him out when there was trouble. In a few hours, his group's lives would rest in the hands of unknown C.I.A. agents working in Wuhan, China, and the staff at the U.S. Mission. The Congressman began to chuckle, thinking they were about to place their very lives in the hands of people working for the United States government. What the Hell are we thinking? Nobody with any sense trusts the United States government. We must all be crazy even to attempt this Mission relying on them.

A half-hour into the flight, Congressman Harris unbuckled his seat belt and walked forward to the plane's cockpit for a route update from Julie. Congressman Harris asks, "Where are we in relationship to the China coast?" Julie reviews the navigation instruments and replies, "From Tokyo to Shanghai is about eleven hundred miles. We are two hundred miles from Tokyo, leaving another nine hundred miles to the coast of China. From the coast of China to Wuhan, it is another five hundred miles, which gives us another fourteen hundred miles remaining for the flight. We may need to reduce our speed once we get over China to allow them to track our flight progress over their territory. They are very protective of their air space. I will try to have us on the ground in Wuhan in another three and a half hours at around two p.m." Congressman Harris replies, "Do everything by the book as we do not want to raise suspicion about this Mission. As far as the Chinese are concerned, we are only going to Wuhan to rotate U.S. Mission staff and enjoy sightseeing in the city." Captain Crossfield replies, "We will do everything by the book, and I will watch over the instruments so as not to raise any issues with the Chinese." The Congressman responds, "I know you two will get this plane there without incident. Forgive me for being a little jumpy." Congressman Harris turned, returned to his seat, sat down, and stared out the window at the waters below.

The blue water below finally turned into a solid mass as the jet flew over the mainland of China. Captain Crossfield's voice came over the intercom, "Less than one hour before we land in Wuhan." Followed by the intercom going silent. Agent Anderson looked at the Congressman and said, "No turning back now, Sir." Congressman Harris replies, "Agent Anderson, there was no turning back two weeks ago."

Congressman Harris closed his eyes and sat deep into his seat. He opened them only when Julie announced that the passengers needed to fasten their seat belts and prepare to land at Wuhan International Airport. The Congressman looked out the airplane's window, and the ground below seemed so peaceful as the plane descended into the airport. He wondered how someplace so beautiful could be the home of so much evil spreading across the world, an invisible virus of death.

View of Wuhan China From the Airplane

With Julie at the aircraft's controls, the engines were reduced to a whisper, and the jet became a large glider surfing the sky above Wuhan. The glider made a sharp left turn, the landing gear deployed, and a minute later, it settled onto the main runway with the familiar thumping of the tires as the plane slowly rolled to a stop. Once again, the engines powered the aircraft down a long taxiway to its final resting point before a security area hangar to be greeted by armed Chinese security.

The Chinese ground crew assisted in opening the aircraft's door, and Captain Crossfield deployed the jet's stairs to allow the passengers to deplane. As Congressman Harris looked out the airplane's door, there were no high-ranking officials, no marching band, no red carpet, only the Chinese ground crew to welcome the Congressman's arrival, backed by two armed Chinese security agents.

Before any Diplomatic staff was allowed to leave the airplane, Congressman Harris made a final statement: "Remember, you all have diplomatic immunity and Chinese security are not allowed to search your person or anything you carry. If there is a problem, signal Agent Anderson or me to intervene before there is an issue. The Chinese respect strength and will challenge weakness. Do not show weakness."

As Julie and Captain Crossfield exited the plane, Chinese security requested their passports or visas. Security quickly looked at the photo on the documents and waved them through with the customary "Welcome to China." Congressman Harris followed them through the line and passed without incident. The Professor and Mrs. Norris exited next and presented their visas as they went through the security line. Professor Norris stopped to chat with one of the Chinese security agents, stating, "I have heard so many good things about China and Wuhan, and I can not wait to experience the sights and sounds of your wonderful country."

The Congressman looked at the blue sky, thinking, 'Great job, Professor, so much for flying unnoticed under the radar.' Next, though, the line was seven of the Diplomatic staff, each showing their credentials as they passed. Agent Anderson exited the plane, showed his passport, and informed security that one staff member had injured her leg, and he was going to mount a ramp and use a wheelchair to remove her from the plane. The security agents nodded, and Agent Anderson re-entered the plane, lifted the folding ramp into place, and wheeled the injured staff member through security as she displayed her visa.

Once everyone was off the aircraft and verified by Chinese security, the U.S. Mission security personnel were allowed to approach the airplane. Agent Anderson met with the two U.S. Mission security personnel, and they helped him fold the ramp and store it in the aircraft. They advised Agent Anderson they would move the airplane into a secure hangar and that it would be guarded by U.S. Mission staff around the clock until they departed China.

Congressman Harris approached the U.S. Mission staff and asked how long before transportation would arrive. The Mission staff advised the Congressman that transportation to the U.S. Mission was already at the airport, and they were waiting for Chinese security to allow them to enter the hangar area. The Congressman was also advised by U.S. Mission staff that Julie and Captain Crossfield would need to take their luggage to the front of the airport and board a shuttle bus to their hotel because the shuttle bus was not allowed in the hangar area.

Agent Anderson walked over to where Julie and Captain Crossfield were standing and related the information to where they needed to go to catch the shuttle to the hotel. Unsure about where to go, one of the Chinese security agents offered to walk with them to the shuttle bus area.

Two vehicles arrived a few minutes later, and the drivers began loading the luggage into the storage areas. Agent Anderson helped the injured staff member into the second vehicle, and the driver secured the wheelchair in the rear. The remaining staff members and the Congressman's group climbed into the transport vehicles, and the two transporters left the airport.

As the transport vehicles traveled along the highway to the U.S. Mission, Agent Anderson said to the Congressman, "Well, that was easy." Congressman Harris replied, "Getting in is one thing. Getting out will be another."

CHAPTER TWENTY-TWO

Welcome to Wuhan China

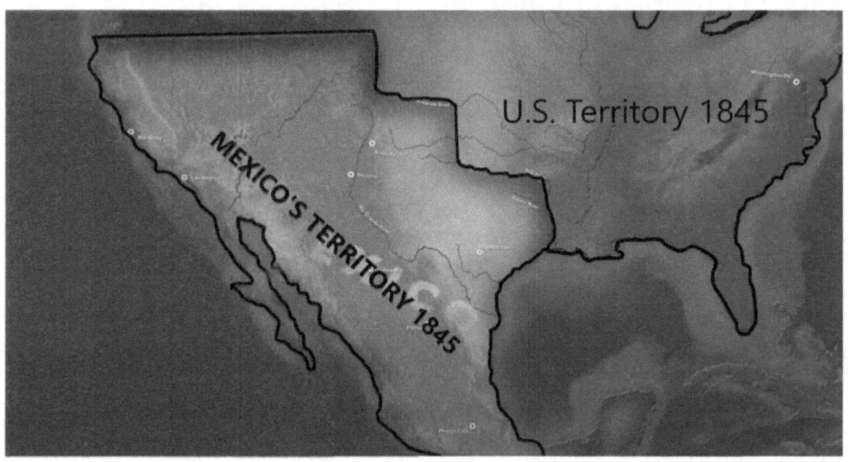

The fifteen-and-a-half-mile trip from the Wuhan airport to the U.S. Mission took over an hour. The two transport vehicles weaved in and out of traffic when possible, but the congestion of the streets of Wuhan rivaled a rush hour in New York City. The only advantage was that the trip gave the Congressman time to evaluate the problems they may encounter when returning to the Wuhan airport with the three women they needed to remove from China.

Professor Norris filled in the fine details as they sat in the lead transport vehicle crawling through traffic. According to the Professor's literature in his hand, "The world's largest experiment in driverless cars is underway on the busy streets of Wuhan, a city in central China with eleven million people, four and a half million vehicles, eight-lane expressways and towering bridges over the muddy waters of the Yangtze River."

The Professor picked up another brochure and continued reading, "A fleet of 500 taxis navigated by computers, often with no safety drivers for backup, buzzed around Wuhan. The company that operates them, tech giant Baidu, said last month that it would add another 1,000 of the so-called robot taxis in Wuhan shortly. As of June of this year, Baidu's Apollo Go has provided over three and a half million rides to the public across China." Congressman Harris says under his breath, "Well, that accounts for why we are sitting here in traffic and not moving."

The only sure thing was that traffic in Wuhan moved very slowly. The Congressman also noticed how many of the cars were electric vehicles. He did not see any cars driving unattended, but taxis appeared everywhere.

Another thing that surprised Congressman Harris was Chinese women's Western dress. Many of the women were wearing what appeared to be light sweatshirts and pants or leggings. The more mature women wore dresses with a high neckline; many had sleeves over half an arm's length. The color black, if black is a color, was as prominent as pink with the more mature women. He also noted that the shoes were closed-toe sandals for many women, and for those wearing hats, they consisted of a woven material with an overlapping brim. What the Congressman thought of as traditional Chinese clothing, loose, bright-colored, floral garments were nowhere to be found on the streets of Wuhan.

The Congressman sat formulating a plan as the transport weaved through traffic. The problem with the entire plan was that damn wheelchair they needed for the grandmother. They successfully used it to remove a Diplomatic staff member from the airplane, and the wheelchair was in the back of vehicle number two. They needed to somehow get the wheelchair into the hotel where the Professor and Mrs. Norris stayed without being obvious. He decided to put Mrs. Norris into the wheelchair when the couple checked in and put the wheelchair in their second rented room. That would get the wheelchair with the 'Diplomatic Staff' label attached to the hotel to move the grandmother when leaving Wuhan.

At that time, the Congressman realized Mrs. Norris would need an update on her wardrobe before she and the Professor registered at the hotel. The hotel was bound to have cameras, and Mrs. Norris's appearance would need to be blended in some way to make her stand out less. The Congressman knew there would come a time when they would need to substitute Mrs. Norris with the grandmother in the wheelchair, and they did not want to make it obvious it was a different person in the chair. Mrs. Norris's appearance was a problem the Congressman must address before the Professor and his wife registered in the hotel.

Finally, the two transports arrived at the U.S. Mission in Wuhan. The U.S. Mission is in downtown Wuhan's New World Trade Tower 1. As expected, the transports parked outside the building, and the Congressman and his staff were greeted by local police who performed security for the Mission. The Congressman informed the driver of the second transport to allow the eight Diplomatic staff members to enter the U.S. Mission. At the same time, Agent Anderson and the Congressman would accompany the Professor and Mrs. Norris to the hotel in the first transport vehicle. While the two transport drivers un-loaded the luggage from the second vehicle and escorted the eight staff members into the building, Agent Ander-son removed the wheelchair from the second vehicle and placed it in the first. A short time later, the driver of the first transport vehicle walked out of the building and re-entered the driver's seat to continue to the hotel where the Professor and his wife would stay.

As the transport pulled away from the U.S. Mission building, the Congressman turned to take a physical description of Mrs. Norris. She is about five foot six inches tall, has shorter sandy blonde hair, and a tanned skin tone like someone who spent much time at the beach. Mrs. Norris, he thought, is probably not the general description of a Chinese woman. She is wearing a green and white low-cut dress, displaying a fair-sized bosom, highlighted by a beautiful necklace, jewelry on both her wrists, and large earrings, all matching gold. By all accounts, Mrs. Norris was attractive, but the Congressman was unsure if Professor Norris ever noticed her beautiful eyes and smile. The Congressman could only see the Professor's eyes and mind buried only in books about history, and he believed a woman's physical being never came into the Professor's view.

The issue was not making Mrs. Norris appear Chinese but instead making her less of a standout among the other women around her. The green and white dress would need to go along with the jewelry. And the sandy blonde hair that highlighted an attractive face would need to be covered. The Congressman calls up to the driver, "Sir, is there a good women's clothing store in Wuhan?" The driver replied, "Wuhan is the fashion center in China, and we have many clothing stores in this city." Congressman Harris responds, "Great, take us to the best women's clothing store in Wuhan so I can make a special gift to Mrs. Norris."

Mrs. Norris's face went blank momentarily before she spoke, "Thank you, but I don't need any additional clothing. I have packed plenty of things to wear while we are here." The Congressman replies, "Nonsense, you are my guest, and I would like to treat you to something special for coming with us." Mrs. Norris responds, "Well, thank you. But you don't need to do it." Congressman Harris looks at the sandy-blonde-headed woman and answers, "Yes, we do. Please trust me. We need to get you some perfect clothing."

A short time later, the transport parked in front of a large women's clothing store. The Congressman instructed the driver to wait while they took care of their special guest. Congressman Harris takes Mrs. Norris by the hand and says, "We need to make you blend in better with the locals. I have noticed that local mature women, like yourself, wear many pink things with high necklines and sleeves. Let's pick out some lovely pink dresses with a touch of black and some closed-toe sandals. And I think a Petite Gabi Fedora hat will cover the sandy blonde hair, and a good pair of sunglasses will protect those beautiful eyes. And someone as pretty as you will not require all the jewelry to reflect your beauty."

Mrs. Norris looks down and says, "You are embarrassing me, Congressman," as she smiles back at him. The Congressman waves to a salesperson for assistance, and he and Mrs. Norris inform her what they are looking for. A half-hour later, Mrs. Norris emerges from the rear of the store dressed in a pink and black long-sleeve dress with a length almost to her ankles, a Gabi Fedora to cover her sandy blonde hair, and shoes to match the hat with a pair of perfect sunglasses. She carried two bags, one with her clothes and jewelry and another with a second set of new clothes.

Professor Norris stares at his wife and says, "My dear, you look beautiful in that color combination. But the sunglasses are hiding your gorgeous eyes." Congressman Harris takes a moment, thinking, 'I guess I was wrong about the Professor. He did notice her beautiful eyes and other features.'

The Congressman paid with his credit card, and the four exited the store and slid back into the transport to continue to the hotel. Congressman Harris leans to Mrs. Norris and whispers, "When you enter the hotel, Agent Anderson will push you in the wheelchair so we can get it to your second room unnoticed." Mrs. Norris nodded, indicating that she understood what the Congressman had said.

The transport arrived at the hotel, and the driver unloaded the luggage from the vehicle. The driver looked surprised when he found the wheelchair in his vehicle but said nothing. While he moved their luggage to a hotel cart, Agent Anderson removed the wheelchair from the storage area, and Mrs. Norris sat in it. The driver again looked surprised until Agent Anderson said, "The new shoes are hurting her feet, and I think this will be better for her." The driver smiled and replied, "That is a good idea; nothing worse than shoes that hurt."

Congressman Harris instructed the driver that they would be there for a short time and to wait in the parking area. Then, Congressman Harris, Agent Anderson, the Professor, and Mrs. Norris entered the hotel. The Congressman and Agent Anderson blocked Mrs. Norris from the cameras as much as possible as they waited for the Professor to sign in and pick up the door keys. When the Professor returned with the bellboy pushing the luggage cart, he informed the Congressman and Agent Anderson that they would be in adjoining rooms in rooms three-zero-six and three-zero-eight.

The elevator moved the group to the third floor, where they all exited into another large hallway. The bellboy unlocked the door to room three-zero-six, and Agent Anderson pushed Mrs. Norris into the room in the wheelchair. The bellboy walked next store to room three-zero-eight and unlocked it to allow the Congressman and the Professor to enter. Once the bellboy unloaded the luggage into the rooms, the Congressman reached into his pocket, took out two dollars, and handed it to the bellboy. As the room door closed, Professor Norris said, "Congressman, in China, tipping is frowned upon." Congressman

Harris replies, "Professor, that was not a frown on the bellboy's face."

Congressman Harris walks over and opens the adjoining door between the rooms to find Agent Anderson has already unlocked the other side of the door. Congressman Harris says, "Quick thinking Anderson when the driver questioned why she needed to be in the wheelchair. What the hell made you think of that?" Agent Anderson replies, "When I was in training, I had a pair of shoes that hurt, and I wished I had a chair to sit in."

The Congressman turns to Mrs. Norris, "I believe you have everything you need to perform your magic on the women." She points to one of the suitcases and replies, "All the things I need should be right in that case." Congressman Harris says, "You guys should unpack and get a good dinner. The hotel has my credit card, and you should not pay for anything. Anderson and I will return to the U.S. Mission and set up things in the private office. You have all the group's telephone numbers on your cell phone, so don't hesitate to call if you need something. I will keep you updated as information comes to me. Later, I will contact you after dinner tonight to ensure everything is okay. The rest of the day belongs to you, so enjoy whatever sites you can. Don't worry about anything, we got this."

Congressman Harris and Agent Anderson leave the room and head to the elevator to exit the hotel. Once outside the building, Agent Anderson sees the transport vehicle parked in the parking area for new arrivals. The two men walk to where the transport is parked and tap on the window for the driver to unlock the doors. The driver awakens, unlocks the doors, and asks if they want to return to the U.S. Mission. Congressman Harris tells the driver to take them back to the Mission, and the driver starts the transport and drives out of the parking area.

Agent Anderson asks the Congressman, "What is your schedule for this evening, Sir?" Congressman Harris responds, "Lots of telephone calls and a meeting with the Consul General at the U.S. Mission to explain why we are here." Agent Anderson replies, "How much will you tell the Consul General at the Mission?" Congressman Harris pauses before answering, "Just enough to give him a plausible denial should things go wrong. The less he knows, the better. We are here to rotate staff and inspect the U.S. Mission facility. We will leave eight new staff members and return five to the United States. I will not tell him much more unless I need to."

The transport arrived at the New World Trade Tower 1, where the U.S. Mission is housed, around ten minutes after leaving the hotel. The Congressman stood outside the building and tipped his head vertically to view the building. The driver comments, "Beautiful building, isn't she? Eight-hundred and ninety-six feet from the ground floor to the top. And the elevator can travel from the bottom to the top of the building in less than one minute." Congressman Harris looked at the ground, thinking, 'My God, another rocket ship ride.'

The driver loaded the Congressman's and Agent Anderson's luggage onto a cart, and they entered the building. The Congressman heard the driver say, "Room 4701, Sir, is where you are going." The three men entered the high-speed elevator, and the driver pressed the button for the fourth-seventh floor. The doors closed, and the elevator accelerated rapidly, like Julie's take-offs in the jet, straight up. The doors opened when the elevator came to rest, and the three men entered a massive hallway. The driver led the way to the principal U.S. Mission office. The door opened, and they entered.

A friendly American smile greeted them: "Hello, welcome to the U.S. Mission of Wuhan. I believe you are Congressman Harris, and I am sorry, I do not know the other gentleman's name with you." Congressman Harris says, "This is Agent Anderson, and he is the head of my security while we are in Wuhan." The smiling face responds, "You won't need much security in Wuhan. Wuhan is one of the heaviest policed cities in the world." The Congressman replies, "Thank you for assuring us of that fact. I hope we do not need the police for any issues that may arise."

A door to an inter-office opened, and the Consul General stepped out to greet the Congressman. "Good to meet you, Congressman Harris." The Consul General said. "And the person with you is?" Congressman Harris repeats his previous answer, "This is Agent Anderson, my security person." The Consul General continues, "Well, it is good to meet both of you. Please come into my private office, and I can answer any questions."

The three men entered the Consul General's private office and were seated at a large desk. The Consul General says, "You will need to forgive me, but I was unaware of this visit and the staff rotation until just a few days ago. Is there a problem I should be alerted to?" Congressman Harris replies, "There is no problem with anything you do. I just needed some time out of Washington and decided to visit China. What better reason than to spend taxpayer money during a staff rotation or inspection? And get a vacation at the same time." The Consul General responds, "Perfect, but I know of only five staff members making a rotation, and you brought eight." Congressman Harris replies, "That is my fault. When I was back in Washington, I had some bad information about the number of people being rotated, and I did not have the heart to tell the three of them that they could not go. Besides, the extra staff will come in handy here in China." The Consul General says, "Extra hands are always welcome when working with the public. If nothing is wrong at the Mission, let my staff show you your lodging and private office space. If you need anything, let my private secretary know, and she will ensure it gets done for you."

The Consul General pressed a button, and his private secretary entered the room through a side door. "Gentlemen, this is Ms. Miller." The Consul General said. "She will assist you in any way necessary during your stay. Ms. Miller, please show the Congressman and Agent Anderson their private office and have a staff member take them to their lodging on the next floor." The private secretary nodded without speaking, and the three of them left the private office.

Once outside the private office, she guided them down the hall to another room where the Congressman could set up his office and handed the Congressman the key. Once the Congressman and Agent Anderson placed some miscellaneous items in the office, the secretary called for another staff member to take them to the next floor for their lodging.

The transport driver, who had been waiting in the hall, moved their luggage on the cart into the elevator with the Congressman, Agent Anderson, and the staff person and pressed the button for the next floor. This time, the elevator accelerated more slowly, and within seconds, the doors re-opened, allowing everyone to exit. Congressman Harris felt relieved as the last thing he needed today was another trip on a rocket ship.

The staff member said, "Here are the keys to your quarters," as she opened the doors. As the transport driver moved the luggage into each room, the Congressman thanked the staff member and bid her a good day. The Mission staff member left, and the transport driver followed her down the long hall to the elevator. As the door to the room closed, the Congressman moved over to a chair and sat down. As he removed his shoes, he closed his eyes and thought, 'So far, so good.'

CHAPTER TWENTY-THREE

The Plan Comes Together

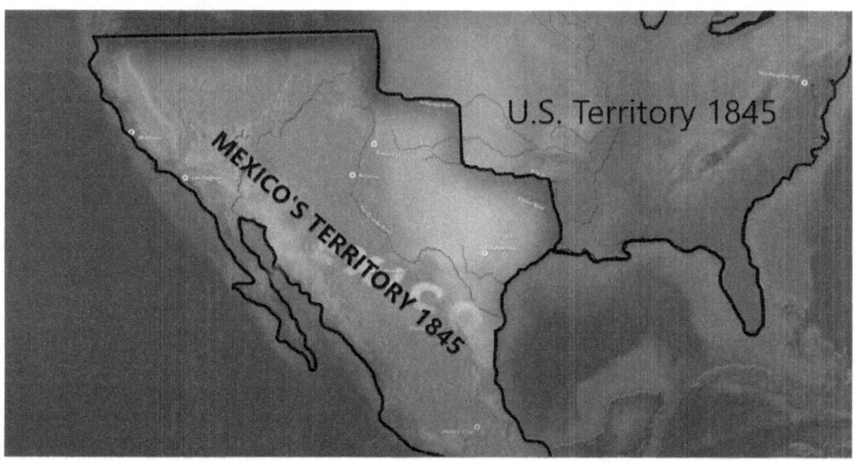

As the Congressman sat in the chair exhausted, his mind drifted back to something his mother had always told him. His mother would say, "Kevin, there is no rest for the wicked." My God, he thought, based on my mother's theory, I must be one of the most wicked people on the earth. His memories were interrupted by a knock on the door and Agent Anderson's voice requesting to come in. The Congressman slowly stood from the chair and walked to the door to open it. He opened the door and said, "Yes, Agent Anderson, I see we have had enough rest. We have been here almost ten minutes." Agent Anderson ignores the sarcasm and replies, "I was thinking, Sir, we probably should get something for dinner before you start your telephone calls. If we don't go and get something before you start, you will probably not get a good meal tonight. Besides, the time difference in Washington is twelve hours, making it six a.m. in D.C. If we take an hour for dinner, that will give Bill and Ken time to wake up, and the calls will be more beneficial for both parties."

The Congressman interrupts, "Okay, I get it. I'm also hungry. Let's go and get a good meal. Do you have any ideas as to where to go for something?" Agent Anderson reaches into his pocket and removes a flyer he picked up at the Marriott Hotel when they dropped off the Professor and his wife. He hands the flyer to the Congressman and says, "What do you think, Sir? It is close to us, and the flyer claims they have the best American-style steak in China."

The Congressman returns to the chair where he left his shoes and says, "Sure, looks like a great place to have dinner." As they left his room and walked down the hallway to the elevator, he thought, "We have come halfway around the world to have an American-style steak in China. Even in China, people don't want to eat Chinese food."

The restaurant was a short walk, and as the brochure stated, they served an American-style steak dinner. Agent Anderson and the Congressman took the liberty to enjoy an after-dinner drink and joked about Agent Anderson's Mrs. Norris shoes hurt comment to the transport driver at the hotel. Congressman Harris repeats, "I must hand it to you, Anderson. That was quick thinking on your part about the wheelchair." Agent Anderson replies, "Yeah, but that incident points out another problem with our plans. We can not make excuses for what we do to the transport drivers without causing a problem. Sooner or later, one of them will say something, and the result of that could be fatal to the task at hand. Did you say there are Marines at the U.S. Mission to handle classified materials?" Congressman Harris replies, "I believe there are several assigned to the Mission, and each has a 'Top Secret' clearance." Agent Anderson responds, "I'll bet two of them would make great drivers for the transport vehicles. And we could trust them not to say anything about our actions in Wuhan. The real advantage would be that when we travel back to the Wuhan airport, they could drive us right up to the aircraft to board and depart China, and there would be no questions about the additional three women with us." The Congressman sat and digested Agent Anderson's statement before speaking, "I think you have a great idea, and I will take it up with the Consul General tomorrow morning. He will probably question why we need two Marines to drive us around Wuhan, but I will think of a reason by morning. It's starting to get late, and I need to make several calls tonight to ensure everything is still on track."

The Congressman signed the credit card bill for dinner, and the two men left the restaurant and walked back to the Wuhan New World Trade Tower building, where they would spend the night. As earlier, the Congressman dreaded the trip up in the highspeed elevator and held on to the handle on the elevator wall when it ascended the forty-plus floors. To state the Congressman was not a fan of flying straight up into the air would be an understatement after the first takeoff with Julie at the controls of the private jet. When the elevator stopped on the forty-eighth floor, he checked to see if he still had his stomach and all it contained from dinner. As the door opens, Agent Anderson says, "You're looking a little ill, Congressman. Are you okay?" The Congressman replies, "I will be fine. I can't get used to rocketing straight up in the air on the highspeed elevators. I will call you in the morning around eight unless something comes up that will need your attention sooner. Have a good night, Agent Anderson."

The two men opened the doors to each of their rooms and entered. Congressman Harris walked directly to the chair, sat, and removed his shoes. The long trip from the United States to China had taken its toll, and he wanted to lie down and sleep, but he needed to make several phone calls before his day ended. The first call would be to Julie to ensure she was okay, and the next would be to his office in Washington for updates with his secretary, Bill, and computer crackpot Ken.

The Congressman picks up the encrypted cell phone Ken provided to the group and presses the speed dial for Julie. Two rings later, Julie was on the phone, sounding worried. Julie asks, "Kevin, Is everything okay?" The Congressman answers, "Everything is going as planned or as close to the plan as possible." Julie says, "Did anything serious happen?" Congressman Harris responds, "Nothing serious; we just needed to buy Mrs. Norris a new set of clothes." Julie responds, "New clothes, why new clothes?" Congressman Harris says, "Julie, I will tell you all about it tomorrow, and then you will understand why the new clothes. Did you get something to eat tonight?" Julie says, "Captain Crossfield and I grabbed a bite at a small restaurant in the hotel. Not bad for hotel food but not the best either." Congressman Harris responds, "I am glad you guys got something to eat, but I must call Washington now. Julie, don't let the bed bugs bite, and get some sleep. Tomorrow will be a big day, and I need your moral support." The soft voice on the other end of the line said, "Good night, Kevin, and please get some rest. We need you, no, I need you. Goodnight." And the cell phone disconnected.

The Congressman sat motionless for some time in his chair. It had been a long time since such a soft female voice wished him goodnight, touching him deeply as he sat. Unfortunately, his feelings would need to wait until another time as he needed to speak with his office in Washington.

Pressing the screen on the cell phone, he finally located his office phone number in Washington. It would be slightly after eight a.m. in Washington, and he hoped someone would answer. After three rings, his secretary's voice, Bill, garbled, "Good morning, Congressman Harris' office. How may I help you?" The Congressman replies, "Bill, it's Harris. Are you okay?" Bill responds, "Sure, Ken and I are okay. We are spending nights sleeping on an office couch and small cot. Why shouldn't we be okay?"

Congressman Harris moves the cell phone away from his mouth, smiles, and laughs. He returns the cell to his mouth and asks, "Has security been in the office with you guys the entire time?" Bill replies, "Security comes in and changes guards in six-hour shifts. A new person replaces the one finishing this shift every six hours." Congressman Harris asks, "Do the guards find it strange you two are sleeping in the office?" Bill pauses before answering, "They did at first, but I told them Ken, and I are partners, and we lost our apartment because the rent was too high, and now we are forced to stay here in the office." Congressman Harris could not help but laugh into the phone while trying to speak, "Do you think they believed that story?" Bill answers, "I think they believed the story because not one of the guards will sit next to Ken or me." Congressman Harris says, "Great, is Ken awake? I need to speak with him." On the other end of the line, Bill's tired voice says, "Let me get Ken for you. Please hold on."

The Congressman could hear Bill shaking Ken in the background to wake him up. Ken answered the phone with a single word, "Hello." "Ken, Congressman Harris here," said the Congressman. "Are you awake enough to talk right now?" The Congressman concluded and waited for an answer. Ken replies, "Sure, I was just resting here waiting for you to call."

Congressman Harris pauses for Ken to wake up and speak with him before saying, "Ken, I have some information that may or may not be helpful. I have learned that a car company in China builds and deploys driverless taxis throughout Wuhan and other parts of China. The company's name is Baidu, and they operate a fleet of five hundred taxis navigated by computers without backup drivers in Wuhan. They may call the taxis Baidu's Apollo Go or something like that, and they are so-called robot taxis. What struck me was that they are computer-controlled, right up your alley. You should check this out and see if and how they are regulated. Would it be possible for you to 'hack' into the taxi control system? Maybe we could also find a way to use it to move the three women. While you are looking at things in Wuhan, the Professor and his wife stay at the Mariott Hotel in downtown Wuhan, which has security cameras. Are they accessible from outside of the Mariott's building? In other words, can you control the camera and security system at the hotel if we need you to take control?" Ken's voice on the phone sounded disoriented when he replied, "Give me a second to write all of this down."

The Congressman could hear Ken's voice in the background repeating the words as he wrote them down, "Mariott Hotel, Baidu Company, Baidu's Apollo Go, robot taxis, downtown Wuhan." Ken finally says, "Okay. Is there anything else you need me to look at?" Congressman Harris responds, "Have you been monitoring our progress with the tag and cell tracking?" Ken replies, "I have been monitoring your locations and every move you have made in Wuhan. The next move will depend on contacting the C.I.A. agents working in Wuhan and locating the three women. From what I understand from Bill, they will contact you tomorrow before noon at Wuhan time. There will not be much for Bill and I to do until contact with the agents has been made and the three women are located. It is early morning here, so it must be early evening in Wuhan. You should get a good night's sleep and start fresh tomorrow morning. By then I should have the information on the things you just gave me to do. Please, Congressman, go to bed so I can get up and go to work." Congressman Harris ends the call with, "Thank you, Ken. I will call you when I get up in the morning." And he disconnected the cell phone.

The Congressman stood from the chair and headed to the shower to rinse off eleven hours of travel. The questions in his head would need to wait until after he had a good night's sleep before he would find the answers. After his shower, he flipped open a suitcase and picked up his nightwear. Looking into the carefully packed suitcase, the Congressman imagined a flashback of how his wife would have packed it differently. She would say that the socks are always packed on the left side of the case to make them easier to find. The Congressman stood as he realized his grave mistake by putting the socks on the right side of the case. As he turned to lay on the bed, he thought changing sides for the socks in the case would be addressed in the future. Tonight, he needed a sound sleep to prepare for whatever issues would present themselves tomorrow. The Congressman laid back and closed his eyes, drifting into a deep sleep.

The alarm on the Congressman's cell phone began to ring at seven a.m. the following morning. As the Congressman lay in bed, he thought about the snooze button on the phone, but instead of pressing it, he sat up and looked around the room, trying to verify where he was. Strangely, he thought, no matter how often you wake up in temporary housing, you still feel lost when you first wake up in unfamiliar surroundings.

Planting his feet firmly on the floor, he placed one foot in front of the other toward the bathroom. The bathroom was the only stop he was sure of this morning, and after that, the rest of the day was an unknown maze. While he was standing in the shower, the shower's hot water started to wash away the drowsiness of the night's sleep, and the reality of the upcoming day filled the void. He remembered what the smiling U.S. Mission secretary said about Wuhan being one of the safest and most heavily policed cities in China. The last thing the Congressman and his group needed was the attention of the Chinese police while they were trying to extract the three women from the city. An old saying goes, 'Where is a policeman when you need one?' When it comes to the police in Wuhan, the opposite was true. 'When you don't need a policeman, they are everywhere and in large numbers.'

He removed his socks from the wrong side of his suitcase and put them on. He slipped his feet into his shoes and looked around the room to see if he was forgetting anything. Once satisfied he was leaving nothing behind, he grabbed his briefcase and opened the door. Standing outside Agent Anderson's room, he knocked and waited for an answer. A tap on his shoulder alerted the Congressman that someone was standing behind him. As the Congressman turned, he came face to face with Agent

Anderson standing behind him. Agent Anderson says, "Good morning Sir. I have been waiting for you to get up." The Congressman replies, "I have been awake and waiting for you, Agent Anderson. I was afraid I was going to wake you."

The two men smiled and walked to the elevator for their morning rocket ride down to the building coffee shop on the ground floor. Standing outside the coffee shop, the Congressman slowly reads the sign "Starbucks" posted over the main door. Congressman Harris tells Agent Anderson, "No matter where you go, 'Starbucks' will find you. Please make mine a black coffee. I will need something to get me started today."

With coffee in hand, the two men rocketed back up to the forty-seventh floor to their temporary private office. The Congressman unlocked the door, and they entered the private office. Agent Anderson sat in a wooden chair in front of the single office desk, sipping his coffee, and the Congressman took the chair behind the desk. Congressman Harris spoke first, "Agent Anderson, I think you should take a transport to the Professor's hotel and make sure everything is ready at that location to receive the women. I will remain here to make calls and deal with any issues or problems. Call me on the cell if anything has changed or we missed something." Agent Anderson replies, "Got it. I will be leaving in a few minutes. Anything else before I go?" Congressman Harris responds, "I don't think so, but this whole thing is very fluid and changes by the minute."

Agent Anderson stands and leaves the private office en route to the Mariott Hotel, where the Professor is staying. Congressman Harris unpacks his laptop computer and sets it up on the office desk. He turns the laptop on, and the computer comes to life, and everything works despite the 'Great China Firewall.' Ken was right, he thought. The 'Great China Firewall' is ineffective on the changes Ken made on the computer. He opened the email program and started to read the emails when a knock on the door was followed by the Consul General entering the office.

The Consul General says, "Good morning, Congressman. I see you have set up your office already," Congressman Harris replies, "Not ready, but there is not much to set up. A laptop and some papers." The Consul General responds, "You did a great job anyway. May I sit down and speak frankly with you?" The Congressman gestures with his hand for the Consul General to sit.

The Consul General leans forward and says, "I am not sure why you have come to Wuhan, and I don't want to know any details about why. And I don't need more information to give me a plausible denial claim. Is there anything you need from me behind the scenes to help you achieve whatever you are doing?" Congressman Harris smiles before answering, "Is it that obvious? I hoped we put on a better show. Does your staff think anything other than what we told them?" The Consul General replies, "The staff doesn't pay much attention to details like I do. I don't think they care why you are here."

Congressman Harris pauses before speaking, "I understand you have at least two Marines at the Mission for classified document handling. I don't want to say your transport drivers have caused a problem, and in fact, they are excellent, but." The Consul General interrupts, "You want me to assign two Marines to drive your transport vehicles." Congressman Harris replies, "Well, yes. That is precisely what I was going to ask of you." The Consul General says, "I have two in mind that will take good care of you. They hear and see nothing. They will drive and take you and the others in your group where you need to go. No questions asked. Please advise my front office secretary when you need the drivers; she will make them available."

Congressman Harris smiles and says, "That is what we need. Please understand that if everything goes well, the five rotation staff members and my group will leave Wuhan on short notice. I will try to give them time to gather their belongings, but it will be short notice. Please advise them."

The Consul General replies, "I will inform the staff to be ready to leave on short notice as you have requested. It will be an emergency back in Washington. I don't know why you are here, but I sense it is crucial. Good luck,

Congressman." The Consul General stood and turned to leave the office. He stops and says, "Congressman, I don't recall speaking with you today about anything." The Congressman nodded to acknowledge what the Consul General had told him as he left the office.

Congressman Harris continued reading his emails, thinking that working with the Consul General behind the scenes had solved the issue of transport drivers. Now, he needed to wait to hear from the C.I.A. agents in Wuhan to arrange to remove the three women from China. His only fear was that one or more of the women would not wish to leave China for whatever reason. He would ask that question of each woman, and they alone would answer it. They could choose to stay in China or leave with them to go to the United States. Whatever their answer was, they would decide whether to stay or leave.

CHAPTER TWENTY-FOUR
The Time Line Details

The cell phone started vibrating alongside the Congressman on the office desk. As the Congressman lifted the phone from the desk, he discovered that he must have turned off the ringer tone, and the cell phone was set to vibrate-only mode. He could not recognize the phone number on the display and hesitated to answer. There was another moment of hesitation before he finally decided to push the answer button on the phone to accept the call. "Hello," Congressman Harris said, "May I ask who is calling?" A voice on the other end of the phone replied in heavily accented, broken English, "Congressman, fifteen minutes, go out the main entrance of the building, turn right, and walk to the first intersection. Put your right hand up in the air for a taxi." And the cell phone disconnected.

Congressman Harris was unsure of what to make of the call. It was apparent that whoever was on the phone knew who he was. But the directions were minimal: out of the building, turn right to the first intersection, and hail a taxi. How would he know if he had the correct taxi? The streets of Wuhan are packed bumper to bumper with taxis. The Congressman felt very uncomfortable filling his briefcase and exiting the office door. Doing this is crazy, he thought as he navigated the building's hallways and rocket ship elevator to the ground floor. I am about to walk out of a secure building into an unknown city, possibly meeting an unknown person or persons for unknown reasons. Even with all the possible things that could go wrong in his head, the Congressman exited the building and turned right, stopping at the first intersection with his hand waving above his head. A car pulled up in front of the Congressman and stopped. The markings were all in Chinese, and as far as Congressman Harris knew, it could have been a food delivery vehicle. Undaunted, the Congressman opened the rear door and slid in. The car immediately pulled from the curb and started down the wide street, going to places unknown. Congressman Harris sat looking at the rear of the driver's short-haired head. Without looking back at the Congressman, the driver began speaking in Chinese, and when the Congressman did not answer, the driver switched to broken English. The driver said, "Welcome to Wuhan, Congressman Harris. My name is, well, call me 'Mr. X,' for a name. I understand you have come to take three women from Wuhan." Without warning, the driver quickly turned and continued down another street.

"We will have the three women with us tomorrow afternoon before one p.m. The authorities are not closely watching them, and collecting them should not be a problem," Mr. X said. After a pause, Mr. X continued, "We saw your tall, dark-skinned man on his way to the Marriott Hotel earlier." The Congressman interrupts, "Have you been watching us all the time we have been in Wuhan?" Mr. X laughs before replying, "We have been watching you since you boarded your private jet in Washington. Please listen and not speak, as this is important. The three women will be at the Marriott Hotel at exactly one thirty p.m. tomorrow. A service entrance at the back of the building leads to service elevators directly inside the worker entrance. Have your dark-skinned man pretend he is lost and wander into this area by mistake. Hotel staff will not question his being in the area if he pretends he is lost." Congressman Harris interrupts, "What about the cameras in that hotel area? Hotel security will surely see the activity on the cameras." Mr. X says, "Congressman, please stop interrupting. The cameras in the hotel service area are not functioning as of this morning. The hotel maintenance staff removed them from that area this morning for service, claiming a communication issue with their computer server. Two of my people will be inside the service entrance, guiding the transfer operation and keeping hotel staff away from the area using whatever distractions are required. I will make the transfer of the women to your dark-skinned man. From there, he can move the three women to where your accomplices are waiting by using the service elevator. The older woman will be in her wheelchair when you receive her, and the other two will be able to walk. Please be aware once the dark-skinned man takes control, we can no longer help you. I believe the authorities will not miss them for about four or five hours from the time you receive them. You will have a narrow safety window to work within to do whatever you must to disguise the women. I suggest you and your people leave Wuhan at six p.m or earlier. I have given you all the help possible, and the rest of the planning depends on you." The Congressman asks, "Please, one question. Do you believe the three women want to leave China?" Mr. X responds, "The Chinese government has imprisoned these women for some time just because of who they are, where they were working, or who they knew. No matter how large the cell is, a prison is still a prison. The women were locked in the entire city of Wuhan, but still, to them, it was a jail cell unable to contact friends and loved ones. You provide a chance for them to leave China, and they will go."

The car stopped abruptly, followed by Mr. X saying, "This is where you get out. Your building is right down the street." Mr. X repeats, "The hotel's service entrance at exactly one thirty tomorrow." The Congressman opened the rear car door and slid out of the vehicle. Mr. X had dropped the Congressman exactly where the taxi picked him up. As he walked back to the U.S. Mission building, he was trying to work out the fine details of the events for tomorrow. There would be no room for error based on the four-hour window to get the three women, disguise them, and leave Wuhan. He began to laugh when he arrived at the main door of the New World Trade Building. He thought, 'If he ever decided to write a book about his life, he would not include what had just happened with Mr. X as no one would believe it. A story like the one that happened today would only be written in a cheap novel and not a biography.'

The Congressman entered the building to ride the rocket ship elevator to the forty-seventh floor. Upon arrival, he entered the U.S. Mission's main office and met the smiling young lady from the day before.

The Congressman said, "Good to see you again. I believe arrangements have been made for two of your security staff to act as our drivers around Wuhan." The young lady replies, "That is correct." Congressman Harris continues, "How long would it take for them to be available to transport my staff around the city?" The young lady says, "One of the men is in the building currently, and the other could be here in about an hour." The Congressman replies, "Right now, I only need one of the drivers. Please inform him I need my staff to move from the Marriot hotel to this building for a meeting. I will call my staff at the Hotel and have them ready to be picked up. And thank you again, pretty lady."

The Congressman walked down the hall to his temporary private office. After entering, he sat in the chair behind the desk, called Agent Anderson, and instructed him to bring the Professor and Mrs. Norris to the U.S. Mission for a meeting and that the Marine substitute driver would shortly arrive at the Hotel with the transport vehicle.

Time, time, he thought. The only thing he did not have was time. It's such short notice to make this all happen. The Congressman would need to lay out the plan for the staff in Wuhan and update Bill and Ken in Washington with the details.

And then, of course, Julie and Captain Crossfield would also need to be updated about the new plan. They would need to be at the Airport before the transport vehicles arrived, carrying the Diplomatic staff being rotated from the Mission, the Congressman and his group, and the three Chinese women. There would be no room for an error or misunderstanding between anyone in his group.

Forty-five minutes later, the door to the temporary office opened, and Agent Anderson, the Professor, and his wife entered. Congressman Harris says, "I'd like to offer you all a chair, but as you can see, we have only two. Mrs. Norris, please take the chair and let the strong men stand."

Congressman Harris continues, "I was in contact with the Wuhan agent we will work with. He called himself Mr. X." Agent Anderson says, "Sir, Mr. X? You accepted that as a name?" The Congressman asks, "Agent Anderson, would you feel better if his name were Smith or Jones?" Agent Anderson responds, "Well, no. I just thought the Mr. X name seemed fake." The Congressman replies, "Of course, the name is fake. They are undercover C.I.A. agents in a foreign country. Let me continue if I may. Mr. X advised me that a service entrance at the rear of the Marriott Hotel leads to an open area inside the Hotel. His people have turned off the cameras in the area, and there is a service elevator to move the women to the third floor.

Mrs. Norris must have everything ready to make her magic. I hate to say this, but you will have about an hour and a half to do all three women and make them look like the photos created by Ken and yourself."

Mrs. Norris looks at the Congressman and says, "How long did you say I have to do all this?" Congressman Harris replies, "An hour and a half, two hours on the outside." Mrs. Norris responds, "That is very little time to cut their hair, adjust their eyebrows, and make up for skin tone correction, and God only knows what else to make them look like a Filipino woman." The Professor says, "Don't forget they will need to try on and get dressed in the clothes we brought from the United States to make them appear more Western." Mrs. Norris looks directly at her husband and says, "Maybe you should be in charge of dressing them." The Professor backed away from his wife as she spoke. The Congressman could see her first name may be Angel, but the Professor knew she could also be a devil if needed and was moving out of Angel's reach.

Congressman Harris intervenes by saying, "Alright, I know the time frame is narrow, but that is what we must work with. Maybe you can combine the things you must do on all three women simultaneously. Besides, Agent Anderson will be there with you to assist with the women." Agent Anderson speaks up, "I will? I will be there?" In a surprised voice. The Congressman replies, "Yes, Agent Anderson, you can assist Mrs. Norris in whatever capacity is required other than personally dressing the women."

The Congressman pauses for questions before continuing, "Your transport vehicle will be at the front of the Marriott Hotel at exactly four p.m. to take you three and the three women to the Airport. Take everything with you except the old wheelchair. Find a storage closet on the floor and place the old chair there. The grandmother must be wheeled out in the Diplomatic Staff marked wheelchair. And don't forget to give each woman their identification papers so they can carry them on their person. The transport vehicle will move to the arrival parking area and wait for the second transport, carrying the five staff members and myself. Once I arrive, Professor Norris will change places with me to entertain the staff members on the way to the Airport. Transferring will allow me to contact the rest of our group members privately to direct the exit from China and receive updates on possible issues from Ken in Washington."

Professor Norris asks, "How will Ken back in Washington assist us here in China?" Congressman Harris replies, "Ken is currently monitoring a great deal of the security electronics in Wuhan. He is also able to access the Wuhan Lab computers and security systems. Ken should be able to warn us if a security alert is issued anywhere in Wuhan during our departure." The Professor responds, "Sounds like 'black magic' to me, all smoke and mirrors."

The Congressman concludes the meeting by saying, "I know the schedule will be tight, but the transport vehicle will be outside the Hotel at four-thirty. I think that is all for now. Mr. and Mrs. Norris, please return to your Hotel and lay everything out, including the clothes we brought from the States. Pack everything and take it with you when the three women's disguises are complete. Agent Anderson, do you want to go with them to help get everything ready?" Agent Anderson looks at the Professor for direction as to what to do. Professor Norris waved his hand to gesture they would need no help getting things ready at the Marriott Hotel.

The Congressman reconsiders and says, "Agent Anderson, on second thought, why don't you return to the Hotel with them and check out the service area today?" Agent Anderson nods his head in agreement.

"As for me," said the Congressman, "I need to tie up the loose ends here to prepare for tomorrow. So why don't you three get out of here and let me do my work." The Professor, his wife, and Agent Anderson left the office to return to the Hotel to prepare everything for the main event.

The Congressman stood and left the temporary office and decided to walk the flight of stairs down to the U.S. Mission office. As he entered the main Mission office, another young lady was at the greeting area desk. The Congressman said, "Hello, I am Congressman Harris, and I need to arrange for our departure tomorrow afternoon."

The young lady replied, "Of course, Sir, I can help you. What is your schedule for tomorrow?"

Congressman Harris begins, "I would like the five Mission staff members who are being rotated to the States in this office at two-forty-five p.m. I would like to have one of the transport vehicles here simultaneously to allow us time to load. At four p.m. I want the second transport vehicle at the Marriott Hotel to pick up the rest of my staff. Advise him he may need to wait a short time for them to gather everything. I plan to travel in the first transport vehicle to the Marriott Hotel and join the other transport so we can all leave together to travel to the Airport. I hope this doesn't seem complicated." The young lady smiled and replied, "Not at all, Sir. We understand the difficulty of moving around in Wuhan with all the traffic, and it only makes sense to keep both transports together." Congressman Harris replies, "Thank you. I will be here tomorrow to pick up the staff and return them to the States." The Congressman turns and leaves the Mission office, walks down the hall, and re-enters his loaner private office.

After sitting in his chair, the next call would be to Julie to advise her about the updated departure schedule. He pressed the speed dial for Julie, and after several rings, Julie answered. The soft voice replied, "Hello Kevin, where have you been?" The Congressman replies, "I will fill you in on what happened today when returning to the States. I must update you on what you and Captain Crossfield must do tomorrow. We are leaving Wuhan tomorrow afternoon, probably around six p.m. I think you and Captain Crossfield should go to the Airport around noon and devise a reason to move the aircraft from the hangar onto the tarmac for 'engine testing' or any other reason you can come up with. Please start the engines several times during the day to keep them warm if we need to leave quickly." Julie interrupts, "Are you expecting trouble?" Congressman Harris replies, "I don't know of any trouble as of right now, but this thing is so fluid that I want to be ready for any events."

Julie replies, "Captain Crossfield and I will be at the Airport by noon tomorrow. I will instruct the ground crew to move the aircraft out of the hangar for engine test maintenance. I will also have the airplane turned around to eliminate the need for a push truck to turn it later." Congressman Harris repeats, "Please have the engines warm for a six p.m. takeoff in case something goes wrong." Julie's response is direct, "Captain Crossfield and I know our job, and we will have the airplane warmed up and ready to fly at six p.m." The phone disconnects abruptly.

Congressman Harris laid the cell phone down on his desk, thinking, 'I believe I just pissed Julie off.' He lifted the cell phone and considered calling Julie back, but his excellent sense stopped him. Telling a detailed woman like Julie about how to do her job was not a good decision on his part. And calling her back right now would only aggravate her more. He laid the cell phone back on his desk and opened his e-mail on the laptop. Sitting there reading the e-mails, he thought, 'Dealing with the Chinese security police would be easier than dealing with a mad Julie.'

He looked at his watch and realized the day was slipping away quickly. The Congressman decided that when Agent Anderson returned from the Marriott Hotel, he, Congressman Harris, would decide what to eat for dinner. Tonight, I am making an executive decision. Tonight, Agent Anderson and I will have Chinese food.

CHAPTER TWENTY-FIVE
The Last Day in Wuhan

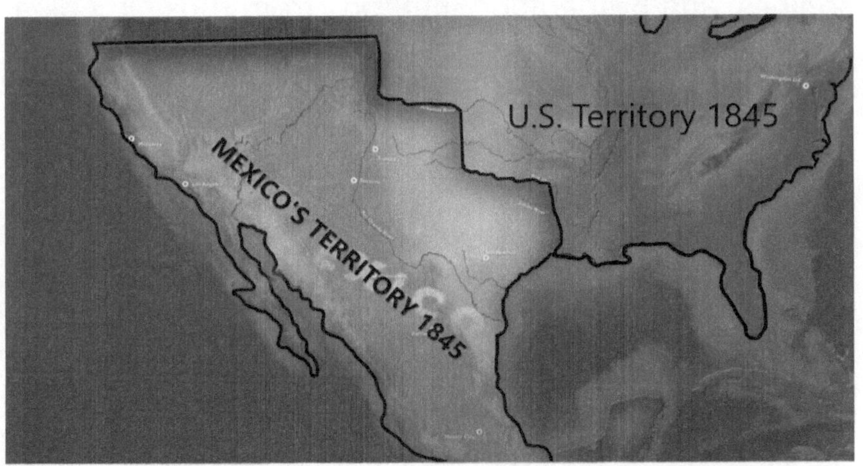

The Chinese food from earlier that evening sounded the first alarm in the Congressman's stomach around eleven thirty. Grabbing his laptop from the nightstand, he headed to the bathroom as the image of not going there would be hard to bear. While sitting on the toilet, he quickly researched American Chinese food and compared it to China's Chinese food.

The search engine displayed the following: 'American Chinese food is different from the food served in China. American Chinese cuisine has been adapted to suit American tastes, often sweeter and more heavily sauced than traditional Chinese dishes. Additionally, American Chinese dishes may differ in ingredients, spices, seasonings, and preparation methods from those in China. Dishes served in China may cause indigestion, stomach discomfort, or severe diarrhea.'

Congressman Harris dropped his head, thinking, 'My God, I wish I had known this before I ate all that Chinese food. The way I feel, I am going to live on a toilet for the entire day.' As he sat there, other noises from his stomach confirmed his worst nightmare. How will I get around today when I can't even get off the toilet?

He quickly traveled to the nightstand and picked up his cell phone before returning to the commode. As he sat on the toilet, he dialed the office in Washington. After two rings, his secretary, Bill, answered, "Hello, Congressman's Harris Office. How may I assist you today." The Congressman takes a deep breath to avoid sounding distressed and says, "Bill, this is Harris. I need to speak with Ken and you. Could you enter my private office, close the door, and put me on speakerphone so you and Ken may hear what I need to say?" Bill replies, "Sure thing, Sir, please give me a moment, and I will be right back with you from your office."

The Congressman could hear the music on hold playing in the background while he waited for Bill to pick up his office phone. Finally, Bill re-answered and said, "I have Ken also here with me on speakerphone. Have there been changes since we last spoke? And by the way, it is almost noon here, which makes it midnight where you are. Why are you calling in the middle of the night?" The Congressman answers slowly, "Well, I was just sitting here and decided to review the last-minute details with you guys. I don't want any shit, no, I mean problems tomorrow with the plans." Congressman Harris closed his eyes, not believing what he had just said. The loudest voice in the bathroom was his poor stomach crying out for help, and he was sure Bill and Ken could hear it. He quickly looked at the cell phone screen for the mute button should it be needed in an emergency.

The Congressman takes another deep breath and says, "I sent you a text message detailing what will happen here in Wuhan. Did you receive and review what I sent you?" Bill replies, "We received the message, and Ken and I have reviewed it." Congressman Harris continues, "Get a lot of coffee and energy drinks, as you both will be up all night monitoring what is happening in Wuhan. Ken, you are both our eyes and ears. Bill, you must support Ken if he needs extra hands." Bill and Ken respond, "We got this, Sir. We are ready." Ken interrupts and says, "By the way. Those taxis we spoke about in Wuhan. The taxis that do not have drivers. I checked it out, and they are all controlled by a central computer in Wuhan's business district. I intercepted some of their communication between the taxis and the central computer and hacked into the system. It works because the central computer accepts a request for a taxi service and dispatches a cab to that location to pick up the passenger. The central computer automatically charges the taxi fare to the passenger's account. Pretty cool, huh?" The Congressman responds, "I am glad you figured that all out, Ken, and if I should need a taxi while I am here, I will contact you." Ken replies, "I thought it was interesting that I could control all the taxis in Wuhan from Washington."

The Congressman says, "It's not that it is not interesting, but I don't know how useful summoning a cab will be tomorrow. More importantly, you can monitor police, city security systems, and traffic controls. We can not afford to get stuck in a traffic jam and not be able to get to the airport quickly." Ken replies, "Yes, Sir. I have your back on this and will not disappoint you."

The phone went quiet momentarily, and Bill said, "Congressman, are you near a water machine or something? We can hear a grumbling in the background." Congressman Harris replies, "Well, no, I am making a cup of coffee, and that noise is from the coffee maker. It must have air in it or something. Okay, that is all I needed to speak with you about, so get rested for the main event." The

Congressman disconnected the phone immediately after finishing the sentence, knowing that Bill and Ken had heard enough.

Congressman Harris remained in the bathroom for another hour before he thought it would be safe to return to bed. First thing in the morning, he must find something to treat the self-inflicted diarrhea caused by the Chinese food.

It was slightly before eight a.m. when he woke, and a quick trip to the shower offered little relief from his still upset digestive system. He dressed and headed to the U.S. Mission office on the floor below for directions to a local pharmacy. Upon entering the Mission's main office, the Congressman was greeted by the sweet young lady from a day prior. He spoke in a low voice to the young lady, "Could you tell me where I can find a pharmacy nearby?" The young lady responded, "The closest one is about four blocks from here. Maybe we have something here to help. Do you have a headache or a cold?" The Congressman replies, "No, the problem is much lower." The young lady smiles and says, "Something you ate?" The Congressman nods his head. The young lady says, "Please wait here for a moment. I have the medicine that you need." She returned shortly with a small box of pills in her hand. She hands the Congressman the box and whispers, "Don't eat the Chinese food. It can be bad unless you grew up on it, you know what I mean.

Whatever it says on the box to take, I would double it." Congressman Harris thanked the young lady and left the Mission office, returning to his room to take the medication. As he opened the package, he read the directions on the box. It said to take one tablet every four hours until you get relief. He stood there and reasoned that he felt at least three times worse than the box of pills thought, so three pills would be the correct dosage. He placed three tablets into his hand, swallowed them, and washed the pills down with water. The Congressman took a deep breath and thought, 'My God, a war with China could depend on three small diarrhea pills.'

The Congressman stayed in his room waiting for the three miracle pills to work. A knock on the door and a friendly "Hello" alerted him to Agent Anderson outside of his room. The Congressman says, "Come on in Anderson. The door is open." Agent Anderson opened the door and walked through it, sporting a big smile. "How are you doing, Congressman?" Agent Anderson said. Congressman Harris replied, "I am doing fine, Agent Anderson; how about you?" Agent Anderson responds, "I feel great today. I was worried about you eating the spicy Chinese last night. I chose the bland items on the menu as some spicy items will give me terrible diarrhea." With a look that could kill, Congressman Harris says, "You are the second person today to tell me that. Thank you for warning me last night." Agent Anderson, looking confused, replies, "Second person today, Sir?" Congressman Harris responds, "Forget it, Agent Anderson. Last night, when you checked out the service area at the hotel, did you see any issues that would interfere with the transfer of the three women?" Agent Anderson moved over to a dresser in the corner of the room and replied, "I don't know how those C.I.A. agents do it, but all the cameras are gone from the service area. I did not see a single worker from the hotel when I was there. I walked the entire area to map the exit path from the entry door to the elevator. After the three women arrive, they should be upstairs in the Professor's room within minutes." The Congressman responds, "That is the best news I have had in a long time. Agent Anderson, you must move the three women as quickly as possible inside the hotel."

The Congressman moved around the room, packing his items for the trip back home. He looks at Agent Anderson and asks, "Are you all packed and ready to go?" Agent Anderson replies, "I started to pack last night and finished early this morning. My suitcase is in the doorway of my room, and I am taking it with me to the hotel." Congressman Harris says, "I think it would be a good idea to take a taxi to the Marriott Hotel instead of the U.S. Mission transport. I would be there an hour before the drop-off time for the women to review the service area again. If something has changed, we need to know before the one-thirty transfer time." Agent Anderson nods and says, "I will be at least an hour early and survey the service area again. Sir, I have this, and I will get the three women up to the Professor's room." Congressman Harris smiles and says, "I know you will, Anderson, I know you will."

Without speaking another word, Agent Anderson turned and left the room. Congressman Harris finished placing his items into the suitcase and secured the locks. He looked at his watch and realized it was almost ten in the morning. Where does the time go, flashed through the Congressman's head. He sat on the bed and evaluated if he felt well enough to meet with the Consul General of the U.S. Mission on the forty-seventh floor. After sitting for a few minutes, he decided how he felt would not change the fact that he needed to meet with the Consul General to thank him for his hospitality. He rose from the bed and exited the room, walking straight to the stairway and heading to the floor below. A quick left turn brought him to the main entrance of the U.S. Mission.

Turning the doorknob, he entered the central area of the U.S. Mission, and the smiling young lady greeted him again. "Feeling better?" She said. Congressman Harris replies, "Much better, thank you." The Congressman asks, "Is the Consul General available for a quick meeting?" The young lady presses a button on her intercom, and the Consul General's voice asks, "Yes, Maria." The young lady responds, "Sir, Congressman Harris requests a meeting with you. Are you busy?" The Consul General says, "Never too busy to meet with Congressman Harris. Please send the Congressman in."

The young lady stands, walks to the private office door, and allows the Congressman to enter the Consul General's office. The Consul General stands behind his desk and extends his hand to greet the Congressman. He says, "I am glad you took the time to see me before you left Wuhan." Congressman Harris replies, "How could I leave this beautiful city without saying goodbye?"

The Consul General sits down and motions the Congressman to sit before speaking, "I hope your trip here was fruitful. The Chinese are a very good people, although I must admit that sometimes government officials leave a lot to be desired. I still have nightmares about the COVID-19 virus outbreak. My staff and I stayed in Wuhan and quarantined in this building for almost a year. The citizens of Wuhan, and China in general, did not fare any better and, in many cases, worse. I can't even relate to the horror stories and the pain and suffering the Chinese endured."

The Consul General stands up and walks over to a small wall safe. He opens the safe, removes an unmarked envelope, walks back to his desk, and hands it to the Congressman. As he hands the envelope to the Congressman, he says, "Please take this back to Washington. I have had it for a long time, and I am glad to get rid of the damn thing." Congressman Harris asks, "What is in the envelope?" The Consul General responds, "The envelope contains humanity's best and worst. It contains answers to questions and brings new questions forward. Please don't open it until you arrive in Washington; you can decide what to do. Slide it into your jacket so no one sees you have it." Congressman Harris replies, "Is the envelope's contents that important?" The Consul General looks at the ceiling and says, "Congressman, I remember an old movie named The Maltese Falcon. The Character Sam Spade spoke a famous line in the movie when asked a similar question. A policeman asked, 'What is it?' Sam Spade replied, 'The stuff that dreams are made of.' Congressman, sometimes dreams can become nightmares, and it depends on where your viewpoint is."

Congressman Harris slid the envelope into his jacket, shook hands with the Consul General, and left the office. He ascended the stairs to the forty-eight floor and entered his room. Congressman Harris removed the envelope from his jacket and stared at it. What could be in a plain yellow envelope that he should not open it while in China? As the Consul General requested, the Congressman unlocked his suitcase and stored the envelope in the case, relocking it.

The Congressman picked up his cell phone and pressed the speed dial to call Julie. On the first ring of the phone, Julie answered. "Kevin, I have been waiting for you to call," She said. Congressman Harris replies, "I've been swamped last night and this morning with something that needed to be done." Julie responds, "I hope everything worked out all right. Captain Crossfield and I have headed to the airport to get the airplane ready to fly. The plane will be ready when you arrive." Congressman Harris replies, "That is what I wanted to hear. I knew I could count on you and Captain Crossfield. And about last night, I want." Julie interrupts, "I will take that up with you once we return to Washington." And she hung up the phone.

The next call was to his secretary, Bill, and Ken, to verify everything was ready. Pressing the speed dial for his office connected his phone to Washington. A tired voice answered, "Hello, Congressman Harris' office. How may I help you?" Congressman Harris says, "It's Harris Bill. Ensure Ken and you are awake and ready for the next twelve hours. Leaving Wuhan may be full of pitfalls, but Ken and you must watch what is happening here. Bill replies, "Ken has two computers running side by side in case of a failure. The office has plenty of snacks, coffee, and energy drinks.

We plan to be with you remotely all night and day if necessary." The Congressman asks, "What do the security guards think?" Bill answers, "Other than Ken and I being lovers who lost their apartment, we told them we are going to do research from the office tonight to support you and your staff." Congressman Harris laughs while speaking, "Well, I can see you two have everything under control. I will call and give you updates as they happen here. Bill, do you need to tell me anything else?" Bill replies, "Not that I can think of right now." The Congressman finishes the call by saying, "Expect updates as long as we are in China. Did you get the direct phone numbers of the Tokyo U.S. Navy and Air Force commanders?" Bill says, "I have those and two other direct numbers in case of an emergency." The Congressman says, "Keep them handy as I do not trust the Chinese in this part of the world. Besides, the last thing I want to do is create an international crisis. Goodbye, Bill, rest, but be ready for anything." The Congressman disconnected the cell phone and pushed it deep into his pocket.

The only thing left was to wait for his departure time with the five Diplomatic staff members returning to the United States. Sitting in his room, the Congressman realized the following hours would seem like an eternity.

Beating the Odds

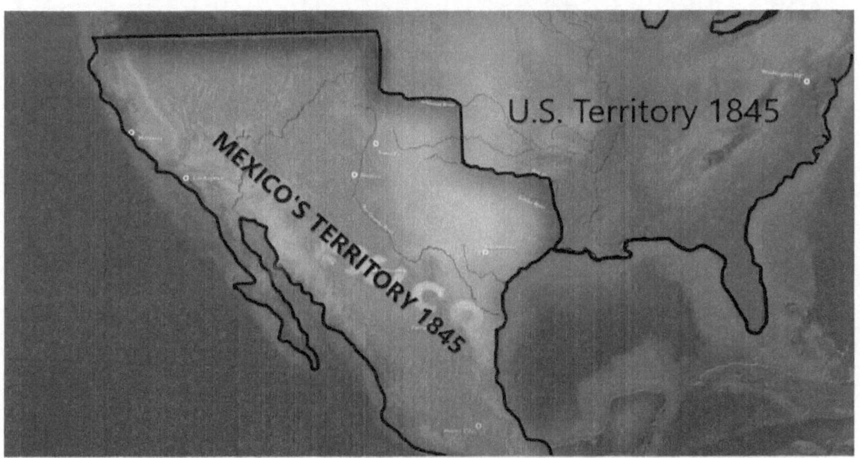

The cell phone rang shortly after one-thirty in the afternoon. The Congressman momentarily looked at the phone, hesitating to answer its ring. He closed his eyes, lifted the phone, and pressed the answer button. If there were ever a case of fearing the worst and hoping for the best, this call would decide which of the two had occurred. He immediately recognized Agent Anderson's voice on the other end of the line as he spoke slowly,

"We have all three of the women in the Professor's room!" The Congressman's head tipped back with relief as Agent Anderson spoke. The Congressman replied, "Get Angel Norris to work immediately, and I will see you at the designated time." Pressing the button on the cell phone, he disconnected and replaced the phone on the nightstand.

The Congressman sat momentarily, thinking the C.I.A. agents had performed a miracle. They convinced the three women to accompany them, promising to be removed from China and move to the United States. He wondered how desperate someone must be to take a chance of this magnitude, as failure would mean certain death. These three women must be courageous and trusting in order to allow strangers to attempt to remove them from China.

The bravery of the three women faded, and his thoughts drifted to how beautiful the city of Wuhan appeared to an outsider. It is overcrowded with people and vehicles but still gorgeous, much like New York City or San Francisco. The main difference is that the authoritarian government completely controlled daily life. He remembered something he had read in a document written by James Madison from college. He believed it was called the Federalist 51, and it stated, 'In framing a government which is to be administered by men over men, the great difficulty lies in this: you must first enable the government to control the governed; and in the next place oblige it to control itself.' In China, the government took control of the governed, but instead of controlling itself, it made the government a deity to which to give homage. Everything comes from the government, and citizens must return everything to the government, leaving incentives only for the chosen few in power. He thought that as the nation evolved, it would likely be China's downfall as the citizens would rebel sometime in the future.

The Congressman looked down at his watch and realized he would meet with the Mission staff traveling to the United States shortly at the U.S. Mission office. The only thing he needed to do before he left his room with his luggage was to call Washington and speak with his secretary, Bill, and computer guy, Ken. Pressing the speed dial button on the cell phone connected the phone to the Washington office. Four rings later, his secretary Bill answered, "Congressman Harris' office, how may I assist you?" Congressman Harris says, "Bill, it is the middle of the night. Who else besides me would call the office in the middle of the night?" Bill replies, "That is a good point." The Congressman continues, "Will you place me on speaker phone so I may speak with you and Ken together." Bill says, "Please give me a moment to move to your private office with Ken."

After briefly listening to the music on hold, Bill picked up the telephone, "I'm back, Sir, and Ken is here also." The Congressman says, "Is the door to the office closed?" Bill replies, "The door is closed." The Congressman contin-ues, "The three women are in our custody. Mrs. Norris is working on them as we speak. It is going to be touch and go from this point forward. We will stay as close as pos-sible to the plan, but this is a fluid operation, and things may change. Ken, do you have a current location of our group using the tracking chips?" Ken replies, "I have each person's current location on my computer screen. And Sir, something new: I have modified a parser program to monitor police and security voice communications." Congressman Harris replies, "That's great, Ken. What is a parser program, and what does it do?"

Ken takes a moment before answering, "A parser takes lists of things and separates them into small linked pieces. I am monitoring voice communications between police and security personnel, translating Chinese into English, and searching for keywords such as Congress-man, Harris, Missing, Huang Yanling, and over a hundred other keywords. If any communications contain one of the keywords, the computer displays the entire message on the second computer screen so I can read what they said and see if we need to be concerned with the mes-sage. This is a second level of information available to us while you leave Wuhan."

The Congressman responds, "Agent Anderson is right. You are the scariest son-of-a-bitch we have ever met. But I must admit that it is a great idea. The bottom line is everything ready to complete this mission?" Bill and Ken reply together, "All set, Sir." Congressman Harris says, "Perfect, stay alert; this will be tricky. I will be speaking with you very soon." And the Congressman hangs up the phone.

The Congressman's wristwatch displayed two-forty in the afternoon. He gathered his luggage and opened the door, exiting his room and entering the hallway. Using the building stairway, he descended to the forty-seventh floor and walked down the hallway to the U.S. Mission office. Opening the door, the smiling young lady again greeted him with, "You're right on time, Congressman Harris. As requested, the staff members will be here in a few minutes." The Congressman replies, "Thank you for that update and all you have done to make my stay pleasant." The smiling young lady responds, "You're welcome, Congressman. Please come back and see us again."

Congressman Harris sat in a soft chair along the central office's inside wall, waiting for the staff members to arrive. The five Mission staff returning to the United States filed precisely through the office door on time at two-forty-five. The Congressman stood and greeted the staff members and instructed them to go down to the ground floor and wait for the transport vehicle. As the Congressman passed the smiling young lady, he stopped and said, "Maria, don't ever lose that wonderful smile." The young lady smiles again, saying, "I did not think you would remember my name." The Congressman smiles and replies, "I will never forget your name or that smile. I promise I will come back someday." And the Congressman opened the door and left the office, heading to the rocket ship elevator.

Once everyone was outside the building, the transport vehicle drove up, and the Marine driver exited the transport. He opened the vehicle's storage area and loaded each Mission staff's luggage. The last piece of luggage to be loaded belonged to the Congressman. Once the driver had all the luggage loaded, the passengers slid into the rear section of the transport for the trip to the hotel, which the journey to the airport would follow.

As expected, the trip to the Marriott Hotel exceeded half an hour. The good news was they left the U.S. Mission early in case of a delay traveling to the hotel. It was not yet four in the afternoon, and the first transport had not arrived. The Congressman instructed the driver to park the vehicle in the arrival parking area and wait for the other transport. The Mission staff agreed to stay with the driver and transport until we were ready to leave for the airport. While waiting, Congressman Harris decided to go up to the Professor's room and see the magic Mrs. Norris had performed. The Congressman entered the hotel and strolled to the elevator. Once inside the elevator, he pressed the number three button for the third floor. The elevator moved slowly from floor to floor, making the Congressman happy that it was not a rocket ship ride.

The elevator door opened, and the Congressman exited, walked down to room three-zero-six, and knocked on the door. Agent Anderson opened the door, and the Congressman stepped into the room. "Where are the three women?" The Congressman asked. Agent Anderson points to the adjoining door to the next room, which is the location where the ladies are. As the two men walk towards the adjacent door, Agent Anderson says to the Congressman, "We have a bonus. The mother speaks both English and Chinese. She can be a translator so that we can speak with the other ladies." Congressman Harris responds, "Perfect, one less problem to deal with."

As the Congressman enters the room, he finds three women who, by all appearances, are Filipino, not Chinese. Angel Norris had performed magic at a new level. Even the Congressman, who knew they were Chinese, was fooled by their appearance.

Mrs. Norris walked out of the bathroom, where she was working on cleaning up the makeup materials. The Congressman looks at her and says, "I don't know how you achieved this, but it is truly magic. You are indeed an Angel, Mrs. Norris. Please let Agent Anderson and I help you clean and pack up everything. And I must say whoever picked out the Western-style clothing and dressed them did an incredible job." Agent Anderson says, "I picked out the clothes and matched the pieces together, and Mrs. Norris helped them dress." Congressman Harris responds, "They look remarkably like the other Mission staff women. Do they have their 'special visas' Ken prepared?" Agent Anderson replies, "They each have their paperwork and are ready to go."

Looking around the room, the Congressman asks, "Where is the Professor?" Mrs. Norris replies, "He is in the lobby gathering flyers and brochures to take back with us." Congressman Harris says, "Okay, we will gather the Professor on the way out of the hotel after the transport arrives. He will ride in the transport parked in the arrival parking area with the Mission staff to the airport."

Agent Anderson and the Congressman spent the following twenty minutes packing the makeup supplies and personal items of the Professor and Mrs. Norris. Agent Anderson placed the old wheelchair in a storage closet on the hotel's fourth floor, delaying its discovery. The grandmother was seated in the wheelchair with the Diplomatic Staff label attached so Agent Anderson could move her quickly out of the hotel and into the transport vehicle. The plan was simple: walk straight out of the hotel's main entrance as if they were checking out of the hotel. The six people, Congressman Harris, Agent Anderson, Mrs. Norris, and the three women, would be in a tight group to exit the building. Agent Anderson would return to the hotel to find the Professor and take him to the transport waiting in the arrival area of the hotel parking lot.

The Congressman's cell phone alarm began to ring at four p.m., indicating the scheduled arrival of the second transport vehicle. The Congressman decided to remove everyone from the hotel and into the transport, and he and the Marine driver would return to gather the luggage after the three women were safely in the vehicle. The Congressman said, "Remember, stay together and go slow. We are just checking out of a hotel like any other guest. Slow and steady."

The group exited the rooms and crossed the hall to the elevator with Agent Anderson pushing the wheelchair with the grandmother in it. As the elevator door opened, the group found the Professor, hands full of flyers, preparing to enter the elevator and return to the third floor. The Congressman places his hand on the Professor's arm and guides him along with the group. Mrs. Norris says, "Come on honey, you need to come along with us now, and the driver will take care of our things." The Professor walked alongside the group like a puppy on a leash, saying nothing.

The group strolled straight through the main lobby, totally unnoticed by anyone. They appeared to be just another group of tourists wandering through the Marriott Hotel. As they left the main entrance, the transport vehicle was ready to receive the group. The Marine driver looked at the three additional women, but his face remained expressionless. Carefully, Agent Anderson moved the grandmother from the wheelchair into the transport and stored the wheelchair in the vehicle's rear. Congressman Harris asked the driver to return to the rooms and recover the luggage. The Marine driver nodded and followed the Congressman to the rooms to collect the luggage from the third floor.

Minutes later, the Marine driver, pushing a luggage cart, returned to the transport and loaded the luggage into the rear. While the Congressman and Marine driver were upstairs getting the luggage, Agent Anderson walked the Professor across the parking area and placed him into the transport with the other five Mission staff. The last person to slide into the transport was Congressman Harris, watching as he entered for anything unusual.

He informed the driver the two vehicles must stay together on the trip to the airport. The Marine driver drove the transport to the arrival parking area and told the other transport driver to follow him and not to get separated for any reason. The driver nodded an acknowledgment, and the two transports left the Marriott Hotel parking area en route to the Wuhan International Airport.

The Congressman took his cell phone from his pocket and called his office in Washington to advise Bill and Ken of their departure from the hotel. The only thing left was to sit back and enjoy the trip to the airport and flight home from China.

The Congressman sat deep into the transport's seat, listening to the road noise as they traveled the streets of Wuhan. They had just beaten the gambling house at odds by getting this far without a problem. The rest would be simple. They would arrive at the airport, board their private jet, and fly home to the United States with the three women they have extracted. What could be easier?

However, Congressman Harris should have realized that gambling houses do not like to lose, that the odds can change quickly, and that things were about to worsen.

CHAPTER TWENTY-SEVEN

Last Stop the Wuhan Airport

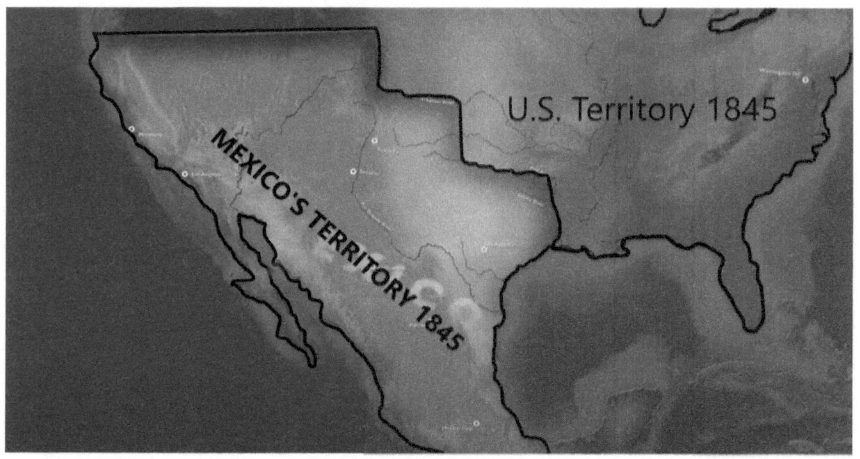

The Congressman's cell phone rang, and he removed it quickly from his pocket. The caller's I.D. displayed the number of his Washington office. He pressed the answer button and said, "Hello, Bill." The voice on the other end of the phone replied, "No, this is Ken, Congressman. I see your transport in traffic and not moving in Wuhan. Is your driver taking the expressway to the airport?" Congressman Harris raises his voice to speak with the driver, "Marine, which way are we going to the airport?" The driver responded, "I am trying to get out of the Wuhan city traffic and enter the expressway to the airport." The Congressman asks, "Any idea how long before we can get on the expressway?" The driver replies, "Not sure, Sir. Typically, we could be at the airport in twenty-five minutes with light traffic, but this is anything but light traffic."

The Congressman responds to Ken on the phone, "The driver is trying to get to the expressway." Ken interrupts, "Congressman, I will set the traffic signals to green along your route as you move. I can make the traffic signal controller think your transports are emergency vehicles. The signals will act like those in the United States and clear traffic for you to proceed to the expressway."

Using his computer, Ken identified the transports to the computer system in Wuhan as emergency vehicles, and the traffic lights switched to green as the transports approached them, which helped clear the traffic jam. After several minutes, the driver says, "About another mile and a half to the expressway. Once on the expressway, about twenty minutes with the traffic to the airport." The Congressman says, "Ken, about a mile to the expressway and maybe twenty minutes to the airport." Ken responds, "I am still monitoring the changing of the traffic lights for you to get you to the expressway. Shit!" The Congressman replies, "What is wrong, Ken?" Ken says, "I just received a message on my second computer screen from my parser and decoder program. Damn." Congressman Harris asks, "Ken, what is the problem?" Ken replies, "Give me a second to think about what has happened." Congressman Harris says, "Ken, what has happened? What is wrong?"

The phone went silent for several seconds, and the Congressman repeated, "Ken, what has happened? Ken. Ken, what is going on?" Ken's voice returned to the phone, "The police have issued an alert." Congressman Harris questions, "An alert about what?" Ken replies in a low voice, "I have sent a screenshot to your cell phone. Please check your messages. I need to do something while you are checking the messages." Congressman Harris opens the message application on his cell phone and reads the message sent to him by Ken:

Voice message input to parser system:

黄燕玲没有回家。她失踪了。找到她

Parser decoded and translated output:

"Huang Yanling did not return home. She is missing. Find her."

Ken's Computer Screen Message

As the Congressman finishes reading the message, he blurps out a single word, "Shit!" Agent Anderson leans forward to view the message on the Congressman's cell phone, and after reading it, he closes his eyes and drops back into his seat without speaking.

The Congressman asks Ken again, "What are you doing, Ken?" Ken responds, "I am calling a cab." Congressman Harris replies, "Ken, we do not need a cab. We need an answer as to what you can do to get us out of here." Ken says, "I am not calling one cab; I am calling fifty cabs and sending them all to the area where the police are looking for Huang. That should slow them down for hours while stuck in traffic. Please get to the airport as quickly as possible while I make the search for her almost impossible. Remember, the police do not know you have her. They think she is just missing as of right now. Get out of China as quickly as possible, as this delay will not work forever, and the Chinese police will soon figure out Huang is with you."

Congressman Harris asks the driver, "How close to the expressway are we?" The driver says, "We will be on the ramp in about one minute."

Congressman Harris speaks into the phone, "Ken, can you tell how the traffic on the expressway is moving?" Ken replies, "It is a little slow but moving steadily." A voice from the front of the transport says, "We are turning on the freeway right now, Congressman." Congressman Harris asks, "Ken, can you buy us any more time?" Ken responds, "I believe I just did, Sir. I triggered a leak alarm at the Wuhan Virology Lab! The Lab is twenty miles south of your current location, which will pull police and security in that direction to see what has happened at the Lab."

Agent Anderson speaks while shaking his head and his eyes closed, "My God, the Chinese are going to lock down the entire city of Wuhan shortly because of another possible Lab leak. We must get to the airport and out of Wuhan as quickly as possible."

The next twenty-four minutes seemed like an eternity while traveling the expressway. The trip turned into a race to get to the airport, board the airplane, and get out of town before the Chinese could shut down the entire area.

Ten minutes later, the driver's voice indicated they had arrived at the airport and were driving through security as he spoke. The diplomatic signs on the side of the transports reduced security, allowing for a wave-through of the two vehicles. The two transports traveled slowly along the taxiway to where the aircraft was parked and stopped parallel to unload the passengers and luggage.

The good news was that the aircraft was outside the hangar and turned around as Julie had promised. Agent Anderson saw that Julie and Captain Crossfield had already attached the temporary ramp to the plane and were waiting for their arrival to board the passengers.

Congressman Harris took a moment and informed Ken, "We are here and going to board the aircraft. I will contact you once we are in the air." And he disconnected the cell phone.

The security guards paid little attention to unloading the luggage from the transport vehicles and the diplomatic staff waiting to board the aircraft. Agent Anderson removed the wheelchair from the rear of the transport and helped the grandmother into the chair. The Congressman slowly began to push the wheelchair toward the ramp to board the grandmother so the ramp could be removed and stored in the airplane. At the same time, Agent Anderson watched the Chinese security agents closely to see if anything triggered suspicion with the activity around the aircraft.

Agent Anderson was not sure what had happened. Still, he could see the two Chinese airport security agents paying particular attention to the grandmother as Congressman Harris started to push her up the ramp into the jet. As he watched, he was sure the Chinese agents noticed something unusual about the woman in the wheelchair. Agent Anderson waited for a moment, and when the two Chinese agents started walking to intercept the Congressman and the grandmother on the ramp, Agent Anderson reached into his pocket and pulled out his 401k report, displaying long rows of printed numbers. Stepping into the path between the ramp and the two Chinese agents, he begins to boast loudly to the Chinese agents, "I can't believe this. My ancestors all came from China. Look here at this ancestry report I received. I am Chinese, and you are my brothers."

The two Chinese agents stopped dead in their tracks, with Agent Anderson blocking their view and path to the ramp leading into the jet. This delay allowed the Congressman to finish pushing the wheelchair up the ramp.

Agent Anderson waves the paper containing all the numbers printed on his 401k, speaking loudly, "Look right here. It says that the belief that all Chinese are short is a myth. China's northern provinces of Liaoning and Jilin are home to the tallest people in China, on average 173.45 cm for men. That converts to five foot nine or taller in the north for men. It also says that Chinese in the northern provinces have a darker skin tone than those in the southern regions. That explains it all. You are my relatives."

Agent Anderson stretched out his arms and tried to hug the two Chinese agents, and they stepped back out of his reach. The two agents stood looking up at a black man over six feet tall claiming to be Chinese based on a report from a genealogy company. The two agents backed up, turned, and began to walk away, with Agent Anderson following closely, arms extended. Agent Anderson repeats, "Yes, you are my brothers, and I am Chinese."

As Agent Anderson followed the two agents, forcing them to retreat from the airplane, he overheard a comment from one of the Chinese agents to the other, "This guy has been watching too many TikTok videos."

Agent Anderson looked over his left shoulder and saw the Congressman had finished climbing the ramp pushing the wheelchair, and the grandmother was now safely in the aircraft. He watched the Marine transport drivers remove the ramp and move it into the airplane.

Agent Anderson took a deep breath of relief, glad he had listened to Professor Norris's lecture on the flight from Washington to L.A.X. Without that information about the Chinese in the northern regions, Agent Anderson had no idea what he would have said to the Chinese agents to divert them away from the person in the wheelchair.

In the following minutes, the remaining staff and the two Chinese women boarded the aircraft, following the grandmother in the wheelchair. Mrs. Norris dragged the Professor up the entry stairs to stop him from wandering away and looking for souvenirs to collect.

Once the passengers boarded the aircraft, Agent Anderson boarded the airplane, finished folding the portable access ramp, and stored it in the back of the jet. Congressman Harris was the last to board and waved to the Chinese security as Captain Crossfield closed the aircraft door. When Agent Anderson joined the other passengers on the plane, Congressman Harris questioned him about what he said to the two Chinese security agents. Agent Anderson replied, "I repeated what the Professor had lectured the Diplomatic staff about on the flight from Washington, D.C. to L.A.X. airport. "Even the Chinese agents did not want to hear it, so they turned and walked away. And you are right about one thing: Mrs. Norris must be an Angel."

Julie fired the jet's engines and ensured they were at the correct temperature for takeoff. The plane began moving slowly down the taxiway, heading to the main runway. Congressman Harris slid his cell phone from his pocket and pressed the speed dial to call his Washington office to update them on their progress. The confident smile on the Congressman's face reassured the other passengers that the mission to remove the three women from China would be a success. His secretary, Bill, answered the phone while sitting with Ken, the computer genius. Bill says, "Wow, that was a close one." The Congressman could hear keys tapping in the background as Bill spoke. Ken's low voice interrupts the celebration by saying, "I don't like what the Wuhan police are saying in their communications in Wuhan. They have managed to clear the traffic jams of the robot taxis and are intensifying the search for Huang. They checked Wuhan's city's cameras to see Huang's last known position. Congressman, it will not be long until they track her to the Marriott Hotel and then to you. Get out of there as quickly as you can."

Congressman Harris yells to Julie, "We need to get out of here. They will know we have the three women very soon. Julie, get this plane into the air and out of China."

Julie replies, "We are almost on the main runway, only a few minutes more. I need only a few minutes more. Everybody fasten your seat belts and prepare for take-off."

The aircraft stopped at the taxiway's end and waited for the tower's takeoff clearance. The seconds ticked away and seemed like hours as the aircraft waited for final clearance from the Control Tower. In Julie's headset, a message from the Control Tower echoed, "U.S. Diplomatic flight 172. Please return to the airport's main hangar for a security inspection of your airplane." Captain Crossfield asked Julie, "What will we do now? They will search the aircraft and find the three women."

The mission of extracting the three women from China now depended on Julie's next decision. Everything was riding on Julie's subsequent actions, and she had only five seconds to decide what those actions would be.

CHAPTER TWENTY-EIGHT

Making a Run for Home

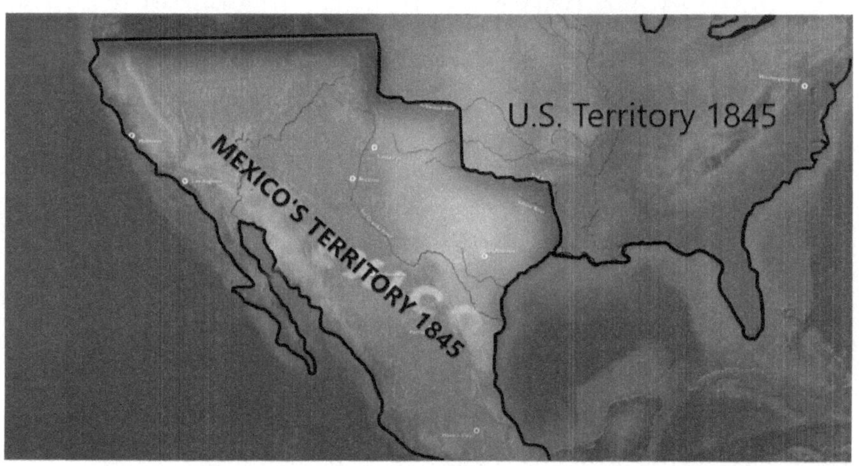

With only seconds to decide what to do about the Control Tower's request to return to the main hangar for a security inspection, Julie picked up a piece of paper and wrinkled it near the headset's microphone. She then begins tapping her headset's microphone and replies to the Control Tower, "Control, your message was garbled. Thank you for giving us clearance to take off." Julie pushed the engine throttles forward, and the two

Pratt & Whitney jet engines began a full-power roar as the airplane turned onto the main runway.

Captain Crossfield sat silent, shaking his head as the plane accelerated down the runway and lifted into the air within seconds. The landing gear retracted with a thump, and the airplane banked steeply to the left as it rose from the runway. Captain Crossfield broke his silence and said, "They will try to shoot us down, Colonel." Julie replies, "The keyword, Captain, is 'try.'"

Julie turns off the aircraft's transponder, which hides the airplane's current location from scanner beacons. Captain Crossfield says, "Colonel, turning off the transponder will not hide this plane from the Chinese radar. This aircraft will be above the horizon and visible to Chinese radar for about thirty-eight miles in flat terrain at one thousand foot altitude." Julie replies, "The higher the altitude, the farther out the radar range, but Nap-of-the-earth should hide this aircraft." Captain Crossfield echos, "Nap-of-the-earth Colonel. This aircraft can not handle a Nap-of-the-earth flight pattern."

Overhearing the conversation, Congressman Harris asks, "What is Nap-of-the-earth?" As she looks forward, Julie replies, "Military pilots practice a type of flying called Nap-of-the-earth for this purpose. Smaller fighters and attack aircraft primarily use this tactic, but a small private jet like this one may be able to use it if it stays together. We need to fly very low at the highest speed possible.

It should work while we are over land as I can fly the contours of the land to hide the plane, but once over the ocean, the Chinese will likely pick up the plane on radar. And another thing, our people will not know where the airplane is either. We will be invisible to everyone, friend or foe."

Congressman Harris responds, "I don't care what you call the tactic. I am concerned about the airplane staying together, but I want to make this plane hard for the Chinese to track. Sooner or later, the Chinese will discover the three missing women and come looking for us. Once we are over the ocean, we can climb to cruising altitude quickly and head directly to International air space.

Captain Crossfield interrupts, "Sir, I don't think the Chinese will honor the twelve nautical mile International limit, especially if they believe we have the three women." Julie says, "You are correct that the Chinese will not honor the twelve-nautical mile International limit. Captain Crossfield, re-route from our flight plan to Tokyo and head to the south until we are over the ocean. That way, it will be hard to locate this aircraft." Captain Crossfield replies, "I am re-routing right now."

Congressman Harris asks, "How long before we are over the ocean, Julie?" Captain Crossfield answers, "On the new coordinates, we will be over the ocean in twenty-five minutes. That is unless we crash into something on the way. After we reach the ocean, International waters will be three minutes after that."

Captain Crossfield says, "Colonel, our altitude is under five hundred feet. Please remember this private jet is not a fighter plane." Without looking up from the instruments, Julie replies, "Today, it's a fighter plane, Captain. It's a fighter plane now." Captain Crossfield unbuttons his shirt and removes a religious medal from his neck. Putting the medal in his left hand, Julie could hear him whisper, "God help us. Please keep the wings on this airplane and make everything before us below less than four hundred feet tall."

Daylight began to wane as the aircraft sped over China's barren terrain. Julie was busy at the airplane's controls as Captain Crossfield played lookout for anything that appeared to be over four hundred feet tall in the aircraft's path. Captain Crossfield's voice broke the silence with, "Colonel, two mountain peaks directly in our path. We must climb to avoid hitting them. Colonel, we will crash into the mountains if we do not gain altitude."

Julie looked stone-faced ahead at the airplane controls, watching the mountains as they approached. Captain Crossfield echoes a last warning, "Ten seconds to impact!" Julie forces the aircraft's left wing ninety degrees, making it vertical with the ground below. The airplane was now flying on its side with both wings vertical. Captain Crossfield blurts out, "Oh my God! Please keep the wings on this thing." The airplane flew between the mountains on its side, and after clearing the hazard, Julie leveled the aircraft to continue the journey.

Captain Crossfield calls back to the passengers, "Is everybody okay back there?" If one of the passengers could have said something, the answer probably would have been a resounding no. Congressman Harris looks to Agent Anderson and says, "I think I have soiled my pants. How about you?"

The Congressman was still holding his cell phone in his hand, but the cell phone had disconnected from his Washington office, and the phone would not redial, possibly due to the aircraft's very low altitude. Using the earth below to hide the airplane would not allow the cell phones to work. The Congressman would need to wait until the plane was over International waters to reconnect to his office in Washington. Should the aircraft be shot down before reaching International airspace, no one would know what happened to the plane or its passengers. The plane's disappearance would become another mystery in the annals of history.

Minutes later, the Congressman caught a glimpse of the ocean from the airplane's window. Julie began a steep and steady climb to a cruising altitude as the aircraft left the land behind and moved over the sea. Captain Crossfield's voice came over the intercom to inform the passengers that the plane was out of Chinese jurisdiction and over International waters. The Congressman thought he could hear relief from the passengers throughout the airplane after the announcement.

The passenger's relief was short-lived when two Chinese J-20 fighters encircled the private jet. One of the Chinese fighter jets on the left side of the private plane and the other banking in front, directing Julie to turn back into Chinese territory. Captain Crossfield suggested they radioed a distress call for assistance when Julie stopped him by saying, "If you make a distress call, they will hear it and shoot this plane out of the sky." Captain Crossfield replies, "But we turned off our transponders. No one will be able to locate us. The U.S. Air Force does not know we are here or, for that matter, where here is."

Chinese J20 Fighter

Second Chinese J20 Fighter

Julie calls back to the Congressman, "Kevin, you should be able to contact your office now. Call Ken and have him locate this aircraft using the attached tracking device." The Congressman nervously presses the speed dial for his office and waits for someone to answer. On the third ring, Bill, his secretary, answers the phone, and the Congressman speaks before Bill can say a word. "Bill, Harris here." The Congressman begins, "Give me Ken. We are in trouble, and I need him now."

The Congressman could hear Bill yelling for Ken to pick up the phone. Within seconds, Ken answered, "What is wrong? Your plane is almost a hundred miles from China and, off course, to Tokyo." The Congressman responds, "That may be correct, but we are being chased by two Chinese J-20 fighter jets trying to force us back to China." Ken says, "I have your location on the tracking device; who should we call?" Congressman Harris replies, "Bill has the direct phone numbers of Air Force Command operating between China and Taiwan. He must call and three-way connect them into this call before they shoot this plane down."

Julie looks out to the J-20 fighters, waves as if nothing seems wrong, and hand signals her radio is not working. The Chinese fighter pilots start using hand signals directing her to turn back to China with the private aircraft. Julie smiles and waves back, trying to buy some time.

A click on the telephone indicates someone has connected to the Congressman's conversation on the cell phone. A deep voice says, "This is Colonel Blanchard, U.S.

Air Force. What is your emergency?" Congressman Harris speaks calmly, "Colonel, this is Congressman Harris. We are being pursued by two Chinese J-20 fighters attempting to force us back into Chinese airspace, and I believe if we do not turn back, they will shoot this plane down." The deep voice replies, "I need your location to assist." Ken's voice interrupted, "Colonel, the airplane is at the location I just texted to your phone. The airplane is currently traveling at five hundred and fifty miles per hour on that course." The Colonel could be heard speaking with someone with him, giving him the airplane's location and speed. The Colonel returns on the phone, "I need to speak with the pilot." Congressman Harris takes the cell phone forward and hands it to Julie.

The Colonel says, "Begin a wide turn right as if you are going back toward the China coast. Reduce your speed as much as possible as you turn and descend to fifteen thousand feet as you make the turn." Julie asks, "How long do I hold this aircraft into the turn, Sir?" The Colonel replies," Until you see the orange glow of the four F-35 fighters, we have scrambled."

As the private jet began to turn back toward China, the two Chinese J-20 fighters stayed alongside the airplane, guiding it back into Chinese territory. The night was approaching, the sky turned blue to grey-black, and the private jet inched back to China. Off to the aircraft's left side, Julie could see a J-20 fighter silhouette against the darkness, highlighted by an orange glow at a distance. She motioned for Captain Crossfield to take a look over her shoulder.

The glow became larger and split into four parts as it approached the private jet. The two Chinese J-20 fighters broke away from the private plane and disappeared into the darkness. Encircling the private plane were four F-35 U.S. fighters directing Julie to turn the aircraft back away from China.

One of the four F35 Fighters

Julie instructs Captain Crossfield to change the aircraft's routing to Tokyo International Airport. She sat back and watched as the four F-35 fighters safely escorted the private jet and its passengers. Sitting there, Julie wondered how much fun it would be to fly an F-35 fighter. Maybe in my next life, she thought, maybe in my next life.

A few things are certain in life, such as taxes and death. And now I can add another. Two Chinese J-20 fighters want nothing to do with four U.S. F-35 fighters. The outcome will be the same as the taxes, and death would be inevitable.

CHAPTER TWENTY-NINE

The Story of Huang Yanling

A voice echoed in the transport jet's radio headset, and the lead pilot of the F35 fighters asked the pilot's and co-pilot's names of the plane they had just rescued. Captain Crossfield answered the request, saying, "My name is Captain Crossfield, and the pilot's name is Colonel Martin." The F35 pilot asks, "Do you have a first name?" Captain Crossfield replies, "My first name is James, James Crossfield. And Colonel Martin's first name is Julie, Julie Martin."

For several long seconds, the F35 pilot did not reply. Finally, he said, "Excuse me, are you Colonel Julie Martin of the U.S. Air Force Weapons School?" Julie responds, "That was a long time ago in another life." Captain Crossfield, with surprise on his face, looks at Julie and says, "You are the Julie Martin from Air Force Weapons. The military compares the Air Force Weapons School graduates against your standing records and achievements. You are considered by many to be the best fighter pilot and weapons specialist in the world." Captain Crossfield pauses momentarily before continuing, "Everybody relates to the movie 'Top Gun' as being the best pilots, but you, Colonel Martin, are the standard bearer for all Air Force and Navy fighter pilots."

The pilot of the F35 speaks again over the radio, "We made a mistake about who we save from whom. Colonel Martin, if that transport jet had any weapons, I am sure you would have taken down both Chinese J20 fighters. Imagine their surprise, the best Chinese fighter jets, shot down by a transport aircraft."

Congressman Harris and Agent Anderson sat quietly, listening to the conversations in the aircraft's cockpit. The Congressman leans toward Agent Anderson and asks, "Do you know anything about this U.S. Air Force Weapons

School they are talking about?" Agent Anderson replies, "I have heard about the school from other pilot friends. Very few pilots are selected to attend the school, very elite. Only the best of the best can even apply. From what I have heard about the school, students are trained to be tactical experts in the art of battle-space dominance. This ability creates such a complete overmatch in combat power in any domain of conflict that adversaries have no choice but to submit or capitulate. Julie is the real guy, or girl in this case, right out of the movie 'Top Gun.' According to what we just heard, she may be the best fighter pilot in the world." Congressman Harris replies, "That accounts for how she was able to fly this plane on its side only a few hundred feet off the ground to avoid two mountain peaks and Chinese radar."

Congressman Harris sits back in his seat thinking, now that explains why Julie is so detailed about everything, as life or death could depend on a decision she must make at any time. Congressman Harris smiles while considering that it appears Julie Martin is much more special than I thought in more ways than one. Congressman Harris smiles, and his thoughts riot as he reviews movies with a fictitious character, Tom Cruise, as 'Top Gun.' And here we are lucky enough to have a real-life Colonel Julie Martin piloting this aircraft. Even the movies could not make something this good up.

As the aircraft turned toward Tokyo, the Congressman's next task could prove more challenging. How would he convince the five Diplomatic staff aboard the airplane that today's events were reasonable? He would need a great story or money to remove the memory of what had occurred. The Congressman balanced the story idea against the money and decided to use the money to remove the memories of the staff. He unclicked his seat belt, stood, and moved slowly down the aircraft aisle. Upon reaching the section where the five staff members were seated, he says, "Tough ride out of China. The Chinese mistakenly identified this airplane as hostile somehow. I hope none of you suffered an injury. I can't change what happened, but I can offer a settlement for your emotional distress. I will authorize my office to pay each of you twenty thousand dollars when we arrive in Washington, provided what happened today is never spoken about. We do not need any more problems with China, and this incident would cause a problem. Will the five of you agree to take the money and let what happened today go by the wayside?"

One of the Diplomatic staff spoke for the group, "Twenty-five each, and you have a deal. As far as we are concerned, the entire trip was eventless and boring." Congressman Harris replies, "Twenty-five it is. I appreciate your understanding."

Congressman Harris returned to his seat, and Agent Anderson greeted him. Agent Anderson says, "Did you make a deal with the staff?" The Congressman replies, "Yeah, twenty-five thousand each to buy their silence." Agent Anderson says, "Cheap, I would have asked for fifty to keep quiet about what just happened." The Congressman smiles and replies, "Maybe the staff likes me better than you and were willing to negotiate, Agent Anderson." Agent Anderson responds, "If they knew what this was about, even fifty would not have been enough."

While the Congressman and Agent Anderson were speaking, Professor Norris walked to the front of the aircraft and stood before Agent Anderson. Reaching into his jacket, he removed a box and handed it to Agent Anderson. "This is for you, Agent Anderson," the Professor said. Agent Anderson slowly opened the box and found a Chinese man's necklace. The medallion was over two inches in diameter, all black, and hanging on a black beaded chain.

Blessed Necklace for
Agent Anderson

Professor Norris continued, "I met with a Chinese Shamanist at the Mariott Hotel, and he blessed me. And after the blessing, he allowed me to purchase this lucky Tai-Chi Necklace with a medallion and blessed it. Strangely, he told me to give it as a gift to my dark-skinned friend as he would need it to protect him. Agent Anderson, please accept this wonderful Chinese gift as a token of our appreciation for all you have done. Please wear it always, as the Shamanist said."

Agent Anderson looked at the Congressman and said, "Well, usually, I do not accept gifts for professional reasons." Professor Norris replies, "I do not think anything about this trip or what happened would be considered usual or normal. Please take the wonderful gift and wear it. If for no other reason, it will make my wife feel better if you wear it. She is very superstitious and believes in that sort of stuff."

Agent Anderson unbuttons his shirt, removes the necklace from the box, and places it around his neck. The Professor motions to his wife to come and see the necklace around Agent Anderson's neck. As she stands before Agent Anderson, Mrs. Norris comments, "That is perfect. It hangs down to his heart, right where it should be." Congressman Harris says, "It looks great on you. Too bad it will be under your shirt, but it still looks great."

As the Professor and his wife walk away, Agent Anderson says to the Congressman, "I feel uncomfortable taking a gift from them." Congressman Harris replies, "Agent Anderson, the Shamanist told the Professor to give it to you, and that is what the Professor did. Look how good it felt to them to give you that small gift. It would help if you enjoy things while you can. Someday, things can change in a heartbeat, and you will be thankful for what you have had, even something as small as a Chinese necklace. Trust me, it is the little things in life that make the biggest difference."

Agent Anderson buttoned his shirt, sat back in his seat for the flight to Tokyo, and decided to wear the Shamanist blessed necklace given to him by the Professor and his wife. The Congressman was right. If it made them feel good, who was he to take that feeling away from them?

As the F35 fighters flew escort for the transport plane back to Tokyo, the Congressman decided to speak with Huang Yanling to find out if she had any credible information about the COVID-19 virus that killed millions of people around the world.

The Congressman moved Huang Yanling into the forward section of the plane to speak with her. He requested Agent Anderson, a Diplomatic staff member who could translate Chinese into English, and Professor Norris to join them. The Congressman was unsure what they would hear from Huang Yanling, but he was sure she could shed a great deal of light on the origins of COVID-19 and whether it came from the Lab at Wuhan or was a natural jump between species.

Congressman Harris said through the interpreter, "We have been looking for you, young lady, for a long time." Yanling speaks with tears in her eyes, "I believed everyone thought I was dead and forgot about me. I lost all hope a long time ago and had resigned myself to living as a caged animal. The government stopped watching me a while ago as they knew I could go nowhere. I was forbidden to speak with anyone who knew me or have contact with my family."

The Congressman reaches out his hand while speaking, "We have you now, and I will make sure things will be getting better for you. Could you tell us what you know about the virus that did so much damage?"

Huang begins her story by saying, "Without question, military scientists at the Lab created COVID-19 at the Wuhan Institute of Virology in 2019. Chinese military scientist Dr. Zhou Yusen researched live animal infections at the Wuhan Institute of Virology in 2019 using the COVID-19 virus. I was still in the hospital when I heard he filed for a patent for a COVID-19 vaccine in February 2020, barely one month after China put Wuhan into lockdown due to the first outbreak.

I believe as part of the cover-up, the Chinese government killed Yusen, who may have caused the COVID pandemic by secretly working on a vaccine months before the global health crisis broke out. Just Three months later, Zhou Yusen died when he allegedly fell from the roof of the Wuhan Institute. Zhou Yusen feared high places, and the last place he would go was up to the roof of the Institute.

I believe that something happened while Zhou Yusen was doing his work, and that was when the virus first emerged. As was I, people at the Lab became infected by his work. I don't know if he was held accountable through some formal proceeding or not, but by July 2020, he was dead. I can't prove it, but I believe officials threw him from the roof of the Wuhan Institute as he would have admitted his mistake to the world.

I have received some information from the outside world through unauthorized sources while the government held me captive. I believe the United States' denial by your head doctor was a way to divert attention from the fact that his agency allocated grant money funding the experiments at the Wuhan Institute of Virology. The Institute used grant money at least partially for the experiments with the COVID. The claim that favored the zoological theory that the virus jumped from bats to humans is a joke. Your doctor cooperated with the Chinese government to hide that he authorized the research money. I hope one day, the truth will come out, and you will see the United States supplied the cash to build this monster virus.

Early on, I had come in contact with the virus and became ill. I believe my youth allowed me to survive the infection. After I became infected, the government moved me to a hospital for evaluation to see if the virus was survivable, and they deleted my entire life from all records. I no longer exist because they are afraid I may tell others where the virus came from and how the government covered it up. My friends worked at the Lab, and many of them are now dead. Those who remain will not speak because they do not want to be thrown off the roof of the building by officials. No one at the Lab wanted the world exposed to that virus. It was a mistake, and the government should have owned up to it quickly and avoided the unneeded suffering and death. But look to your government also for what happened. Officials in the United States knew what the Wuhan Lab was doing and that they should also be held responsible."

Huang Yanling looks at the Congressman and says, "I am so tired. May I rest briefly back in my seat before we land wherever our destination?" Congressman Harris smiles and says, "Huang, thank you for sharing your story. Agent Anderson will walk you back to your seat so you can rest."

The Congressman watches as Huang and Agent Anderson make their way down the aircraft aisle. He thanked the diplomatic staff member for assistance and reminded her that she knew nothing about the day's events, including the conversation with Huang. As she got up and started down the aisle, the Congressman's voice echoed, "Twenty-five thousand reasons to forget." The staff member stopped, turned, and presented the Congressman with a thumbs-up sign before continuing down the aisle.

The Congressman waited for Agent Anderson to return before speaking, "What Huang told us is in line with the report I received weeks ago concerning the virus." He reached into a folder in his hand and withdrew several sheets of paper. He handed the documents to Agent Anderson and Professor Norris for reading.

The report states:

"In November of 2019, less than a month before the COVID-19 pandemic took off and spread to nations worldwide, several scientists working at the Wuhan Institute of Virology in China fell seriously ill from an unknown virus. One of the researchers was Ben Hu, a scientist who received significant funding from the U.S. government and whose research focused on how coronaviruses infect humans.

At Wuhan Institute, Hu oversaw the gain of function research. The controversial scientific field involving mutating viruses to make them more deadly and more contagious involves coronaviruses. Gain-of-function research, banned in the U.S. until 2017, is typically used to develop vaccines. Hu and other scientists, now identified as Chinese researchers Yu Ping and Yan Zhu, were sickened by something in the fall of 2019 while working at the Lab. It is unclear precisely what made Hu and other researchers ill. The trio was sickened by "symptoms that American officials claimed were consistent with either COVID-19 or a seasonal illness" to the point where they needed to be hospitalized.

Officials reported the illness in 2021, with researchers becoming sick at the Wuhan lab; the story was based on information received by U.S. intelligence but did not identify who was impacted by the illness. The identities of the affected researchers remained a mystery until last week, when Public and Racket, two blogs on Substack, published a story about the incident. The story claims:

According to multiple U.S. government officials interviewed as part of a lengthy investigation by Public and Racket, the first people infected by the virus, "patients zero," included Ben Hu, a researcher who led the Wuhan Lab's "gain-of-function" research on SARS-like coronaviruses, which increases the infectiousness of viruses.

Details about Hu and the other researchers were revealed by a transparency advocacy organization known as the White Coat Waste Project.

The project filed a Freedom of Information Act lawsuit against the government to pry loose documents detailing the United States funding of research that was going on at the Wuhan Institute of Virology.

The documents reveal the grants were used to fund the Wuhan Institute of Virology's research into gain of function. President Trump shut down funding the experiments in 2020.

One of the distributors of grant funding for Hu's research was the U.S. Agency for International Development, while the other was the National Institute of Allergy and Infectious Diseases.

Altogether, the documents and the new reporting raise more questions than they answer, only deepening the mystery around the origins of the worst pandemic in memory.

During the early days of COVID-19, scientists rallied around as the most likely cause of the virus, with high-placed public health officials claiming it likely originated in the more unsanitary regions of a Wuhan wet Market. Speculation about COVID-19 having escaped from a lab or being the result of bioengineering was discouraged by officials as the terrain of cranks and conspiracy theorists. However, this conversation has notably shifted. Today, the "lab leak" hypothesis seems increasingly likely. Government agencies have even admitted that it's the most plausible explanation for the virus's start.

End of report.

Professor Norris returns the report to the Congressman and says, "That is why the Chinese government disappeared, Yanling. She knew many people at the Wuhan Lab who conducted the experiments and got infected. Huang Yanling directly witnessed what occurred and removed the wet market theory the Chinese had put forward. She will be the most wanted woman in the world by the Chinese, and the Chinese will not stop until she is killed and silenced."

The four F35 fighters escorted the transport into Japanese airspace before leaving. The Congressman felt sure the Chinese would not allow one of their fighters to infringe on Japan. Forty-five minutes after entering Japanese airspace, the aircraft prepared to land at the Tokyo airport. The familiar sound of the landing gear extending and the tires bumping on the runway gave way to the sounds of the aircraft rolling to a stop. Moments later, the airplane traveled along the taxiway into a refueling area. Captain Crossfield and Julie exited the plane, oversaw the aircraft's refueling operation, and did a visual inspection.

After refueling, the airplane was airborne again and heading to L.A.X. for its next stop. Congressman Harris sat in his seat and thoughts of everything that may still go wrong entered. Over the Pacific Ocean, the aircraft would be difficult to locate with the transponder turned off. Still, as the plane approached the West Coast of the United States, its location would become more readily determined, making it easy to locate. The Chinese could draw a straight line from Tokyo to L.A.X. and be close to the airplane's true flight path.

Congressman Harris looks up and says to Agent Anderson, "I am putting Huang Yanling's safety in your hands. Her life will depend on the actions you take from this point forward. She is possibly the only person who can explain what happened and how the COVID-19 virus occurred. Without Huang Yanling, everything reported and said is nothing more than a conspiracy theory. By the time we land this plane, every Chinese operative in the United States will be looking for her. Anderson, if needed, contact some other agents you can trust, and I will assign them to assist you." Agent Anderson replies, "I will not let anything happen to Huang Yanling."

The Congressman responds, "We are going to change plans right now. We are supposed to land at Los Angeles Airport and stay overnight. I need to check with Julie. However, I believe this aircraft can easily make it to Denver International Airport, refuel, and fly first to Florida to secure the three women in the Black Ice facility before we return to Washington, D.C. That will throw off any Chinese agents who are trying to track us.

Those Chinese fighter jets did not find us by accident. They know we have the women, and the Chinese can check our original flight plans. The Chinese will stop at nothing to make sure the women do not arrive alive, whatever the cost. Let me speak with Julie about flying to Denver."

The Congressman moves forward in the plane and sits in the co-pilot seat unoccupied by Captain Crossfield before speaking, "Julie, is this plane capable of flying directly to Denver International on the remaining fuel." Julie looks at the fuel indicator and replies, "Denver is about eight hundred and fifty additional miles from L.A.X., but this plane has enough capacity for the trip. Why?" The Congressman responds, "I am sure the Chinese know we have the three women with us onboard. I am also sure they can figure out if we are going to L.A.X and land for a layover or refueling. They would not expect us to fly to Denver. Are you okay flying to Denver and then directly to Florida to get these women to a safe place?"

Julie answers, "I will not have a problem making the trip to Denver and Florida. Why don't we add a little insurance to this adventure?" The Congressman says, "Insurance, what insurance?" Julie says, "Kevin when we approach the Western air defense corridor, Because we have already had a problem with Chinese fighters, I am requesting a fighter escort to protect our valuable cargo. They will pick us up as we approach the United States and follow us to Denver and Florida. Since we have the transponder turned off, I will give them our correct location. Anything approaching this aircraft will cause the fighters to shoot it down as hostile."

The Congressman says, "Can a fighter fly that distance? We are still almost fifteen hundred miles from the West Coast of the United States. Then, we will refuel this plane in Denver, followed by flying to Florida." Shaking her head, Julie says, "Kevin, fighter jets refuel in mid-air with tanker jets. They do not land for fuel. Once they are here, they can fly all over the country. They will stay with us to Florida." Kevin looks back at Julie and replies, "I knew about the air refueling. I was testing you. What are you waiting for? Get on the radio and get the fighters here."

Julie presses on the radio microphone and begins to call for assistance as the Congressman returns to the cabin area of the aircraft. As he passes Agent Anderson, he says, "Julie is calling for an escort as we speak." Anderson responds, "That makes me feel better already as he slides deep into the seat."

The Professor stands and moves to the rear of the aircraft. Sitting with a big smile, the Professor softly says, "This is possibly the most wonderful trip one could imagine. When my wife returns from the restroom, I can't wait to tell her we will have a fighter escort and find her camera. She will want to take a picture of it from the airplane window."

As Julie had advised Congressman Harris, the transport jet was soon to be escorted by two F-35 Lightning fighter jets. Any aircraft or other vehicle approaching the transport jet would need to deal with two of the most potent combat fighters on the planet.

Hours later, the Congressman could see the fighters from his airplane window, and he sat back in his seat, feeling more relaxed. Finally, they had an escort of armed aircraft to protect them from an enemy that knew no bounds or limits.

While the fighters circled, the transport plane landed at Denver International Airport to refuel for the trip to Florida. The ground crew in Denver had the transport jet refueled in forty-five minutes and ready to depart. As the transport jet left the ground, the two fighters were alongside for the long flight to Florida.

The Congressman carried a cup of coffee to the cockpit and handed it to Julie. He asked, "Are you okay?" Julie looks back at him, "Of course, I am okay. I rested while they refueled the plane. I must sit here for the next few hours and let this thing fly on autopilot. How are the passengers doing?" The Congressman responds, "The only ones I am worried about are the Professor and his wife. They may exhaust themselves from all the fun and excitement of the trip. The Diplomatic staff wants to return home, and Agent Anderson is alert and ready for action. The man is a machine."

Julie says, "Well, we have about three hours more flight time before we land in Florida. Is the Black Ice facility ready for the special guests?" The Congressman replies,

"I spoke with them a short time ago, and they are ready to welcome the special guests. I am sure the living quarters at the facility will be far better than what they had in Wuhan. They will also be safer at the facility as security is beyond belief. No one can get near the guests once the Black Ice group takes custody. They will be safe at the facility and well taken care of.

F35 Photo Taken by Angel Norris

During the flight, Julie could see the fighters, one at a time, move away to refuel and return to formation. Over three hours later, the transport landed in Florida, and the Black Ice agents were already waiting in a private taxi area. Fully armed and ready, they took custody of the three women. The Congressman spoke to them through the Diplomatic interpreter, "Ladies, the men are here to protect you. They will take you to a safe place where no one can harm you. I will be back in a few days to ensure everything is satisfactory and that you are doing well. I am asking you to trust me. Do you trust me?" Each of the women nodded their heads, indicating they trusted the Congressman.

As the Black Ice vehicles drove away, the Congressman felt a great relief. They had done the impossible, and the only thing left was the flight back to Washington, where everyone could finally go home.

CHAPTER THIRTY

Safe Back Home

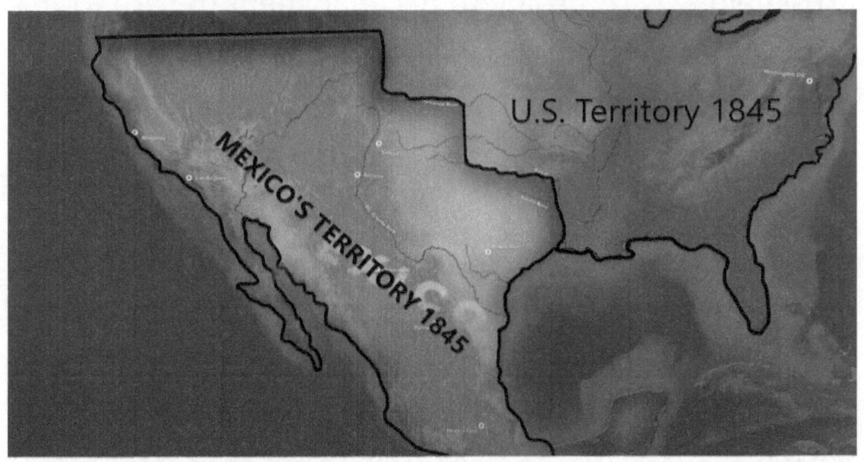

The flight from Florida to Washington was uneventful. More likely, everyone wanted to get back home, and excitement was the last thing on the menu. The events of the previous several days had taken their toll on everyone.

After landing at Bolling Air Force Base, deplaning and unloading everyone's luggage, Julie returned the aircraft to its hangar, where the Air Force maintenance crew could inspect it. The five Diplomatic staff were transported to a local hotel for the night, leaving the Congressman's group at the Air Base.

Congressman Harris decided that the professor and his wife would be the Congressman's guest for the next three days and remain in Washington at a local hotel. Captain Crossfield was returning to his apartment to care for his cat Mildred, and Julie, exhausted from the long flight, decided to go home. The Air Force supplied courtesy transportation for the entire group to each destination.

Congressman Harris was the last to board a transport and driven to his home in Washington. As the Congressman sat in the rear of the transport, he relived the events of the previous few days. Little wonder the world is in such a mess, he thought. Unsure if it was power or greed, but whichever it was, it was spiraling out of control across the planet. It would come down one day to the 'haves and have-nots' sooner or later. How long can a government suppress the masses before they rise against it? How long?

The transport braking alerted the Congressman of his arrival at his home. The driver unloaded his luggage and placed it at his front door before bidding him a good evening. When the driver pulled away, he left him fumbling for his keys, but he somehow unlocked the door. As the door swung open, he saw familiar things in the distance. Standing there, he felt he was looking into the past without a plan to go forward. That is when he decided that he would begin to look forward to the future tomorrow. He could not change what had already taken place, but he would take control of each day forward.

He dragged his luggage into the house and closed the door, slowly ascending the stairs to bed, carrying only his briefcase as he went. Laying on the bed, fully dressed, he fell asleep and drifted into the world of nothingness.

Congressman Harris did not awake until shortly after seven the following day. Hurriedly, the Congressman unpacked his suitcase, showered, dressed, and drove his car to the office. Upon arrival, the Congressman reached over to pick up his briefcase and found he had left it on the chair in his bedroom at home. The Congressman began to laugh, thinking that would be one last thing to deal with today as he walked from the parking area to the office door.

As the Congressman entered the office's front door, he did not know what to expect or who would be there. To his surprise, Agent Anderson, Julie, Bill, and Ken were waiting for him to arrive. Bill says, "Traffic jam, sir?" Congressman Harris responds, "Terrible, just terrible the traffic getting here." And he headed for his private office.

When he opened the private office door, the door slammed against the safe they had installed for the classified documents, and looking down, he still saw the damaged carpeting from the safe's installation. He smiled, thinking nothing had changed here since I had gone.

The private office was still in disarray, with Ken's computers occupying two desks with soda cans and potato chip bags on his large desk. His private office was a mess, but it was good to be home.

Ken poked his head in the private office and asked, "Would it be alright if I clean my stuff up later today? My car needs service, and I must take it to the dealer." The Congressman replies, "Ken, not a problem. See you tomorrow. Go and get your car serviced." Within seconds, the front door closed behind Ken as he left the Congressman's office.

Julie walked into the private office and closed the door behind her. She moved over to the large desk, sat on the corner, and said, "Is there something you would like to say to me, like Julie, I am sorry for what I said in Wuhan?" Congressman Harris' thoughts returned to his comment about telling Julie how to do her job while in China. Choosing his words carefully, the Congressman says, "Well, I overstepped, no, I underestimated, no, I misspoke. Okay, I screwed up when I said that, and I am sorry." Julie smiles and replies, "Apology accepted, but don't let it happen again."

The Congressman says, "Julie, please take a chair and sit down if you can find it under all this stuff." Julie moves the furniture until she locates the office chair and sits beside the large desk.

In the background, they could hear the office telephone ring in the center office, and the Congressman's secretary, Bill, answered. And before he can say hello, the voice on the other end of the line says, "In one hour, a diplomatic pouch will arrive for Congressman Harris. He needs to review the contents immediately." And the telephone disconnected.

Bill hangs up the telephone and presses the intercom button to inform the Congressman of the call. "Sir," Bill says, "We just received a call." The Congressman interrupts, "From who?" Bill continues, "I don't know from whom, Sir." The Congressman interrupts again, "Are you telling me you received a crank call and are wasting my time to tell me about it?" Bill responds, "Well, no, Sir, the voice on the phone told me to expect a diplomatic pouch in about an hour, and you should read it immediately." The Congressman replies, "When it arrives, have Anderson look it over for anything dangerous, and if there is any question of its safety, call in the bomb squad." Bill replies, "Yes, Sir, I will have Agent Anderson look it over before we open the pouch."

An hour later, the knock on the door alerted Agent Anderson of someone's arrival at the Congressman's office. As the Agent opened the door, a man handed a pouch to Agent Anderson, turned, and walked away without speaking. Agent Anderson watched closely as the man walked away, watching his every movement. He noted the person's height, about five foot six inches tall, the slender build of the man, and most notably, the way he moved like a well-trained athlete. His observations and training told him this was not a courier but a military person and, based on his height and build, a man of Asian descent.

Agent Anderson smelled the pouch and then laid the pouch flat on Bill's desk and slowly moved his hands along the surface to check for anything other than the papers inside. Satisfied it only contained papers, he informed Bill the pouch was safe for the Congressman to open. Bill lifted the bag and carried it to the Congressman's private office for review.

Congressman Harris unlatched the pouch and removed the papers, trying to imagine what could be so crucial in a small pile of documents.

The documents were dated only days before and consisted of several small reports and photos of the Japanese Yokosuka Naval base.

In the photos, the J.S. Izumo, originally a massive helicopter carrier, is currently in the last stages of being to carry VTOL (Vertical Take-Off Landing) F-35Bs, to be converted into a 'Lightning carrier.' A need for smaller carriers to bring pure fifth-generation stealth fighters like the F-35 has emerged, surging strategic and military tensions with China in the Indo-Pacific.

Photo From Documents

The report continues with a photo taken by the overhead drone of Japan's largest destroyer that triggered 'grave concerns' about the Japanese military's ability "to detect potential threats." NCIS (Naval Criminal Investigative Service) "investigated their authenticity, but the investigation revealed no indication that a drone flew over the Ronald Reagan carrier. This claim is weird and likely untrue as the images, later confirmed to be genuine, seem to confirm the drone flew, if not directly over the U.S. aircraft carrier, but close enough to take some pretty good shots of the ship's defenses.

A drone is far from being able to cause significant structural damage or sink the ship. But had it been carrying explosives, it could have quickly exploded near one of the delicate radars, communication systems disabling the system. The systems have a host of microelectronics, processors, and electrical circuitry that is tedious to manufacture, assemble, and replace. The damage assessment and repairs would have taken months, removing the ship from service in that area of the world.

But the incident reveals a massive techno-commercial dimension. The rise of global private technology and the drone sector has made a variety of commercial off-the-shelf drones available for leisure use. The war in Ukraine showed how such small UAVs could be retrofitted for military use, for everything from simple battlefield surveillance to artillery fire correction to kamikaze attack roles by being strapped with explosives.

The drone could fly close enough to aircraft carriers and warships at the Yokosuka Naval Base, exposing security failures. Shortly after the photos were taken, the person who had shot the images left Japan and returned to China.

The person who took the photos was not an amateur having a little fun with his drone. The recovered images clearly show a scan of secret protective armament. Intelligence has confirmed the person who shot the photos is a member of the CCP and not a rogue amateur.

Julie says, "That's all the pages in the pouch. It does not give much direction as to what to do with all of it. And they were all taken recently within the last ten days. What does all of this mean?"

Congressman Harris replies, "The Chinese are not fools, and Japan and Taiwan must be vigilant after this incident. The Chinese are trying to provoke either or both of them aggressively to see if the United States will step up and help defend them." Julie responds, "Still, it does not indicate what you are supposed to do with this stuff."

The Congressman sits back in his desk chair and says, "This is the Chinese way of letting everybody know nothing is safe from their eyes. Balloons drifting over the United States, Chinese police stations in the U.S., power outages in India and Mexico. Their fingerprints are all over this, and they want the world to know it. The pouch contained puzzle pieces but not the key to what was going on. Something is missing."

Julie and Congressman Harris reviewed it a second time, and they sorted it into piles but still could not understand what it meant. They placed these documents in the giant safe and would work on them later when more information became available. The missing puzzle pieces must be somewhere, but somewhere is a vast place to search when you have no idea what to look for.

Despite the crazy previous days, the atmosphere in the Congressman's office that morning was festive. Agent Anderson and Bill joked and laughed about the events of the China trip. Bill repeats Agent Anderson's story: "You tried to convince Chinese security agents your ancestors were Chinese. You are a six foot two African American." The laughter was interrupted by a loud knock on the main office door, and Agent Anderson rose from his chair to answer. As the door opened, a muffled sound filled the room, and Agent Anderson stepped back and dropped to the floor. Still unseen by the lone man in the doorway, Bill ducked quickly down behind his office desk. The man in the doorway steps over the still body of Agent Anderson, closes the front door, and methodically moves forward directly toward the Congressman's private office. As if a machine, his steps were as steady as those of a trained dancer as he moved. Slowly, without making a sound or expression, he advanced toward the door.

Placing his left hand on the private office door latch, he pressed it and forced the door open. Standing in the open door like the reaper of death, motionless, holding his weapon and pointing it directly at Congressman Harris and Julie. Congressman Harris stands from his chair in defiance of the threat and speaks clearly to the intruder. "I knew they would send someone sooner or later. So, you are the Chinese government enforcer I have heard so much about. I expected more of a man, not a punk with a gun."

Congressman Harris pauses momentarily and says, "Professor Norris was correct; Chinese honor far exceeds Chinese bravery." The intruder stood silent momentarily before speaking, "Congressman, you and your people have caused the Chinese great pain and embarrassment. Your Western world ideas have caused untold suffering worldwide, and you stand, pompous, trying to take the high ground in life. You have stolen land from your southern neighbors without honor or remorse. So little do you understand about the correct way to live. People need to be controlled, guided, and managed, and they are sheep to be used to advance their main objective and strength. The Chinese will rule the world, and that is our destiny.

You have something that belongs to the people of China, and I am here to recover it."

Congressman Harris interrupts, "You mean the three Chinese women. They are all safe and out of China's reach and control."

The Chinese assassin smiles and replies, "The three women. I don't want the three women. We will find and deal with them another time. I want the documents delivered here today and the ones taken from China given to you by the Consul General in Wuhan."

Congressman Harris' thoughts return to the plain envelope given to him by the Consul General while he was in Wuhan. The same envelope he had forgotten to remove from his briefcase upon his return from China. The case, with the envelope still within it, on his home bedroom chair was the target, not the three women. All along, the Chinese wanted the envelope given to him by the Consul General and were willing to shoot down an aircraft to get it. The three women were only collateral damage should they be captured or killed. The real question was how the Chinese knew the Consul General had given the envelope to him. Someone at the U.S. Mission in Wuhan must have informed Chinese security that the Congressman had it, or the Chinese electronically bugged the U.S. Mission office.

The Diplomatic pouch delivered earlier today must also be part of the puzzle. That's it; you need both pieces to assemble the information to make sense of the complete action plan. The Chinese used the same scheme of two parts in the book 'We Are The Dragons.' Whatever is in the plain envelope must be combined with the Diplomatic pouch documents to find the answers. But, right now, Congressman Harris had another problem in the form of an assassin preparing to kill both of them.

The Chinese assassin continues, "And before you die, I want you to see and feel the pain of the millions of Chinese people your ideas have imposed." The intruder points the weapon directly at Julie and finishes his words, "Watch, Congressman, feel what it is like to see the person you love die because of the things you have done to dishonor the Chinese people."

As the intruder carefully aims at Julie, a loud explosive echo comes from the center of the main office area. The intruder stands motionless without expression, and his face fills with surprise. His head slowly turned back to where the Congressman stood, and he started to smile as his weapon slowly lowered and dropped from his hand onto the floor. Like in a movie or as described in a cheap novel, he gradually settled onto his knees and fell forward on the torn carpet, lifeless and no longer a threat to anyone.

As the intruder fell, the Congressman and Julie could now see Bill standing in the open door, holding Agent Anderson's gun in both of his hands and staring straight forward as if he were in a state of shock. The gun was still smoking from the discharge, and rings of smoke were still rising into the air. Bill did not move. He just stood and stared for several moments as if nothing had happened.

Finally, Bill lowered the gun and dropped it on the floor, and sanity returned to his face. He quickly turned and moved to where Agent Anderson lay wounded. Touching Anderson's face, he said, "Anderson, Anderson." Two green eyes opened, and Agent Anderson mumbled, "Shit, I was trained never to answer a door that way. I hope the Congressman doesn't write me up." Looking down at the Agent, Bill says, "Don't worry, I handle the paperwork and will toss it into the waste basket. Now, we need to get you some help."

Agent Anderson moans, "Damn, that hurts." Bill replies, "Of course, it hurts Anderson; you have been shot. You are lucky you're not dead." Bill rips Agent Anderson's shirt open to inspect the wound, stops, and stares at the center of Anderson's chest. Agent Anderson asks, "How bad is it, Bill? Give it to me straight." Bill smiles and responds, "Looks like you're going to die."

Before Bill could stand to seek help, the Congressman had already alerted security, and they could hear the sounds of sirens as they approached.

Within minutes, security personnel and other federal officers swarmed the office. Medical staff were treating Agent Anderson on the floor before attempting to move him to a hospital, and investigators had secured and bagged both weapons for evidence as to what had occurred.

As the medical staff reopened Agent Anderson's shirt to inspect the wound, a stunned look came over their faces. Lodged in the center of a Chinese medallion was the bullet intended to kill Agent Anderson. The Medallion had blocked a direct shot to the heart, and his injuries were more like someone in a nasty fight and not a gunshot to the chest. The medical staff removed the necklace and informed Agent Anderson how lucky a man he was for wearing it.

The Medic said, "That injury is a one-in-a-million chance of survival on a near-range heart shot." Agent Anderson looked at the Medic and said, "A friend of mine got it from a Chinese Shamanist and told me to wear it to protect me. Crazy as it sounds, he told me that on the day he gave me the necklace."

*Bullet Lodged in the
Blessed Medallion*

As the medical team removed Agent Anderson and transported him to the hospital, Congressman Harris requested that any needed questioning be delayed until after the office was again under control, and the lead investigator agreed to honor the request.

Julie remained in the private office, sitting in a chair alongside the Congressman's desk. Congressman Harris takes a moment to comfort her as she sits. Julie, speaking softly, begins, "You know, Kevin. When I was flying those F-16 fighters and shooting at aircraft and even people, this may sound strange, but it was not personal, if that is a good word. You do not see up close the actual damage your actions are taking. I guess you could almost consider it a video game of sorts. But to stand close and point a weapon at someone, knowing you are about to take their life, is a different type of engagement. Bill stood there and placed his life on the line to save ours. He could have stayed out of sight and let it all happen, but he chose to go it alone. Had he made a sound when retrieving Agent

Anderson's weapon, the gunmen would have turned and shot him dead. Maybe I am just getting soft, but I needed to say that."

Congressman Harris places his arms around Julie and speaks, "I was thinking the same thing. I was thinking the same damn thing. I hate to say this, but we may need to get Bill his gun."

Congressman Harris says, "Julie, I think I have figured it out. We now have the puzzle pieces, and we must pull the group back together to see what it all means." Julie responds, "Another adventure, Kevin?" The Congressman smiles, "Not sure right now, but I never want to say never. But not today. Today, we must verify Agent Anderson is okay, and then we must stay out of here for the rest of the day so security can do their job. I will have Bill take you home as I must do something I have neglected for too long."

An hour later, Congressman Harris walked the stone-covered path to the place where his wife and daughter had been laid to rest over a year before. As always, he sat on the corner of his daughter's head marker and relived better times when the family was still with him. He looked down and began to speak softly, "I need to try and get up here more often, but I needed to travel to China, and you know how that goes. Honey, do you remember Julie, the girl I took to the prom? The one you said was only cute and not pretty. She is a pilot now and a

Colonel in the Air Force. I was lucky enough to have her fly my group to China and then back to the U.S. She lost her husband in a terrible accident. Julie reminds me of you, honey, always paying attention to minor details. Nobody could replace you, but she is fun to be with when she isn't correcting me. I want to spend more time here but must go home now and get something I forgot in my briefcase. I promise I will return soon."

Congressman Harris immediately climbed the stairs to his bedroom as he arrived home. Still lying on the chair was his briefcase containing the plain envelope given to him by the Consul General in Wuhan. He slowly opened the case and removed the envelope, thinking about what this could include that the Chinese were willing to shoot down a United States aircraft to recover or destroy.

He scanned the pages as he removed the documents and thumb drive storage devices from the envelope. The main thing that caught his attention were the words. 'Mexico, distribution, drugs, accounts, and Cartels.' He did not know how this puzzle piece fit the other documents, but he would find out. One thing for sure is that the events in China were somehow related to Mexico and the cartels. These were the same people the Congressman believed were responsible for the death of his wife and daughter.

I told Julie that I would never say never about another adventure. Well, I guess I was right.

The End

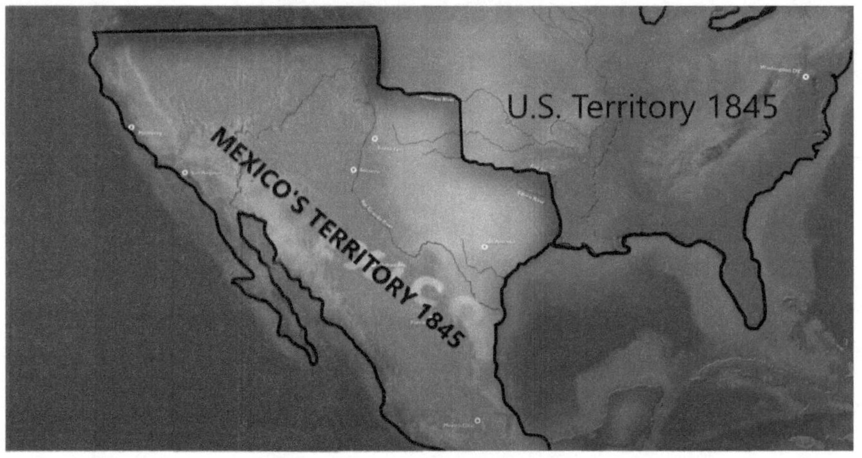